Take Me

Take Me

Bella Andre

POCKET BOOKS

New York   London   Toronto   Sydney

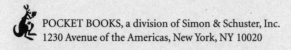
POCKET BOOKS, a division of Simon & Schuster, Inc.
1230 Avenue of the Americas, New York, NY 10020

Library of Congress Cataloging-in-Publication Data

Andre, Bella.
    Take me / Bella Andre.
      p. cm.
    ISBN-13: 978-1-4165-0957-8
    ISBN-10:   1-4165-0957-7
      1. Overweight women—Fiction. I. Title.

  PS3601.N5495T34 2005
  813'.6—dc22

                        2005053466

This Pocket Books trade paperback edition November 2005

10 9 8 7 6 5 4 3 2 1

For information regarding special discounts for bulk purchases,
please contact Simon & Schuster Special Sales at 1-800-456-6798
or business@simonandschuster.com

Interior book design by Davina Mock

Manufactured in the United States of America

For Jami and Monica, who informed me with utter certainty that this book was "the one," and my amazing husband, Paul, for his love and support.

Big kisses!

ACKNOWLEDGMENTS

I'd like to say thank you to everyone in the San Francisco RWA for teaching me the ropes; my parents and mother-in-law for being so darn proud of their erotic-romance-writing daughter; my agent, Jessica, for believing so strongly in this book; and my editor, Selena, for being such a joy to work with.

Take Me

1

*M*E? A MODEL? You've got to be kidding."

Janica Ellis's lower lip trembled. "Please, Lily. Sonia has the stomach flu. She was my only plus-sized model. You're my last hope." Gesturing to the skimpy, colorful dresses hanging from the rack beside her, she added, "This is my big break. My first big fashion show with major buyers in the audience. You just need to model one dress for me."

Under most circumstances, Lily Ellis would do anything to help out her little sister. But not when "anything" included showcasing her un-model-perfect size-sixteen body under glaring lights while tottering down a runway in stiletto heels. Already she could hear the baffled whispers from the audience of, "What is that cow doing up on the stage?" She would pass out from humiliation.

She already felt painfully uncool among this cutting-edge crowd of designers and artists. Just walking the two busy city blocks from the parking garage to the Moscone Center in the very hip San Francisco, South of Market area, was enough to make Lily feel like she had the word "boring" stamped across her chest.

Shaking her head forcefully, Lily raised her voice over the din of the models, makeup artists, and designers backstage. "I came to sit in the audience and applaud your incredible clothes, not to put on a skintight, see-through dress and parade around like a lumbering elephant."

So then why, Lily wondered moments later, *am I being poked with pins and made up by an androgynous makeup artist?*

A sarcastic inner voice wasted no time in replying, *Because you're a lily-livered pushover, that's why.*

How apt the name Lily was. Even among flowers, lilies were overly large. If she had been named Petunia or Violet, would she have been petite and cute, with a button nose and straight brown hair? In her daydreams, Lily was a reed-slim, perfectly toned size six, with straight blond hair and sparkling blue eyes, who everyone gazed at with envy. Just like the women on the Pilates infomercials that she watched late at night alone in her apartment. As it was, all she had going for her was the blue eyes. But given the fact that they were on *her* face, Lily figured they might as well have been mud brown. And as far as Lily was concerned, her out-of-control curly red hair and pale skin didn't help matters any. She slumped her shoulders in defeat.

Janica grunted with displeasure and forcefully pushed Lily's shoulder blades together. "You need to keep your back straight for me to get the fit right."

But when Lily looked in the mirror and saw nothing but a huge pair of breasts encased in a wildly printed sheer mesh fabric, she choked on a hysterical laugh.

"Janica, stop," she pleaded. "My chest looks like the spinnaker of a large ship."

Her sister glanced into the mirror, and insisted, "It does not."

Because of the barely masked worry in Janica's eyes, Lily wished she had kept her mouth shut. Trying to make her baby sister laugh, Lily said, "Don't worry, Jan. Swashbuckling pirates always hightail it toward small, cute girls with twenty-inch waists and French manicures, so your dress should come through the salty seas just fine."

Around a mouthful of pins Janica giggled. "Lils, you've got an overactive imagination. Pirate ships and salty seas. Your creative talents are definitely wasted at Barker's Furniture. Besides, most women would kill to have boobs like yours." Janica gestured to her A cups. "Like me, for instance. Besides, who wouldn't want your gorgeous curls and your peaches-and-cream coloring? Which, if you hadn't already noticed, is perfectly highlighted by this fabric." Janica took a step back to study Lily more closely and sucked in a breath. "Wow, you look incredible. You're going to blow all of the other models away up there. It's as if I made this dress just for you."

Lily opened her mouth to disagree with her sister's compliments when the makeup artist bit out, "Hold your head still. I'm doing your lip line now."

Hardly daring to breathe, Lily decided that a few minutes of extreme public humiliation was worth it if it could make the person she loved most in the world happy. Lily thought back to the day Janica had made her first dress, nearly twenty years ago, when they had gone to live with Grandma Ellen after their parents' death. Only ten years old herself, Lily had been so proud of her talented, sparkling five-year-old sister. Every now and then when it felt like Janica was growing up and getting further and further away from her, Lily pulled the soft red-and-white gingham sundress out from the dusty box underneath her bed and rubbed the fabric against her cheek.

You are going to have to suck it up and pull yourself together,

Lily told herself in a firm voice, when a size-zero model skipped by, all long legs and pouty lips.

Lily promptly lost hold of her false confidence. Her legs trembled, and the dress fluttered around her knees, mimicking the quivering in her stomach.

"Would it help if Luke was here to cheer you on?" Janica asked with concern.

Lily stopped chewing on her lip. No question about it, her best friend Luke was exactly the right person to see her through this terrible ordeal. He would make some silly joke about the whole thing, and she'd forget about how big and jiggly and stupid she felt wrapped up in high fashion, like Jell-O in cellophane. Maybe they could go see that new Queen Latifah movie when the whole thing was over. Lily loved any actress who had a full figure. It proved that other women had curves, too.

Feeling slightly calmer, Lily nodded and pinned a falsely bright smile on her face as she grabbed Janica's cell phone and dialed Luke's number. She quickly explained the situation to him and felt a thousand times better after she hung up.

Thank God for her best friend. He would never let her down.

LUKE CARSON closed his cell phone with a snap, stood up, and threw down a twenty. "Sorry to drink and run, bro, but I've got more important things to do right now."

"Gotta get on your white horse again?" Travis Carson asked, his full mouth twisting at the corners.

Luke ignored Travis, like he had ignored him for the past thirty years whenever he was being a total jerk. So, as he had for the past three decades, Travis kept digging away at his younger-by-sixty-seconds brother.

"You never should have rescued her cat from up in the tree

in first grade," Travis drawled. "It set a bad precedent. A really bad precedent."

Travis took a slug of his beer but kept his eye on his twin brother to gauge his reaction to the ribbing. Luke had been best friends with Lily for nearly twenty-five years. Travis wondered why they weren't married yet.

Or at least doing the nasty on a regular basis.

Because even though they almost never talked about Lily, and Travis made it a point to avoid her whenever possible, more often than not Luke couldn't hang out with the guys because he already had plans with Lily.

"You might as well admit that she's your girlfriend, already."

"I would if she was," Luke said, not the least bit bothered by Travis's jibes. "I'll see you for some one-on-one basketball tomorrow," Luke added, but before he walked away from the table he was interrupted by the insistent ring of his cell phone.

Luke flipped open the cover. "Now? You're kidding? No, don't worry, I'll be there in ten." He turned his bright green eyes to Travis.

Travis put down his empty beer bottle and shook his head. "You know I hate it when you look at me like that. And the answer is no."

Luke gave Travis a conciliatory smile. "She needs me, Travis. And since I've got to be in the ER, you need to be me." At Travis's skeptical glance, Luke said, "Remember how often we pulled this off when we were kids? Besides, I'm sure it'll be dark in there. Sit close enough that she'll be able to see you."

"But not close enough that she gets a good look at me," Travis finished for him. "I still know the drill."

"And be sure to wave when she looks over. Hopefully, it'll be dark enough in the audience that she won't realize that I'm you until the show's over."

"Sounds like a good plan," Travis said, then shook his head. "But I've got a date."

"I'll personally call Bimbos Are Us and cancel for you," Luke said. "And to sweeten the deal, tomorrow afternoon I'll let you beat me at hoops."

Travis thought about what being stuck with Lily all night would be like. Definitely boring. Especially compared to what he had been planning to do with the stacked brunette bartender who had already given him her number. Now there was a woman who a guy could have a good time with.

But another glance at his twin was enough to convince Travis that he needed to do it in the name of brotherhood. Even though they didn't always see eye to eye, Luke was the one person Travis would do anything for. Travis considered himself to be a pretty nice guy, all in all. He did volunteer work building homes for the needy, and no matter how busy he was he always kicked the soccer ball around with whatever kid was hanging out on the street in front of his house.

Feeling noble, Travis agreed to step into his brother's shoes for the night. "Okay. I'll do it. But I'll beat you tomorrow on the blacktop fair and square."

Luke slapped him on the shoulder. "I knew I could count on you. In any case, this should be right up your alley. You're going to a fashion show downtown. Moscone Center."

Travis laughed out loud. "Lily is in a fashion show? She barely has the guts to walk down the street, let alone a runway."

"Watch it, Travis," Luke warned, his hand already in a tight fist.

Travis took a step backward. Luke didn't have much of a sense of humor when it came to Lily. "I'm kidding," he said. He might have been a minute older than Luke, but his twin had a mean right hook.

Luke uncurled his fingers and took a step back. "I hope she'll forgive me for sending you in my place tonight." Luke ran his fingers through his dark hair. "Although I have a feeling that if she figures out that I'm you, she may never speak to me again."

Travis tried to ignore the sting of being told just how much Lily disliked him. What did he care? After all, he was the one who had broken ties with her long ago. When they were ten years old Luke had tried to ask Travis why he didn't want to be friends with Lily anymore, especially since they had all been such good friends up until fifth grade. But since Travis never answered, Luke stopped asking.

"I'll bet her spoiled-rotten little sister is using and abusing her again," Luke said. "She needs someone on her team tonight. I wish I could be there, but the ER is jammed."

Travis felt a twinge of sympathy for Lily, but then caught himself and quickly squashed the sentiment. Women were great for a night out on the town and getting sweaty with between the sheets. Not for emotional entanglement. Travis couldn't imagine being shackled to one woman for the rest of his life.

"Try to be nice for once, Trav," Luke added, his eyes promising serious consequences should Travis do anything to upset Lily.

Travis gave his twin a look of wide-eyed innocence. "Don't worry about it. With all of those models around, I'm definitely going to be on my best behavior."

"I'll bet," Luke muttered as he led the way out of the bar and hailed a cab to the hospital. Travis grinned at his brother's back, as always delighting in irking his twin. But then Travis thought about watching Lily make a fool of herself in a fashion show, and his delight disappeared.

He hopped into the next available cab and fifteen minutes later he was smack-dab in the middle of the unbridled sights and sounds of downtown San Francisco. He soaked up the chaos on the streets, the traffic jams and loud stereos booming from the markets and upstairs apartments.

I haven't been living wild enough lately, he realized. Too many nights burning the midnight oil over blueprints in the office were to blame.

Not that he was complaining about the success of his architectural firm. On the contrary, Travis thrived on the competition and cutting-edge creativity entailed in building worlds for his clients to live in. A natural-born salesperson, Travis had never had a client say no to him. He loved the precision of designing and building the perfect structure and was known for clean lines and sweeping vistas.

The cab stopped in front of the Moscone Center, and Travis paid the driver. He gave his brother's name to the bouncer at the door and walked onto the huge dance floor, taking a moment to get used to the rainbow of lights and earsplitting Electronica booming from the speakers on the ceilings. Three lithe women walked past him, the boldest one in the skimpiest dress eying him up and down, making it clear that she liked what she saw. Travis grinned. Maybe tonight wasn't going to be such a waste after all.

After he was done pretending to be Luke, he was going to take home a cute little thing in a thong. Models weren't the greatest lays—they were too busy putting themselves in flattering positions to get really steamy in the sack—but they sure were nice to look at. And Travis greatly enjoyed looking at pretty things.

He grabbed a martini from a passing waiter and looked for an open seat far enough from the stage for Lily to think he was his twin brother if she glanced in his direction. No one had ever been able to tell them apart, so Travis wasn't worried about fooling her. In any case he was pretty sure her nerves would turn the audience into one big blur of faces. How could she possibly pick him out of the crowd? Regardless, as soon as she made it back-stage in one piece he was out of there. And then Luke could go back to his seemingly full-time job of picking up Lily's pieces.

Spotting an empty chair between a petite blonde and a built brunette, Travis made his way over to it. He took off his leather jacket and propped one jeans-clad leg up on the back of a chair, letting the gin work its way down his throat.

Travis watched the tiny blonde to his left take in his well-defined biceps and triceps, the washboard stomach beneath his thin T-shirt, and long-past-five-o'clock shadow. He knew he looked like he visited the gym on a daily basis, but the truth was he'd been blessed with good genes. The only reason he ever hit the gym was to convince some hot young thing to swap reach-ing her target heart rate on the treadmill in favor of exceeding it as she came beneath him. He much preferred playing a game of pickup basketball to any kind of organized exercise regime.

"Hi, handsome," the blonde said, her gaze on the bulge be-tween his legs.

You should see how big it is when I'm turned on, he thought silently as he cocked an eyebrow and raised his martini glass in greeting.

Coyly, she asked, "Are you with one of the models?"

Taking his time to answer, Travis ran his tongue over his lower lip to lick off the lingering liquor. The blonde watched the progression with obvious hunger.

"Not exactly," he said.

She leaned in close, giving Travis the chance to look straight into her cleavage.

She's a B cup, maybe C, Travis thought with disinterest.

Travis noted his apathy with surprise. Not interested in a hot, perfect specimen of a woman who was offering him exactly what he wanted? Not jumping at the offer of no-holds-barred, anonymous sex?

He had definitely been putting in too many long hours in the office.

The music jumped by ten decibels as the first model hit the stage. Travis slumped farther down in the chair, already counting the seconds until the show was over and he could get the blonde or the brunette—or both—into bed.

Luke's voice played in his head, saying, "Try to be nice for once." He didn't know why Lily pushed all of his wrong buttons, just that she did. It was everything about her, from her round body to her meek mouth and fluffy red hair. Even her blue eyes seemed too big on her face.

But most of all, Travis couldn't stand the way she hung all over his twin. Not to mention the fact that Luke didn't seem to mind. Travis shook his head and drained his martini glass. How his brother could be such close friends with such a Goody Two-shoes he'd never understand. But then again, Luke had always been the caretaker, the kind of guy who supported the underdog. Somehow Luke had gotten all of the nice genes in their mother's womb.

Travis smiled and relaxed back into his seat, perfectly comfortable with who he was, inside and out. The only thorn in his side was Lily. For some reason he was always ill at ease when she was in the same room with him. He could feel her eyes on him, almost as if she were seeing things he didn't intend for anyone to see.

Which was ridiculous, he knew. Travis didn't have any secrets. As far as he was concerned, he was an open book. He worked hard, played hard, and made no apologies for anything he did, because there was nothing to apologize for.

Regardless, for the next hour, he had to pretend to be on Lily's team, or his brother would have his butt on a spear. He composed his angled jaw and green eyes into a mask of interest and support, all the while thinking about how good the blonde's silicone-injected lips were going to feel wrapped around his cock.

LILY'S FEET WERE KILLING HER in the four-inch spike heels, and she wished she could sit down, but she was afraid she'd wrinkle the dress. And then Janica would definitely kill her. She leaned against the wall, her heart pounding a mile a minute.

Lily, who never, ever drank—she was sure she'd say or do something she couldn't take back in the morning if she let her guard down for even one night—knew that she shouldn't drink any of the plentiful alcohol backstage. But she was so nervous that when the makeup artist thrust a glass of champagne into her hands, and ordered, "Drink this or you'll look like a ghost out there with such a white face," all Lily could do was gulp it down. The empty glass was instantly replaced with a full one.

She still couldn't tell if the makeup artist was a he or a she, but as the fizzy liquid made its way down her throat into her flip-flopping belly, Lily hardly cared anymore. She took another large swallow of the sweet, tart champagne and felt infinitely better.

"Luke's here," Janica said after popping her head from between the curtains. "He's on the right side of the stage, four rows back."

Lily smiled and tried to give her sister a thumbs-up, forgetting that she was holding on to the champagne glass. Her head buzzed and she looked at the upside-down empty glass in surprise.

Janica rushed over. "What are you doing? You're not getting drunk are you?"

"No," Lily said, her cheeks flushing. "I didn't even want to drink it," she insisted as she handed the empty glass over, her every move overly precise.

"That's funny, 'cause your glass is empty," Janica said, sarcasm dripping off every word. "You know you can't hold your liquor."

"Oh," was all Lily could say.

Janica looked like she was going to scream with irritation, but instead she threw her arms around Lily, opting for a pep talk instead. "Thanks so much for doing this for me. I know how much you hate being in front of crowds, but you are going to do so great out there tonight. Have I mentioned lately how you're the best big sister in the whole world?"

Lily sobered up a little and put on a brave face. "Don't worry about me, honey. I'm going to do you proud. I promise." She shooed Janica off. "Go on. Your line is up next. Get back to work."

Janica dropped a light kiss on Lily's cheek and scurried off to make sure her lead models were ready to walk. Lily started to rub her eyes wearily, but remembered at the last minute all the makeup she was wearing. A waiter rounded the corner with a tray of champagne and her hand shot out, seemingly of its own accord.

"One more couldn't hurt," she said as she brought the rim of the glass to her lips. Besides, all of a sudden being a runway model for a night didn't seem so bad. She only had to make it down to the end of the plank to pose for pictures. It would take sixty seconds, tops, then she'd go find Luke and they would have a good laugh about it all.

Just so long as he didn't bring his twin brother with him.

When Travis gave her one of his disdainful looks, or worse yet, ignored her completely, it made her feel like dirt. Less important than dirt, even.

Lily didn't know how two people could be less alike. It was especially strange considering Luke and Travis were identical twins. Luke was warmhearted, fun, and nonjudgmental. On the other end of the spectrum, there was Travis, with his piercing verdicts. Lily had been watching him from afar for long enough to know that all he cared about was pleasing himself and looking at pretty things. And that, Lily knew, was the crux of the problem between her and Travis.

She wasn't pretty enough for him. Or thin enough. Or perky enough. And none of those things were ever going to change.

As kids, she and Luke and Travis had been inseparable. The three musketeers. But then the boys' mom died when they were ten, and everything changed. *No,* she thought with a sigh, *not everything.* She and Luke had remained incredibly close, best friends to this day. But Travis had never been the same after that. And no matter how much she wanted her old relationship with Travis back, no matter how much she tried to let him know she was there for him, Travis kept rejecting her. Turning his back on her. Lily told herself she had given up on him, but in her heart of hearts, she knew it wasn't true.

Could you ever completely give up on someone that you loved? From her painful experience with Travis, Lily didn't think so.

Janica ran back to Lily, breathless, and stuck something in her free hand. "I almost forgot to give you this."

"What is it?" Lily said as she grasped the edge of a purple feather.

"It's your mask. Actually, I should probably put it on for you so that you don't mess up your hair or makeup." Janica slid the mask down over Lily's riot of red curls, gently laying it against her face and tying the ribbon behind her head.

"Wow," Janica breathed. "I thought you looked amazing before, but now you look . . ." Her words fell away, and Lily's heart raced with renewed panic.

"Like an old lady on Halloween?" Lily said, mocking herself.

Janica shook her head. "God no. Not at all. You look like royalty. Like a queen!"

The words were no sooner out of Janica's mouth than the stage manager grabbed her by the shoulder. "You're on in sixty seconds," he said, and Janica turned and ran to get her first model ready to walk.

I look like royalty? Like a queen? The words swam around in Lily's already muddled-by-bubbly brain. A part of her wanted to turn around and look in a mirror to see if her little sister was telling the truth, but the other bigger part of her that never ever shut up was scornful, like always.

More like queen-size, that part of her said.

On any other night, Lily would have believed the voice. Being beautiful was laughable. She had spent a lifetime with her shoulders hunched to hide her too-big breasts and her hair hanging over her face to hide blue eyes too bright and red lips too big. But suddenly, an unfamiliar feeling of boldness swept through her from the tips of her toes to the feathered mask on her made-up face.

Grabbing another glass of champagne off the tray of a passing waiter, she swallowed it in one gulp, letting the now-familiar warmth and easiness flow through her. Without giving herself another moment to doubt, she turned around to the full-length mirror behind her.

Lily gasped. The woman staring back at her was a stranger.

A beautiful, stunning, sexy stranger.

Her hands flew to her hair, which had been brushed and lacquered until her curls looked better than those in any hair commercial ever did, shiny and glowing as they cascaded past her shoulders. Behind the mask, her eyes shone like the blue of the Caribbean, and her lips looked full and kissable.

She looked just right. Not too big. Not too small. Curvy in all the right places, her large breasts and round hips nicely offset by her waist.

But even as she surveyed herself in the mirror, Lily knew that Janica's dress was responsible for the amazing change. She had always known that her sister was incredibly talented, but to see how Janica's dress had turned Lily from supersize to just right shocked her to the core.

One of the models in Janica's show stepped up behind Lily in the mirror, the model's long, ultrathin limbs showcased by the short, strapless dress she was wearing. "Wow, you look amazing," she said to Lily.

The words "thank you" popped out of Lily's mouth, and she bit her lip in surprise. When was the last time she had actually accepted a compliment?

More to the point, when was the last time she had actually *believed* a compliment?

The model walked away, and Janica called to Lily from several feet away. "You need to get in line behind Ellen."

Lily took a deep breath and a crazy thought popped into her head. What if she acted like a model while she was out on the runway? What if she decided to be supersexy for a few minutes in her life? Who would it hurt?

Maybe with some help from The Dress she could be invincible.

She had seen the rehearsals and knew that the original plus-sized model had planned on shimmying and swaying to the music as she made her way down the runway. Janica hadn't asked her to try it, knowing that Lily would have definitely said no.

The Dress would really shine if the audience saw how well it moved over the curves and valleys of a *real* woman's figure.

With only seconds to go before she walked out onto the runway, Lily made up her mind. She would do it.

For as long as she had The Dress on she would behave like a queen.

A sexy, take-no-prisoners queen.

And then when the night was over, she would go back to being the same old Lily she had always been, having had a taste of something dangerous and wild to savor for the rest of her life.

2

THE EMCEE ANNOUNCED, "Spring Collection by Janica Ellis," and Travis slid down deeper into his seat. He dreaded the moment when Lily would plod onto the runway, stuffed into a sheer, skin-baring outfit.

He could hardly believe that Lily had let her little sister bully her into taking part in a fashion show. Lily couldn't find her spine if it bit her in the butt, but saving Janica by modeling in a fashion show was pushing things *way* too far. Even for Lily.

Travis had often wondered how Lily and Janica could have possibly come from the same gene pool. Janica was the perfect opposite of Lily—a tiny little brunette with a big mouth and a sharp wit. She was Lily's fiercest protector, and definitely hated him.

Several models had already made it down the runway, and he was finally getting comfortable when the music fell away and a redhead appeared from behind the curtain, a sparkling mask of feathers and sequins covering the top of her face. Her plump, red lips caught the spotlight. The lights changed from wild greens and blues to a deep, warm red, coating the woman in a sexy haze. Rich melodies from a Spanish guitar and a lilting tenor, promised sex to everyone in the audience.

Hot, slick, pounding sex.

The woman hadn't even moved yet, had made no effort to slink down the runway to showcase her outfit, and yet chatter fell away in a hush. The front of Travis's jeans grew tight, and every nerve came to life as he waited for her to slink down the runway.

She didn't disappoint. The mesh Asian print fabric molded lovingly to her every curve as she made her arousing progression down the catwalk. Her hips swayed side to side, one red-tipped, jeweled hand finding its way past her waist, stopping at the curve of her breasts, while the other caressed the curve of her hip.

Travis was leaning forward in his chair, all of his practiced ease gone. He needed to have this woman. It didn't matter that she was the polar opposite of every woman he had ever been with. Where he craved bones and angled lines, she was lush curves and soft promise. He had thought that small and blond was perfection, but the red-haired, full-bodied goddess consumed him with wanting.

The flamenco guitar grew more and more frantic the closer the beautiful model got to the end of the catwalk. In perfect time to the passionate music, the model began an exotic dance, throwing her head back in delighted laughter. Travis waited for her unveiling, holding his breath for the second time that evening.

The woman stopped dancing and reached for her feathered mask. She brought her tongue out to taste her lips, and a low sound came from deep in Travis's throat.

She threw the mask to the floor, and the applause was fero-cious. She was even more magnificent than she had been be-neath her disguise.

Travis stopped clapping, unable to trust what he saw.

Lily Ellis, his twin brother's meek best friend, was staring him straight in the eye.

And even though he tried to deny it with every fiber of his being, he wanted her.

THE FASHION SHOW ENDED, and the party began. The music kicked up another notch, and with the chairs put away every-one was moving and dancing. Maybe it was the champagne, maybe it was the daring outfit that made her feel so powerful, so hungry, so restless. For the first time in thirty years, Lily felt in control and ready for action.

As long as she had The Dress on, she could do all of the things she had always wanted to do but had always been too afraid to do.

Travis was out there in the audience. As soon as she stepped onto the runway and looked four rows back to the right, she had known that it was Travis. She had always been able to tell him and Luke apart, even if nobody else could. They were both tall and lean and muscular. They both had thick black hair that fell over their eyes. But Travis made Lily sizzle. Whereas Luke only made her feel warm.

Lily wished she could have fallen in love with Luke. He was so gentle and kind. Knowing that her attraction to Travis was futile from the first stirrings of arousal she'd felt for him, Lily had made a concerted effort to see Luke as sexy, boyfriend ma-terial. But it was impossible. She cringed remembering the kiss she'd given Luke in high school, late one night when they were talking under the huge apple tree in her grandmother's front yard. He had been still as a stone, but then, not wanting to hurt her feelings, he had kissed her back.

Luke's kiss was perfectly pleasant, but the awful truth was she hadn't felt anything. No tingles. No shivering with need in his arms. It was yet another thing she couldn't do right. She wasn't even smart enough to fall for the brother who was nice to her. Instead, she had harbored an insane lust for someone who would never return her feelings in a million years. Not unless one day she woke up as a size-two supermodel.

Lily cursed herself up and down for being stupid enough to keep holding out hope that the nice Travis would come back. That the fun-loving boy she had been friends with as a child would one day reemerge from within the cold, distant man he had become.

Her heart raced in her chest, and Lily was more than a little shocked about what she was about to do. She didn't know why Travis had come to the fashion show instead of Luke. On any other night she would have been furious with Luke for doing the twin-switcharoo on her.

But this wasn't any other night. Tonight was special. And even though it was crazy, even though she might as well take a knife and drive it into her heart to save herself time, Lily thanked God that Luke had sent his sexy-as-sin twin brother.

She had wasted thirty years waiting for him to notice her. She wasn't about to waste another second. Not when she and The Dress had plans for him. Big plans that made her heart beat triple time and the vee between her legs pulse with need.

The Dress was going to make Travis want her.

It had to.

A sudden surge of doubt overwhelmed her as she reached out to part the thick red velvet curtain. She couldn't ignore the mighty chance that Travis would take one look at her and laugh. Or worse, turn away as if she were invisible. It was more than a chance, she thought with dismay. A professional gambler would have to be crazy to bet on Lily, not when Travis could have his pick of any skinny, perfect woman in the room.

She closed her eyes and moistened her lips. *No,* she told herself, *you're not going to give in to these fears. It's either now or never. Are you going to take the chance? Or are you going to continue to be a wimp for another thirty years?*

That did it. Pushing past the curtains, Lily stepped out onto the dance floor, her eyes trained on what she wanted. Travis stood surrounded by women, each one more gorgeous than the next, all vying desperately to get his attention.

But she knew he was waiting for her.

At least she hoped he was.

On the runway, instead of making her want to dive for cover, Travis's presence had emboldened her. Lily had reached deep inside herself to bring forth the sensual woman she had kept so well hidden.

Finally, she was going to show Travis what he had been turning his back on for so long, what he had been missing.

Pleasure.

Lily knew that most people saw her as mousy and timid. She rarely offered her opinion, and people were always cutting in front of her in line at the movies. It had hurt at first, but once she got used to being overlooked, it almost became a comfort. Lily could always disappear into the background, and she used her invisibility like a suit of armor to protect herself.

So the one thing that no one would have ever guessed in a million years, the secret that she had never shared with anyone else, was how much she liked to touch herself.

And how good it felt.

On cold nights Lily's favorite thing was to lock herself in the bathroom with a hot tub of water and her waterproof vibrator. Lying in the warm rose-scented water, she invented elaborate scenes in her head, all of which featured Travis in the starring role.

She often relived her first orgasm, at fourteen, which happened the night after her first high school football game. She had pretended to be watching the game, but all night her eyes never left Travis, who was hanging out with the tough crowd. Every time his fingers brushed across the shoulders of the cheerleader he was with, a shiver shot up Lily's spine. Halfway through the game he disappeared behind the bleachers, the cheerleader in tow. Quietly, Lily slipped away from the crowd. Standing in the shadows, she watched Travis fondle and kiss the girl, finally bringing her to orgasm with his mouth. A warm rush had settled between Lily's legs, and her fingers had found her breasts, sensitive from the slightest brush of her fingers across them.

Since that night, whenever she masturbated, Lily dreamed that Travis's tongue slid across her nipples, drawing circles across her skin. She would slide her fingers between her slick folds, sometimes slipping one finger into her tight canal, all the while picturing Travis's large fingers touching her, caressing her. When she couldn't take it anymore, she would pick up her vibrator and turn it on low, barely pressing the tip of it against the top of her mons. Again and again she would bring herself to the edge, pulling the whirling machine away, gasping for air in the cooling water of the bathtub. Finally, she would switch the machine to high and press it hard against herself as waves and waves of spasms rocked her, Travis's name on her lips.

By the time she had dried off and gotten back into one of her big tent dresses, no one could have ever guessed what she had done to herself in the bathtub. No one could have known how hot she got, how naughty her fantasies were.

Lily could never look beyond her lust for Travis to see herself in love with another man. But even though she wasn't looking for love, she wasn't opposed to having a lover. After exploring all the different and better ways to bring herself to orgasm, she had been overwhelmed with the need to feel a cock deep within her. Yes, she wanted it to belong to Travis—oh how desperately she wanted that—but ever the realist she recognized that she would have to take what she could get. Over the past decade she had shared a bed with several men, and while the experience of a thick penis pumping into her was nice, while the feel of a tongue lapping at her clit was pleasant, none of the men she had dated and slept with had ever taken her to the thrilling place she dreamed of.

No one would ever know how much she wanted Travis to be her lover, the one man she could never have because he had decided she wasn't there anymore one day in fifth grade.

But in The Dress, everything had shifted. Lily felt as if she were in the bathtub, her cunt wet and plump and ready for Travis's cock to slide into it. Ready for him to show her what it truly meant to be a woman.

Lily moved toward him, holding his gaze, forcing herself to walk slowly, to push back the sensual anticipation that caused her nipples to grow taut, that caused the heavy and full feeling between her legs.

What if he doesn't want me?

Lily shelved her persistent doubts. He would want her, she decided, as a wave of arousal edged up her spine. No matter what she had to do, no matter who she had to be, she was going to claim Travis that night.

Travis's eyes marked her as his, and only his. For once, they understood each other as a man and a woman. And then she was standing just inches from him, her full breasts pressed up against his T-shirt, his heat burning through her.

Twenty years of hurt fell away. The only thing that mattered to Lily was the lust coursing through her veins.

Needing desperately to touch him, Lily's hand caressed his hard jaw, memorizing the lines of his face, before moving up to run her thumb along his lower lip. His tongue found the sensitive pad of her thumb, and she stilled, unable to do or focus on anything other than the sensation of his tongue on her skin. She was slick and already as close to an orgasm as she had ever been. His hand was on hers, callused and strong and warm, and he was pressing a hot kiss into the pulse at her wrist.

His lips moved away, and her skin felt cool and bereft. His face came down toward her and she could feel the warmth of his breath on her lips.

"Travis," she whispered, and she felt his surprise.

His lips tightened, and a swift strike of fear passed through her that he would leave her high and dry and desperate for him.

"You know who I am?"

"I've always known," she said boldly. "And now it's your turn to find out who I am."

She slid her hand along his taut, well-muscled arm, reveling in the feel of the light dusting of hair against the tips of her fingers. Every inch of her skin was on fire as she wrapped her fingers around his.

Travis read her mind, and before she could lead him to the dance floor, he was moving them toward it. She loved the way the other women in the room looked at her. She knew the look of jealousy too well. She knew how it felt to watch someone else press close to Travis. She had been watching girls throw themselves at Travis since first grade.

At last it was her turn. *Wouldn't it be heavenly,* she thought, *if he threw himself right back at her?*

It would be a dream come true.

Lily breathed in the faint scent of his cologne. She could drown in him. The crowd of dancers parted for them. Lily was shocked to realize that Travis wasn't the only one getting admiring glances.

Straight out of her fantasies, it seemed that all of the men in the room were looking at her with desire radiating from their eyes. In one of her favorite fantasies she was in charge of a group of prisoners—the naughtiest one, of course, being Travis. She would whip them into sexual frenzies, not letting them touch her until they were about to explode with wanting her. The other men could lick her and stroke her, but only Travis could thrust into her with his huge, hard shaft.

In The Dress, maybe all of her dreams would come true. Especially the part where Travis braced his heavy weight over her and slid into her wetness, hot and relentless.

Lily had to resist pinching herself to see if she would wake up as she moved in Travis's arms, to see if it really was just a dream. *No,* she thought, *if it is a dream, I don't want to know.*

Travis stopped in the middle of the dance floor and pulled her into his arms. One of his hands slid to the curve of her hips while the other was alarmingly close to her breasts.

"Lily," he said.

She looked up at him, her blue eyes bright with longing. "Travis," she whispered, then ran the tip of her tongue along the edge of her upper lip.

He groaned and started to lean down for what Lily hoped was a kiss, the first of many if she had her way. Her eyelids fluttered closed, but then she felt Travis pull back ever so slightly. Her eyes flew open.

"Lily," he said, "I . . ."

Bolder than she ever thought she could be, Lily laid a finger on his perfect lips. "Don't speak," she said. It was a command, not a request. "Tonight is not for talking."

Relief flashed across Travis's face, but Lily didn't care. The last thing she wanted was for their time to be ruined with apologies and second-guessing. She didn't forgive him for the way he had treated her for the past twenty years, but at that moment, warm and aroused in his arms, none of it mattered.

All she cared about was kissing Travis and licking Travis and, oh God, hopefully coming beneath Travis, too.

His mouth was on hers and his hands were in her hair and he was stealing all the breath from her lungs. Lily wanted to memorize this kiss so that she could play it back to herself in her lonely bathtub on cold nights, but she was so stunned by the sensations washing through her that her brain was on the verge of shutting off completely.

First hard, then unbearably soft, his lips ruled hers, coaxing a whimper of ecstasy from her core. Lily had been kissed before but not like this. Not by someone who could teach a course on the art of kissing.

Travis plunged his tongue ruthlessly into her mouth, letting her know in no uncertain terms that he was going to be in charge of their lovemaking, that he was going to take her over completely. He ravaged every last corner and crevice of her mouth with his own, and in the exact moment that she gave in to him, he changed the tenor of his kiss.

Instead of showing her who was boss, Travis backed off, slowed down. Lily reveled in how he took the time to learn her taste, to study the ultrasensitive plump center of her lower lip, to find out how much her tongue loved to mate with his.

One of his hands began to roam, first gently kneading her

shoulders, then the small of her back, sending goose bumps everywhere, centering at the tight tips of her breasts. Lily could hardly concentrate on anything but Travis's kiss, but still she cried out, silently, for him to touch her breasts.

So what if they were in the middle of a crowded dance floor? If Travis didn't squeeze her breasts right then, right there, she would die with wanting it.

His hands moved around her waist to the bottom edge of her rib cage. Lily shook with need. She had never been so turned on in all her life. Her thong was soaked with her juices.

The pad of his thumb ran across her aching nipple, and she cried out into his mouth. Before she could clamp down on it, the first haze of an orgasm shuddered through her as she danced in his arms.

Travis, amazingly, seemed to know that she was coming even before she did. So subtly that no one but the two of them would ever know what was happening, he pressed one of his hard thighs between her legs. Using his hand on her bottom for leverage, he pumped her mons with his muscles, pushing her clit into his thigh in the perfect rhythm to send Lily all the way over the edge.

His kiss was possessive and so hot she felt scalded by it. She cried out in his mouth as the first waves began from the tips of her breasts and worked down her abdomen to her pussy. Travis swallowed her scream, and his fingers tightened on her nipple.

In her haze she felt the huge evidence of his arousal pressing against her stomach, but she was trying so hard to breathe, to stay on her feet, that she barely spared it more than a passing thought of *later*.

Lily's orgasms had always been powerful. They were one thing about herself that she truly, unabashedly loved. But this explosion was more than she had ever experienced with her vibrator or her previous lovers. Being with Travis was even more thrilling than she had imagined it to be. And yet, a little voice in her brain asked, wasn't that why she had been holding out hope on Travis for so long? Because deep within she knew that coming together with him would be this explosive?

She forced her crazy theories away to focus on the here and now, in Travis's arms. The mere thought of Travis's thigh rubbing up and down against her made even more blood flow between her legs. She wondered if one could have a heart attack from lack of blood to anywhere but the clit. What would she say in the emergency room?

Doctor, I was coming so hard against the thigh of my dream guy that my heart stopped for a moment.

Lily clung to Travis as he held her upright and ground his thigh into her throbbing pussy. She felt limp and useless as her orgasm came to its end, but Travis didn't remove his thigh from between her legs. Like a sleepy cat she continued to rub herself against him, only waking up when he whispered, "Let's get out of here," in her ear. He grabbed her hand, pulling her through the throngs of people and out onto the street.

They got in a cab and his mouth was on hers again as he pulled her onto his lap. The sensible part of her, which had miraculously not been permanently put to sleep yet, made her pull back, and say, "Travis, the cab driver."

Chuckling softly, Travis slid her slightly off his lap and nuzzled her neck. "Thank God it's a short ride to my loft," he said.

Lily barely sucked in her gasp of surprise. His loft? Lily had never seen his loft. Except in magazines, that is. And from what Luke had told her over the years, Travis rarely, if ever, took women home.

Her eyes ran over his tall frame, so perfectly set off by his white T-shirt and faded jeans. She saw the wet patch on his thigh, and the gasp finally escaped.

Travis's eyes followed hers. Lily cursed herself for dropping her worldly veneer. She wanted him to think that she left marks like that on all the men she came against while out dancing, but even then, even amid the red haze of their sensual connection, she knew it was ridiculous.

Outside, in the evening light that streamed in the windows, she felt the familiar pangs of self-consciousness. She was afraid to let Travis look at her. They weren't kids anymore, and she needed to face facts: The Travis who liked her wasn't ever coming back. Though he'd made her come like a bomb, that didn't alter the fact that he always acted like she wasn't there, like she wasn't the least bit important. She knew that he had no respect for her whatsoever and, now that they had left the magic of the fashion show behind, she was certain he would realize what a huge mistake he was making. She wished she were strong enough to protect herself against him. She wished she was tough enough to say, "Thanks for the orgasm, Travis, but I've got to get home now."

But, of course, she could never say something like that. Instead, she held her breath as she waited for him to tell the cab driver to stop the car to pull over and dump her out.

She looked into the green of his eyes and tried to think of something to say that would get him off the hook, so he would know she didn't expect him to follow through with his teasing and actually sleep with her—something like "Don't worry, Travis, I won't mention this to anyone, so no one will ever know that we were together"—but nothing came.

But instead of running as fast as he could away from her, Travis gave Lily a hot look and ran his thumb from her neck down to the top of her breasts.

"You are very wet," he said in a low voice.

Lily nodded, unable to do anything else but agree with him. Would he think she was disgusting for getting so soaked from his kiss on the dance floor? One of his hands ran beneath the fold of her skirt along her bare leg, and Lily was amazed to find out that her fears were unfounded. Flicking a glance to the front seat, she whispered, "The driver," again, but the truth was he could have ripped off her dress and taken her right then and there in the backseat of a moving cab, and she wouldn't have so much as made a whimper of protest.

But before any of that could happen, the vehicle stopped. Travis threw some money at the driver. Once again her fingers were wrapped in his, and Lily marveled at how good it felt to have Travis hold her hand.

She remembered how in first grade, Travis was her cross-the-street buddy. He had looked out for her, holding her back on the curb if she stepped out when a car was coming at them too fast. She had never forgotten how safe he had made her feel.

Breathless, she followed him as he opened the large steel front door to the loft and pulled her inside. Closing the door gently, he turned and pinned her against the door with the weight of his gaze.

Before she knew what he intended, Travis dropped to his knees.

"Travis?" she said, the question more breath than solid word.

"Shh," he commanded as he lifted the hem of her skirt, pushing it up past her knees, past her thighs, to her waist.

Her small black purse dropped from her fingers to the floor and she held her breath as he gazed at her. She was nearly naked from the waist down, clad in only a sheer silk thong. He drew one finger up the inside of her knee, and Lily's breath blew out in a hiss. Every inch of skin he touched felt inflamed. His finger slid against the wetness on her thigh and Lily's legs began to shake so hard that she wondered how she could possibly stay on her feet.

Straight from her fantasies to real life, a warm tongue lapped against her thigh. Lily forced herself to still her shaking legs. God forbid she collapse on the man who was about to make her deepest, most wonderful, dreams come true.

Hot breath blew against her silk-covered mound, and Lily moaned as she threaded her hands into Travis's thick black hair.

"Please," she begged, unable to keep the word from spilling out of her lips.

Wordlessly, Travis obeyed her plea, cupping her soaking-wet silken mound. She felt his teeth on her clit and cried out, pressing her hips against his mouth.

Lily wanted to come against every single part of Travis before the night was through. His thigh, his mouth, his hand, his cock.

Especially his cock.

He slipped a finger beneath her thong and Lily reared into it. "Oh God," she moaned as she leaned into his mouth, leaned into his finger as it circled the base of her vagina.

His finger slid into her, penetrating her, and the tremors began in earnest. "Travis," she cried, holding tightly to the back of his head. She moved her hips up and down on his finger, taking in one inch, then another.

"More," she demanded in a thick haze of desire.

Travis was ready to do her bidding, but he had to, of course, do it his way. Midorgasm he pulled his finger from inside her and backed his mouth off her mons.

"No," she cried, desperate for more of him. But she should have known that he knew exactly what he was doing. In less than a heartbeat he had ripped the small patch of silk from her and begun to suck her clit in earnest.

His warm lips and tongue sucked and pulled at her as he rammed one long finger all the way in, sliding and pumping it in time to her ongoing explosions. She was delirious with pleasure.

He licked her pussy with long strokes that only inflamed her further. Somehow he knew that she didn't want him to lightly flick her clit, she didn't want him to be measured.

The last of the tremors subsided, and Lily slowly realized that she had been grinding her pussy lips into Travis's mouth.

Travis!

Suddenly it was all too much for her. Unable to process any more of her fantasies turning into reality, Lily did the only thing she could do.

She passed out.

The next thing she knew, she was lying on a bed, cool sheets beneath her overheated skin. She felt far too tired to ever open her eyes again, but even with her eyes closed Lily noticed how tender her skin was. The fine, tightly woven fabric against her back practically hurt as she shifted.

Groggy, she wondered why she was sleeping without a sheet to cover her nakedness. She always slept in the nude, but never completely on parade for anyone who might surprise her by walking into her bedroom. Janica and Luke both had keys to her apartment, and she would be mortified if they ever saw her naked.

Lazily, she slid her fingers to her breasts. They felt full and heavy. She sank back into the best dream she had ever had. In it, she was on a dance floor with Travis, and he was kissing her.

The fantasy kiss was so real, so hot. She ran one hand down from her breasts to between her legs and stroked herself. She didn't want to rouse herself to get her vibrator from the bedside table. She wanted to keep dreaming about Travis kissing her while she slowly rubbed her clit.

Her fingers slipped and slid between her folds. Lily drowsily smiled at how wet she already was from a dream. Travis had always been able to do that to her, she mused.

She felt his name upon her lips and knew that as she came she would say it and it would be almost as if he were there with her. She spread her legs and opened her thighs, plunging her fingers in an out of her slippery cunt, bucking into her hands.

"Travis!"

The orgasm was short but oh so sweet. Her hands fell to the bed, and she stretched her sated body all the way from her head to her toes.

And then she opened up her eyes and nearly fainted again from shock.

3

TRAVIS DIDN'T KNOW what had consumed him. All he knew was that from the moment Lily had stepped out on the runway in that dress, he had been unable to think of anything but getting her into bed.

And now, as crazy as it seemed, he wanted nothing more than to plunge into her pink wetness. Travis couldn't have asked for anything more arousing than watching her writhe on his bed while she made herself come, her thighs spread, her finger wet as it slid in and out of her incredibly tight cunt.

Travis watched her stretch and admired her curves, curves that he had always thought were too big. He grew another impossible inch behind the zipper of his jeans as Lily opened her eyes.

"Feel better now?" he asked.

Lily's big blue eyes were wide with shock, as if she hadn't known that he was sitting inches away on the edge of his bed watching her finger herself. She tried to cover her breasts and the thatch of red hair between her legs with her hands.

He grinned at what a good actress she was. "I don't think you're going to be able to hide those from me," he said, looking at her breasts, the plump flesh spilling over her forearms.

"Travis, I didn't know . . ." she said, but he leaned over and silenced her with a kiss.

"Enough games," he said. "You've got me so hard I'm about to blow in my pants."

Lily's eyes grew even wider as she lay beneath him. "It wasn't a dream?" she said, her words barely louder than a whisper.

Travis grinned. She was good at pretending innocence. Really good. "It's a dream if you want it to be," he said, bending his head down to her breasts. "I'm going to suck on these for a while," he added, "so feel free to come again if you need to."

Lily gasped as he grazed her hard nipple with his teeth. He used both of his hands beneath her breasts to push them together, sucking first one nipple, then the other, then both.

"Take me, Travis," she said, and he lifted his head.

Just hearing those words come out of her mouth made his cock nearly explode. Lightning fast, he ripped off his jeans, boxer shorts, and his T-shirt.

He followed Lily's eyes to his penis.

"You like?" he asked, knowing what her answer would be but wanting to hear it anyway.

She reached for him. "It's huge," she said, "even bigger than I thought it would be."

A thick spurt of precome emerged from his engorged cock. Travis pushed her hand away. She reached for him again, and he said, "If you touch me, I'll blow."

She shook her head. "No. I want to feel you inside of me. Like that. That big."

Travis quickly sheathed himself in a condom and positioned himself atop Lily on his bed. He had never had sex with a woman on his bed before, but if it was always this hot, he was definitely going to have to rethink his have-sex-at-their-house rule.

Lily was soft and warm beneath him. Her smell, vanilla mixed with sex, was both comforting and exciting.

Travis propped himself up again and settled the tip of his shaft between her legs. He slid his head into her wet heat and had to pull out immediately. He hadn't come so close to premature ejaculation since he was sixteen in the backseat of his souped-up Chevy with the head cheerleader.

But then Lily pressed her hips to his, and he did what he had wanted to do since the moment she walked out onstage: He plunged all the way into her.

"Oh God, Travis, don't stop," she said as she flexed her inner muscles against the length of him.

Even if he wanted to stop, he couldn't have. She was too hot, too wet. He could taste her on his lips, feel her wetness still on his thigh. The only choice he had was to explode in her willing cunt.

Leaning down until her full breasts rubbed against his chest, Travis moved in and out of her in long, intense strokes. Lily watched him, her eyes a deep, dark blue, her plump lower lip between her teeth; then her eyes fluttered closed.

He marveled at how responsive she was. She was eating him up and begging for more. Well, he thought with a groan, she had come to the right place.

It took every ounce of will to hold himself back so that Lily came again before he lost it. He dripped with sweat, causing them to slip and slide against each other. Her nipples raked across his chest. Her hands slid on the hard planes of his shoulders, his narrow hips, then back up to the back of his head.

Her moans merged with his, and her cunt squeezed him.

All thoughts of control gone, he plunged in and out of her, a rabid beast with only one thought: to claim the woman beneath him.

Travis exploded into an orgasm so big that pins and needles surged through his limbs. From within a deep fog, he thought he heard Lily cry, "Travis," but all he wanted was to keep coming like this forever.

He took her lips roughly, sure that he was hurting her with his savagery but unable to do anything else. Lily took as good as he gave, thrusting her hips into his so hard that there would be bruises.

At last Travis fell against her, his heart beating an out-of-control staccato. Holding her in his arms, still nestled between her legs, he rolled over to one side. Incredibly well sated, Travis fell asleep.

BEING WITH TRAVIS had been so much better than any of her dreams. Lying in the crook of his arms as he breathed deep and even, Lily was tempted to let herself fall asleep with him. In his bed. In his loft.

In a perfect world he would wake her up, kissing her all over, until he slipped his huge shaft between her legs again and made love to her with agonizing slowness.

But Lily knew the time for dreaming was over. All of her dreams had already come true. She was going to have to be happy with her memories of Travis's mouth on hers, of his hands on her breasts, of his penis hard and perfect inside her.

Come morning light, if he woke up with her beside him, he would see the real her.

The Lily who had cellulite.

The Lily who was a size sixteen on a good non-PMS-bloat day.

If he had ignored her before, he was going to darn near erase her after he woke up.

With a minimum of movements, she slid out from beneath his arm. He reached for her, and she stilled. He smiled in his sleep, and Lily's heart broke from simply witnessing his incredible male beauty.

She was going to have to be happy with one incredible night in the arms of a god. Especially since it was more, far more, than she had ever hoped to experience.

Sliding off the bed, she reached for The Dress, that miraculous swatch of fabric that had enabled her most impossible dream to come true, and tiptoed out of Travis's bedroom. She took one last look around the loft, at Travis's perfect tanned limbs on the twisted white sheet. She wanted to commit all of the details to memory.

With a quiet sigh, she turned around and put her dress back on. Not bothering to look in the mirror to fix her hair and makeup, she picked up her shoes and purse from beside the door and walked outside into the cold night air to catch a cab.

Too soon she was back in Noe Valley, letting herself into her tiny rental house. She should have showered, but she didn't want to wash away any part of her evening with Travis. Stripping off The Dress, she reverently laid it on the back of the sofa chair in the corner of her bedroom and crawled under the covers, wishing that Travis's warmth was pressed against her instead of her ratty old teddy bear, JuJuBee.

"HEY, LILY!" Luke got up out of their usual booth at the Fog City Diner and gave her a warm hug. "You look great," he said, holding her at arm's length, taking in her flushed cheeks and the "I've-had-great-sex" glow that infused her very soul.

"Thanks," she said with a blush as she slid into the booth and picked up the menu. She was dreading the moment when Luke would ask her about Travis. She had nearly canceled their weekly Sunday brunch in a fit of wussiness.

Luke studied her closely. "Did you get a new haircut?"

Lily shook her head and read *Bacon Cheeseburger with blue cheese* again and again until the words swam in her head.

"Different makeup?"

"The same old me as always," she insisted as she closed her menu.

"I've got it," he said, pleased as punch with himself for figuring it out.

Lily smiled at her best friend, even as nerves fluttered wildly in her belly. She did her best to project a calm and unworried aura.

"You got laid," he said, his eyes twinkling. "And based on that glow you're wearing, he must have really been something this time."

Alarm flashed in Lily's eyes too quickly for her to tamp down on it. She had never been wary of discussing her sex life with Luke before, but the situation was so awkward this time that she didn't know quite how to roll with it.

"Do you think you could say that any louder?" she asked, looking around the full restaurant.

Luke raised his ice tea in a toast. "Do you want me to?" he teased.

"God no. I was kidding." Maybe if she changed the subject really fast, he'd forget all about it. "Did I tell you what Mr. Slimy Boss said to me last week?"

"So, who was it?" Luke asked, his mind alarmingly single track.

Lily tried another tack. "I'm mad at you," she lied.

Luke sat back into the plush leather booth, knowing exactly

what she was talking about. "I'm really sorry Lily. I got called into the ER right after we got off the phone. I didn't know what else to do. Was Travis a class-A jerk?"

She fought back the blush that threatened to overtake her again. "No," she said, "not really. He was actually pretty, um . . ." Lily searched desperately for the right word. "Nice."

"Nice?" Luke raised an eyebrow. "That doesn't sound like my twin. Not at all."

Oops, Lily thought silently. She should have said he was a jerk. But last night he had been so far from a jerk, he had done such wonderful things to her, that she couldn't blaspheme him like that.

Lily kept her expression bland. "You know him. He had all of the models swarming around like flies."

"Uh-huh. And what did he do to you?"

Lily swallowed, but her mouth had gone completely dry. She downed half of her ice tea in one gulp. She slammed the glass down a little too hard on the retro fifties Formica tabletop.

"Oh you know, the usual," she said, but it was hard to lie convincingly as she was faced with vision of Travis's hard, slick body above hers, his tongue in her mouth, his cock so deep within her.

"I'll kill him," Luke said.

Lily gasped with alarm. "No really, Luke, he was fine."

Luke didn't look happy, but thankfully, he let it go. "So," he said, leaning over conspiratorially, "tell me about your new lover boy."

Lily couldn't stop the smile that stole across her face. "Nothing much to tell," she said, trying for nonchalance. "Just a one-night stand."

"You? A one-night stand?" Luke said, clearly incredulous. "That's a first, isn't it?"

It was unreasonable, but Lily felt slightly insulted by that. "Oh, I see. I'm the have a dozen kids, bake a zillion chocolate chip cookies for PTA meetings, drive a minivan to soccer practices type, aren't I?"

Luke's eyes widened, and he backed off the table a couple of inches. "I didn't mean anything by it, Lily."

She immediately felt guilty for laying into him. Luke had to be shocked by her strange behavior.

"Sorry about that. I didn't mean to snap at you. I guess I'm a little tired from the late night. Can we talk about something else?" Lily pleaded.

Besides, if Luke ever found out about her and Travis, she wasn't sure whom he'd kill first—her or Travis. Unfortunately, Luke's sixth sense that something was irrevocably changed about Lily was too strong for him to ignore, and he was like a dog on a hunt for a bone.

"Okay, I'll stop bugging you. But only if you tell me the guy's name. Just in case I know him. That way I can see if you need to make it a two-night stand or if he's a loser, and I need to get rid of the guy for you."

Lily flushed a thousand shades of red as she desperately tried to come up with a name. "Um, it was, um . . ."

Luke looked shocked and not a little concerned. "You don't even know the guy's name? What happened to you last night?"

"Tony," she blurted out. "His name was Tony."

Luke stared at Lily with the oddest look on his face. Any second he was going to see through her lie.

Five, four, three, two . . .

"Oh no," Luke said. Lily's heart sank to the shiny black-and-white checkerboard floor. His voice dropped low and scary. "You slept with Travis."

Lily looked up at her best friend, caught just like he had

caught her passing her test answers to Melanie Frost in sixth grade in a bid to be accepted by the popular girls. Bright stains of pink on her cheeks, she tried to shake her head in denial, but she couldn't pull it off. She nodded and waited for the fireworks.

"How could that have—" Luke began but broke off when he clearly realized how it might sound to Lily.

"What?" Defensive was so much better than guilty. "You don't think I'm pretty enough for Travis to want to sleep with me?"

"Lils, you know I think you're beautiful. Too beautiful for my brother, in fact." Back on the offensive, Luke said, "How could he? How could you?"

Lily bit her lip. "It just happened."

"Don't lie to me, Lils. Look," he said, reaching for her hand across the table, his eyes gentle, "I know you've had a crush on him for a long time."

Lily snatched her hand back as if Luke had burned her. "Shut up," she hissed.

Going on as if she hadn't spoken, Luke said, "But you know how he is. He's never going to settle down with one woman. Ever since our mom died . . ." He let his words drift away and looked her in the eye. "I don't want to see you get hurt. You deserve better than Travis. But now that you've gone and had sex with him, we'd better figure out what we're going to do about it."

"Nothing," she snapped. "We're going to do nothing. I had fun, and I never thought for one second that he would want to date me or be my boyfriend or anything. It was a crazy, one-night, fluke. So don't make such a big deal out of it, okay?"

Luke looked stunned by her monologue. Lily knew she wasn't usually so forward, but maybe something inside of her had really changed. Maybe it was something bigger than The Dress.

Unexpectedly, Luke changed tacks. "I've got an idea," he said.

Lily groaned. "I don't think I want to hear it."

Her best friend smiled. "I think you do, Lils. It's time to beat Travis at his own game. And now I can see that you're exactly the one who can pull it off. He'll never see it coming."

Curiosity might have killed the cat, but Lily couldn't help herself from asking, "How?"

As their bacon and eggs were delivered, Luke talked while Lily listened with a laserlike focus to his advice, committing everything he said to memory.

TRAVIS HAD BEEN on the basketball court for thirty minutes by the time Luke showed up. He hadn't been able to think straight all day, and the only thing he could come up with to fix it was hard physical exertion.

Too bad it wasn't working. All he could think about was Lily.

How good she had tasted.

How kissing her had stolen the ground from beneath his feet.

When he woke up and realized she was gone, he was angry. Angry with her for leaving before he could take her again. Angrier at himself for caring.

Travis was always the one to leave, never the woman, who was always begging him to come back. He couldn't believe he had actually considered getting on his motorcycle and riding to her house. He didn't chase women.

And he certainly wasn't going to chase Lily.

All of a sudden Travis was back in fifth grade, trying to make it through another day. His mom was dead, and the world had gone from yellow and blue and green to black. *I don't care,* he had told himself, over and over, which seemed to work. Except around Lily. Those blue eyes of hers saw right through him, and it killed him. The more uncomfortable she made him, the more he closed himself off from her. He needed her to leave him alone before he did something childish like cry. No one, not even his brother, was ever going to find out how much he had cried alone at night. Lily's mom had died, too. Travis knew that, but it didn't mean he had to be friends with her anymore. It didn't mean he had to accept her comfort.

Comforting was for babies.

Travis emerged from his memories as a picture of Lily naked flashed before him. *Forget her,* he told himself. Sleeping with Lily had been a humongous, idiotic lapse of judgment on his part. He hated how uncomfortable he'd been in his own skin since he'd been with her. He needed to get back on his usual in-control even keel.

The more he tried to erase her from his mind, the harder he played. By the time Luke joined him on the court, Travis was soaked with sweat, and his legs felt like jelly. Without a word, Luke grabbed the ball from him and started the meanest game of one-on-one they had ever played.

No shove was too hard, no foul was too big. It was every man for himself on the court. In the back of his mind, Travis wondered if Luke knew about Lily. Was he trying to make Travis pay for it? But Travis was glad for the distraction of gasping for breath and getting his limbs to obey him, because it meant he didn't have time to think about *her.*

Luke sank the final basket, thirty to twenty-nine, and headed straight for the showers. Travis picked up the ball and stripped off his dripping T-shirt. A woman on the treadmill on the way to the locker room licked her lips, and said, "You have the most amazing six-pack I've ever seen."

But Travis couldn't have cared less what the woman thought about his abs. Without sparing her a glance, he pushed through the thick locker room door. Stripping off his shorts and shoes, he stood next to Luke in the communal shower stall.

"What's your problem today?" Travis asked.

Luke shrugged. "Nothing. Just whupping your ass like I promised." Silence fell between them. "So, you screw any hot babes last night?"

Travis couldn't miss the venom dripping from Luke's verbal blade. He knew he had to step very carefully or he was likely to get his skull cracked on the tile of the locker room. "Why do you ask?"

Luke pinned him with a glance that let Travis know he was being laughed at. "I had brunch with Lily this morning at Fog City."

Travis tried to look like he didn't care. "So?"

Luke washed away the rest of the soap and turned off the faucet. Reaching for a towel, he said, "Looks like her debut as a model turned out pretty good."

Travis put his face under the faucet so that Luke couldn't see his expression. What would he normally say to Luke about Lily? Travis tried to get his muddled mind in gear as he turned off the water and reached for a towel.

"She didn't fall down or anything, if that's what you're talking about."

Instead of looking like he was going to punch Travis, Luke looked suspiciously like he was trying to hold back laughter. "That's for sure," Luke said. "Turns out Lily went home with some guy in the audience."

Travis dragged a clean T-shirt over his head. He couldn't tell yet if Luke knew it was him or not. He wanted to inquire without coming right out and asking, but he couldn't think of anything better than, "Anyone we know?"

Luke shrugged. "She didn't have much to say about him."

Travis spun around. "Some guy took Lily to his place for sex, and she didn't have much to say about him?"

"She didn't mention going to his place," Luke observed, with a raised eyebrow.

Covering his mistake, Travis said, "Whatever. His place. Her place. She didn't say *anything* to you about it?"

"Well, since you're so curious about Lily's sex life, I guess I can tell you that she didn't seem that impressed with the guy."

"What?" Travis exploded. If he continued to behave like such a moron, he was going to give himself away. As nonchalantly as possible he turned to pack up his gym bag. "Why not?"

Luke snorted. "She says the guy thought he was God's gift to women, but"—he gave Travis a cocky half grin and lowered his voice—"she said the guy wouldn't be able to find a clit if a million bucks rested on it."

A growl rose up from Travis's throat. "I'll bet she's lying."

"I doubt it," Luke said. He slung his duffel bag over his shoulder. "She told me all about how she had to fake it three times before she finished herself off. The guy sounds like a major loser."

Travis wanted to slam his fist into the wall. Had Lily faked her orgasms with him? No way.

She couldn't have faked her explosion against his thigh. Could she?

What about when she passed out against his door? That wasn't just to get away from him so that she could play with herself, was it?

At least when his cock was in her he knew she had really come, he reassured himself. Then again, he was so far gone he wasn't exactly sure what had happened. It wasn't inconceivable that she had just clenched her muscles a few times and moaned so that he would fall asleep, and she could get away from him.

He'd never before doubted his abilities with a woman. Based on their ecstatic screams he had always been one hundred percent certain that he had left them satisfied.

But now that the doubts were stuck in his mind, there was only one way to find out if she was telling the truth. He'd have to see her again.

And this time he'd make sure she came so hard that there would be no doubt in either of their minds who was a good lover and who wasn't.

Then he'd be done with her. Once and for all.

4

TRAVIS STOOD AT THE ENTRANCE to Barker's Furniture, in the setting sun, hardly able to believe that he was about to set foot in the grubby store. As an architect who designed multimillion-dollar homes for movie stars, investment moguls, and foreign royalty, Travis had never considered working with an interior designer from the Barker's furniture department. His clients wanted only the best, so he found them hot new furniture designers who sold plastic couches for twenty thousand dollars a pop.

He had spent half the night trying to figure out how to get near Lily again without giving away his true intentions. He didn't want her to think he was interested in dating her. Because he wasn't. He just needed a palatable excuse to be alone with her again. Once he was, he would pull the best orgasm in the world out of her.

He was planning to hire her to furnish a room in the new San Francisco hilltop home he'd designed for a very wealthy couple. What the heck. He figured he could donate the furniture to charity later if he needed to. Nonetheless, he'd already wasted most of Monday in his office putting off this visit, wondering if he was just being a fool. Of course Lily had been satisfied by him. Of course he had made her come. Multiple times.

But that voice in his head, the one that kept saying *Are you absolutely sure?* just wouldn't shut up.

An elderly women opened the door for him. "Are you going to come in or stand outside scowling at our potential customers all day?"

Travis turned his lips up at the woman, but the smile didn't reach his eyes.

"No need to bare your teeth at me, young man," she said, and Travis couldn't help but feel like a bad-tempered idiot. "Now that we've got you inside the store, is there anything I can help you with?"

"I'm looking for Lily Ellis."

The gray-haired woman eyed him up and down, stripping him naked with her gaze, so he added, "I've got a business proposal for her."

The woman cackled like the Wicked Witch of the West. "I'll bet you do, sonny. What I wouldn't have done for a business proposal from you in my day," she said, using her bony fingers to make quotation marks around the words "business proposal."

Inwardly, Travis recoiled from the sexual implications in the woman's words as he waited for her to tell him where Lily was. "She's in the back of the store by the dining tables. And good luck," the woman said, before walking off toward the storeroom, snickering all the way.

"Crazy old lady," Travis muttered as he weaved through the couches, lounge chairs, and coffee tables. A few seconds later he caught sight of Lily bending over a long pinewood table, dusting it in smooth strokes.

For a moment the only thing he could see was the two of them naked and writhing on the table.

Travis shook the image out of his head, forcing himself to look at Lily objectively. From his vantage point hidden behind a large armoire, he studied her in the light of day. Her hair was redder and shinier than he remembered it ever being before. Although the truth was that he had never really hated her hair. Sure, he preferred straight blond or brown locks to such a bright red, but all in all, her red curls weren't the worst thing about her.

She was wearing a well-tailored red suit and he'd have to be blind not to notice the way the fabric tapered in at the waist before flaring out to cup the curve of her ass.

He couldn't remember Lily ever wearing such a vibrant color before, and even though he hated to admit it, the crimson fabric nicely offset her creamy skin. He could only imagine how blue her eyes would look today.

Travis caught himself seconds before he started quoting a Shakespeare soliloquy to her beauty. *For God's sake,* he told himself, *this is Lily.*

Big, boring Lily.

His perspective firmly back in place, he stepped out from behind the armoire and called her name.

Lily jumped, dropping her dusting rag on the floor. She turned to him, shock painted across her face. "Travis, what are you doing here?"

As if he were approaching a skittish, hungry dog that needed reassuring, he held up his hands and moved toward her. "Don't look so worried, Lily. I've come to you with a business proposition."

With each step that he took, Lily took a step back, until she was pressed tightly up against the table. Her voice shaky, she licked her plump red lips, and asked, "A business proposition?"

Travis nodded absently, busy doing a thorough perusal of Lily's figure. How was it that practically overnight she seemed to have blossomed? Surely she hadn't been this ripe, this sexy before.

Or had she?

Crossing his arms across his chest, Travis got down to business. "I want you to work with me on a new house that I designed."

Lily's hand went to her throat. Travis wondered how her skin would taste at the pulse point that was beating so rapidly in her neck.

"You want me to work with you?"

"I need an interior designer. That is what you do, isn't it?"

Lily nodded.

Travis shrugged. "If you don't think you're up to it, I'll understand."

Responding to his goading exactly as planned, Lily took a step forward, a new flush on her cheeks. "Of course I'm up to it. What do you need me to do?"

He bit back a grin of victory. There would be plenty of time to savor the sweet taste of success after he had made her come so hard that she was begging for him to suck and lick and finger her again and again.

Throwing her words of his sexual incompetence back in her face was going to be well worth the wait.

"Why don't you come with me to the house right now, and I'll show you?"

Lily looked over her shoulder. "I can't. I don't get off work for another hour. And my boss is standing right over there."

All Travis could see was a greasy car salesmen type in a brown polyester suit. "That guy's your boss?"

Right then, the beady-eyed man looked over and frowned at them.

"Go away. We can talk later," she hissed, looking desperate.

"May I help you?"

Travis held out his hand. "I'm Travis Carson." He handed the man one of his business cards.

In an instant, Lily's boss went from snide to obsequious. "Oh my. Carson Architects. It is an honor to meet you, sir." He bumbled and stumbled all over himself, saying, "Albert All. I'm the head of this department." He puffed out his chest so far that Travis was afraid his inflated stomach was going to pop and shower them with furniture-salesman guts.

"How may I be of service to you?" Albert asked, shooting Lily a clear sign to get lost.

Lily began to scoot out of the way, but Travis reached out for her elbow and held her firmly by his side. "I was speaking to Lily about a large decorating job I need taken care of."

Albert nodded so fast that his many chins threatened to overtake the rest of his face. "How wonderful, sir, that you thought of Barker's. I would be happy to introduce you to my top designer."

Travis had an unreasonable urge to defend Lily. "I've already found her," he said, delighted to watch Albert stutter with outrage.

Lily turned to Travis, her mouth a soft "o," and he couldn't help but want to kiss her, her boss be damned. But he reined in his impulses. There would be time for kissing later.

Turning back to the purple-faced Albert, Travis said, "I'd like to take her to the job site right now, if you don't have any objections." The greasy man opened his mouth, and Travis knew he had to shut him down with the promise of money. Lots of it.

Leaning in closer to Albert as if they were talking man to man, and trying not to hurl from the putrid smell of his onion breath and nicotine-stained teeth, Travis said, "It's much easier to see an eighty-thousand-square-foot house in person than it would be for me to describe it to her. You understand, I'm sure."

Without waiting for a response from Lily's railroaded boss, Travis turned to Lily, and said, "How about we take my Jag?" as he propelled her toward the door.

They walked through the store and out onto the sidewalk without saying a word to each other. Travis opened the passenger door, and Lily woodenly sank into the plush leather seat.

"How did you do that?" she said in obvious amazement.

"Easy. How do you put up with that pompous loser every day?"

Lily giggled, and Travis was surprised by how easy it was to be with her. *Just like when we were kids,* he thought before he shut down that part of his brain.

"Just barely," she said.

Travis started the engine and shot out onto the street. "Why don't you quit?"

"And do what?"

He shrugged. "Start your own business."

Lily laughed again, but this time it carried a strong dose of self-deprecation. "Yeah right. Like anyone would want to hire me." She turned to him with a look of suspicion. "You don't even know what kind of decorator I am. I know you're not really hiring me to work on a house. And Albert is going to kill me when he finds out he's not getting your business. What's going on, Travis?"

Travis was having a heck of a time keeping his eyes on the

road. His hand kept wanting to move off the stick shift to Lily's thigh. And the soft, slick bounty that lay beneath her skirt.

"Nothing is going on," he insisted. "Look, you're right, I've never seen your work. But Luke said you're great and that you should open your own shop. So how about we'll start with one room, and if my clients like it, we'll see about the rest of the house."

Lily studied him carefully for a long moment, and it took all the manliness he possessed not to squirm under her gaze. He held his breath, waiting for her reply. If she didn't go for this, he had no idea how he was going to get her alone again.

And if he couldn't get her alone, he couldn't get her naked.

And if he couldn't get her naked, he couldn't make her come.

Travis had to make her come. That day. No one had ever questioned his virility, least of all himself.

Lily blew out a breath. "Fine. I'll work with you." Brushing back a springy curl from her cheek, she said, "What styles do your clients like?"

"I think you'll get an idea when you see the house." He pulled into the long driveway and drove beneath thick canopies of hundred-year-old oak trees, parking in front of a huge Italian-inspired villa, high in the hills of San Francisco.

"Wow. What a beautiful house." Lily stepped out onto the brick pavers that lined the driveway and walked toward the front door with her mouth hanging open. "You want me to work with you on this house?"

Travis smiled, pleased that she was so awed by his work. "Wait until you see inside. And the view."

He opened the front door with his key, and they entered the empty house. "My God," she said, her eyes wide. "This is straight out of the Tuscan countryside. I see murals and bright blue tiles. Mustard walls with a faux finish and soft fabrics.

Rugs, the most glorious rugs atop the wood floors. And with the way the sun is setting through the oak trees . . . " Lily's voice fell away. "This house is a perfect extension of nature. From the outside, in, and back again."

Not bothering to mask his surprise, Travis said, "I was thinking along those exact lines when I designed the house."

Lily bit her lip, and the worried look came back. "There's no way that I can get your clients what they need at Barker's. Whoever furnishes this house should be combing through trunks of furniture shipped straight from Italy. The designer should probably even fly to Italy on a buying trip for textiles. The truth is, Travis, you're wasting your time with me."

Travis stared at her as the fading sunlight through the huge windows covered her in a soft, warm glow. He had a hallucination of the two of them lingering over a bottle of Chianti in a sidewalk restaurant on cobblestone streets before he took her back to a villa and made love to her all night long.

Before he was wise enough to stop himself, he said, "Quit your job. I'm hiring you to furnish this house. It'll be your first big commission."

Lily spun around. "No," she said, stepping backward toward the door. "I don't think I could . . . "

"You can."

"The entire house? Every room?"

Travis took another step toward her and spoke quietly, suddenly sure that she was the only person right for the job. Even though he'd pretty much gone out of his way to avoid her for the past two decades, and certainly never thought that he'd become her champion, Travis found himself saying, "Go for it, Lily."

Somewhere in the back of his brain Travis realized that working together on a long-term basis was completely at odds with his plan to take her just one more time and be done with her. Clearly, the hot sex they'd had after the fashion show had messed with his usual clear thinking in a serious way.

Lily squared her shoulders, and her look of doubt transformed into an excited smile. "Oh what the heck. I'll do it!"

She held out her hand. Travis wrapped her long slim fingers in his own, and yet again he was surprised by how soft her skin was.

He couldn't let her leave, not yet. Somehow he had to figure out a way to seduce her before leaving and make her think that it was her idea.

Still holding her hand, he said, "Do you want to see the rest of the house?"

Her blue eyes sparkled. "Oh God, yes."

Travis smiled and headed into the kitchen, vowing that the next time she said, "Oh God, yes," it was going to be from the spasms racking through her as he pumped hot and hard into her.

LILY COULD HARDLY BELIEVE the gift Travis had given her. She followed his trim, buff form from room to room, nearly salivating at being so close to him for so long. Now that she had accepted this job she would get to see more of him, wouldn't she?

At the same time she was a bundle of nerves, sure that at any second, the other shoe was going to drop. She wasn't naive enough to believe that Travis asked her to come see this house because of her interior-decorating skill. Something else was going on; she just hadn't figured out what it was yet. It likely had something to do with him punishing her for daring to think she was worthy of sleeping with him. If she had had any concern for self-preservation, Lily would have refused his offer to decorate the house and kept herself as far away from him as she could. But she couldn't resist being so near to him.

Things were no different in high school when she had followed Travis around the halls, hiding behind her books. He always had his arm around at least one of the cute little cheerleaders, and Lily knew without a shadow of a doubt that she had been completely invisible to him. Utterly unimportant.

But still, she couldn't keep from wanting him. As crazy, as irrational as her lust for Travis was, she had never been able to let go of it. And now that she had been given a taste, she wanted him for every meal. She was as pathetic as she had always been.

As a teenager, stolen glances were all she could get. Why did she think it would be any different now? Sure, she had come apart in his arms. Yes, his body over hers had felt so right. But that didn't mean that things were any different than they had been in high school.

Luke's plan from their Sunday brunch popped back into her head. She tried to accept her role in all of it, but she was having no better luck now than she had during brunch.

"Travis is lucky to have even gotten to be with you once, especially after the way he's treated you. You are an incredible woman, and it's up to you to show him that he's going to need to treat you really well if he wants you to be with him ever again. And this is how you are going to do it: You are going to rip him apart, then put him back together. But only after he earns it."

It wasn't that she couldn't see the truth in what Luke was saying. Playing hard to get was likely the best plan of attack with a womanizer like Travis. But it was hard for her to think about ways to make Travis chase her when she didn't feel worthy of him.

Travis was beautiful, brilliant, confident.

She would never call herself beautiful. Or brilliant. And certainly not confident. Thank God she had splurged on the new red suit at the mall after brunch with Luke. If she had been wearing one of her regular shapeless pantsuits, she would have felt even more inferior.

It was crazy for Luke to tell her that she needed to break down Travis's confidence. She had treated him like a sex god on Saturday night—after all, he had been a sex god, an orgasm-generating machine—and she was supposed to recant all that? She sincerely doubted that Travis would buy her act.

They entered the most lavish master bathroom that Lily had ever seen outside of a glossy magazine spread for *Architectural Digest,* and she sighed.

"Is something wrong, Lily?" Travis asked, his voice as smooth as butter.

She forced a bright smile and tried to tamp down on the voice in her heart that was telling her she was lucky to have stolen so much as a kiss from this man. *Don't forget,* she coached herself, *he dropped you from his life for no reason and has looked right through you for twenty years. You should be demanding an apology for how unworthy he tries to make you feel, not mooning over him.*

"Everything's great. Wonderful in fact." Running her fingers over the cool blue tiles that lined the enormous Jacuzzi tub, she said, "You did an amazing job with this house, Travis."

Travis grinned, and Lily had a moment's surprise at the fact that her words of praise obviously pleased him. She hadn't thought that her opinion would matter to him.

Was Luke right about his twin brother? Was Travis's ego more fragile than it seemed? Was his heart not a bulletproof, steel-lined fortress?

Because even though she'd had a major crush on Travis since they were ten, she had never fooled herself into thinking that she could ever be a part of his life.

They were so different. She was soft and couldn't help but

look for the good in everyone. He was all harsh, unforgiving angles. She was quiet, afraid to speak up because she knew people would laugh at her dumb ideas. He was a storm that erupted in a hundred different ways, assailing any- and everything.

Looking up into his eyes, she saw the storm beginning anew. Taking a step back from him, warring with her own anticipation, Lily said, "I should probably start doing some research this afternoon. After turning in my resignation at Barker's, of course."

Quitting her safe job would be the next-riskiest thing she had ever done—right behind being a sexy queen on the runway and seducing Travis, of course—but it made her smile to think about telling Albert that she quit and was never, ever going to buy a single thing for her clients in his store.

Yeah right, like she'd ever be able to stand up to Albert, even though he deserved it. She really was letting her imagination get the best of her. Although Lily wished she had enough guts to tell Albert what she thought of him, she knew she'd meekly hand him a letter of resignation and let him browbeat her. Oh well, at least a man who had treated her like dirt wouldn't get any commissions from her.

Travis moved toward her, shaking her out of her thoughts. She started, feeling like a gazelle being stalked by some big wild thing. He must have seen the panic in her eyes at being so close to him in such a sensuous bathroom, because instead of cornering her he ran a hand through his jet-black hair, and said, "I'd like you to see the property before we go."

"Why?" Lily asked, increasingly suspicious of his motives. It wasn't that she didn't want him to touch her, of course, it was in fact just the opposite.

She desperately wanted him to touch her. And she was sure

that she wasn't going to be able to pull off the ruse of being un-affected by his touch like Luke had told her to do. If Travis so much as ran one finger down the side of her face, she was going to start pleading with him to take her right there, right then, heedless of the consequences.

Travis gave her a coaxing smile. "Just like you said when we walked in, I've always felt that it's important for a designer to see how the inside of the house interacts with the environment surrounding it."

Lily narrowed her eyes, trying to read between the lines on Travis's face, but it was completely, professionally blank. Suddenly she felt foolish. Here he was giving her the biggest opportunity in her career, and she was being distrustful and apprehensive about it.

What a fool she was. He hadn't even mentioned their night together. Why did she think he would ever want to touch her again?

After all, she was just Lily.

And Travis would never dream of sleeping with just Lily. She was sure of it. He had made a mistake on Saturday night, one that she was sure he would never deign to repeat.

Wanting to cry, but forcing a smile back onto her lips, she said, "You're right, Travis. I would really like to see the property." Digging for something at least partially professional to say, she observed, "From what I can see through the windows, there are some wonderfully mature trees on the acerage."

Inwardly she rolled her eyes. Wonderfully mature trees. Like she really cared about the trees. All she wanted to do was get away from Travis before she did something really stupid, like throw herself at him.

The back of the house was dotted with olive and lemon trees. Travis pointed to the far right of the property, toward a thick grove of oaks. "There's something you've got to see back here."

Stepping carefully down the winding path in her heels, Lily gasped with pleasure when she saw what the trees were hiding. "What an incredible pond," she said, taking in the reflection of the red-gold sunset on the surface of the water.

"It's not a pond," Travis said, "it's a swimming pool." Travis shrugged off his jacket and kicked off his leather shoes. Sitting on the edge of a large, flat rock, he folded up his Armani suit's pant legs. "Let's relax for a minute by the pool before we head back."

Lily was about to say no, but something inside her told her to go for it. In the past forty-eight hours her life had gone from lackluster to crazy to simply unbelievable. First making love to Travis, now being hired to decorate a villa in San Francisco. Surely sitting by the pool with the man she had lusted after her whole life paled in comparison to all that.

She sat on the rock and slid her feet out of her shoes.

"Why don't you take off your stockings?" Travis asked innocently. "Feel the grass under your feet."

Lily shook her head. She couldn't do that. Travis would see her big, white legs and immediately start thinking about elephants.

Travis raised an eyebrow. "Afraid that I won't be able to keep my hands off you?"

Something churned in Lily's gut at Travis's taunting. She'd show him. If it killed her, she was going to make him so hot he would be screaming for release. And then she'd leave him cold and desperate for her.

"No, you're right. I'd like to feel the breeze on my bare skin," she said, working hard to pitch her voice in a sensual manner. After all, the sun was almost down. Didn't everyone always say that sunset was the most flattering time of day?

She pulled up the hem of her skirt and unhooked one side of her garter.

"Do you need any help with that?" Travis asked nonchalantly.

Lily forced herself to reply as carelessly. "Not unless you want some help with your pants."

Trying to still her trembling fingers, she unrolled her stockings down her thigh. As unbelievable as it might have been that the prom king was lusting after the original wallflower, Lily knew it with every fiber of her being. Now was the time for what Luke had instructed her to do: She needed to whip Travis up into a sexual frenzy, then leave him before he got the upper hand.

Could she do it?

Lily looked up at Travis from beneath her lashes, and what she saw in the green of his eyes took her breath away.

He wanted her.

Badly.

Licking her lips, she said in a husky voice, "Is your offer of help still good?" In less than a second, he was kneeling at her feet, his hands on hers at her knees. "I'll take that as a yes," she said, laughing softly at the new feeling of feminine power that was coursing through her.

"Don't forget, my pants are next," he growled. With painstaking slowness he slid the silk stocking off her leg. With every inch of skin that he uncovered he lightly nipped at her skin until wetness soaked her panties.

She bit her lip to stifle a whimper of pleasure. Somehow she needed to act like she was doing him a favor—at least that's what Luke had said she needed to do—but it was so incredibly hard to think of that when Travis was touching her, kissing her.

With one of her legs bare, he gently massaged the arch in her foot. "Oh God, yes," she said, and Travis surprised her by coming up to seduce her with a hot kiss.

His mouth tasted like sweet lemons and sunshine. She blinked uncertainly when he pulled away from her, but before she could protest she was lost in the sensation of his fingers on her skin as he reached under her skirt to undo the clasps on her other garter. He freed the silk from its binding and began the delectable task of sliding it from her other leg. With every nip of his perfect white teeth on her skin, Lily felt herself melting further and further into him.

"Your turn," he said, getting to his feet. Standing before her, she could see his enormous erection jutting out from beneath his expensive navy blue trousers.

Lily reached for his leather belt with shaking fingers. She undid the clasp, then her fingers were on the top button of his slacks. She popped open the button and unzipped him, letting his pants fall to the ground.

She sucked in a breath. His huge, perfect penis jutted toward her, and as her hand came up of its own volition to touch it, a drop of Travis's arousal coated the tip.

That settled it. She needed to taste him, and she needed to taste him immediately. Her mouth covered the thick head of his penis and she licked every last drop of his precome before more coated the inside of her cheeks. She sucked down his cock into the back of her throat, wanting to swallow him whole.

She had spent years wondering what it would be like to blow Travis, wanting to know what it felt like to be holding his balls with her hands while she sucked at his velvety skin.

Running her tongue over the ridges of his enormous shaft, she understood that everything she had ever dreamed about doing with Travis was so much better in real life. His cock grew impossibly bigger within her mouth, and before she knew what was happening he stepped back and pulled her to her feet.

"Take off your clothes," he said, his words a command as he took off his shirt.

In that moment it didn't matter that they were on the private property of Travis's clients, that they could be found at any minute by a pool man or a gardener. It didn't matter that she was supposed to be in control, that she was supposed to be telling Travis what do, and not the other way around.

The only thing that mattered was obeying Travis's command if it meant finding the release that she so desperately needed.

Heedless of their clothes, strewn across the flagstone terrace that surrounded the magnificent pool, Lily stood naked before Travis. She barely resisted the urge to cover herself with her hands, to hide her totally imperfect body from him, to flee.

Conjuring up the invincible queen that she had been at the fashion show only days before, she asked, "Is this what you want?" He growled his response as he pulled her body against his.

"I want more than that." He captured her mouth in a kiss that left no doubt in her mind that he intended to claim her, to brand her as his own. The friction of his skin against hers, of the hair on his thighs against the soft, aroused skin between her thighs made her want to scream out with pleasure.

She rocked her pelvis into the hard planes of his body again, but instead of taking her to the place she needed to go, Travis moved them to the edge of the swimming pool, without breaking their kiss.

His hot breath tickled the curls by her neck. "Come into the pool with me."

"Now?" she asked, shivering at the thought of what he might do to her underwater.

"Now," he said, his green eyes nearly black with passion.

He walked down the wide steps into the cool water, and Lily followed his lead. Her nipples grew hard as the water covered first her feet, then her calves, then her thighs.

"Are you cold?" he asked, staring straight at her rock-hard nipples. "Should I warm you up?" he said as he leaned his head in to her breasts.

His hot breath covered her as he nipped and sucked at her. Her knees gave way, but his strong hands held her up, refusing to let her sink all the way into the water. "I need to taste you again," he said in a low husky voice; then his mouth was on her clit, his tongue lapping in long, hot strokes. His hands moved up her body to play with her breasts, cupping them, massaging them, letting the flesh rest heavily on his big, callused palms.

And then he moved her deeper into the water, and the cool water rushed over her silken heat, making her cry out with wonder at the two so different sensations. So hot. So cold. And then hot again as his fingers slid in and out of her.

"I want to see you come."

Lily looked into his eyes, powerless to stop herself from giving this man whatever he wanted. "Now, Lily," he said, his thumb swirling insistently over her swollen nub. "Now."

His eyes bored into hers as she obeyed his order. "Travis," she moaned against his lips.

"Come, Lily," he urged, even as the contractions became too much for her to handle.

"Come, Lily," he growled as he shifted her in the water and thrust his cock all the way into her ready body.

Travis's thumb never stopped its perfect pattern on her clit as Lily wrapped her legs around his waist and slid up and down on his hard, thick shaft.

Her pleasure was so intense, she was barely able to say, "We need a condom."

Later she would admire his force of will in pulling out of her, spilling his seed on her belly in several quick thrusts. But at that very moment she was heartbroken. She had wanted nothing more than for him to explode in her, to complete her with his essence.

But even in her lust-filled haze, Lily wasn't stupid enough to risk getting pregnant.

Travis's warm body was wrapped around her in the cool swimming pool, but Lily felt a shiver work its way up her spine. A baby with Travis. She knew without a doubt that it would be the most wonderful child in the world, maybe even twins, a little Travis and a little Luke.

Oh no. Luke had told her not to do this. Under no circumstances was she supposed to have sex with Travis. She was supposed to get him hot and bothered, then leave him wanting more.

She knew she couldn't resist Travis. But she also knew that Luke would crucify her if she didn't at least stick to part of the plan. Steeling all of her soft feelings, she prepared to do battle.

Travis gently kissed the top of her head. "That was some amazing orgasm, wasn't it?"

Lily couldn't believe how smug he sounded. As if he thought that all he had to do was be near her, and she'd explode into a million pieces. Tamping down on the truthful part of her that said that was precisely the case, she said, "It was fine, Travis."

In his shock he let go of her, and she swam to the side of the pool.

"It was fine?" he said through clenched teeth.

Lily shrugged. "Yeah. It was fine." Looking up at him all innocence, doing her darnedest to pretend that she was worldly and had sex with men in strangers' pools all the time, she said,

"Oh, I don't mean to hurt your feelings, Travis. I really did like it, you know."

He followed her out onto the flagstone patio. *"You really did like it?* What the hell does that mean?"

Ignoring the racing of her heart—who was she to mess with a man like Travis?—she said, "Any towels out here?"

He reached beneath the seat of a wood bench and threw a towel at her. Pinning her with his green eyes, he said, "You loved what I did to you. Don't try to deny it."

Lily kept her expression as bland as she could, but inside she was incredulous. Luke seemed to be dead on target with his brother. Travis wasn't sure if she had actually enjoyed herself with him. She had come all over the place, and he actually thought that she might have faked it.

Wow.

It was hard for Lily to believe, but it seemed that, for the first time in her life, she had the upper hand with Travis.

Letting her mouth curve up into a small smile that barely hinted at the secrets inside her woman's mind, she got dressed, ignoring his words completely. "I'd really like to get started on the project now. Could you please take me back to Barker's so that I can leave a note of resignation and pick up my car?"

Lily fought back a laugh as he stalked up the path to his car. Following behind him, her hips swaying to a new, all-female rhythm, Lily thought that maybe, just maybe, her life wasn't quite as predictable as she had thought it to be.

"IT WAS FINE."

"I liked it."

"I don't mean to hurt your feelings, Travis."

Travis pulled up to the curb in front of the store and stared straight ahead as Lily fiddled with the seat belt. He could feel her big blue eyes on him, making him feel things he never wanted to feel. He was ten years old again and on the playground trying not to cry, trying not to be a big baby just because he didn't have a mom anymore.

"Thanks for this opportunity, Travis. I won't let you down."

He grunted, knowing she was waiting for him to say something. Finally, she gave up, saying, "I'll be in touch in a few days once I've done some research at the design center downtown," before slamming the door.

Travis intended to burn rubber as he peeled away from the curb, but his foot wouldn't obey his command. Instead, he watched Lily walk up the short pathway to the front entrance of the store, hating how turned on he was by the sway of her hips.

Utterly disgusted with himself, he peeled out from the curb and broke at least ten traffic laws on the way back to his office in the trendy South of Market area.

A new receptionist sat at the front desk. When he walked in, she stood up in all of her twenty-year-old blond-and-nubile glory.

"Mr. Carson?"

Travis nodded and gave her his most devastating smile. "And you are?"

"Megan. Your partner hired me." She shook her blond hair over her shoulder and stuck her chest out slightly, her nipples perky beneath her thin silk shirt.

Travis shook Megan's hand and waited for the usual rush to come from touching a beautiful young woman. He held her hand a few seconds longer than normal and looked deeply into her blank brown eyes.

Nothing.

Dropping the girl's hand like a pile of hot coals, Travis bit out, "I need two first-class tickets to Rome for Wednesday."

If he couldn't fight Lily's lure, he was going to have to do the next best thing.

He was going to have to drown in her until he was completely, totally sick of licking her, kissing her, sliding in and out of her incredibly tight pussy.

Until he never wanted to touch her again.

5

THE NEXT MORNING, Travis made a beeline for Janica's design studio. If he was going to take Lily to Italy, he wanted her to look good. Apart from her red suit and Janica's dress, Travis couldn't remember ever seeing Lily in something that didn't make her look frumpy. So he needed clothes. Incredible clothes. And from what he had seen during the fashion show, even though she was just starting out in the business, Janica was going to be one of the best.

He found her J Style studio in a refurbished warehouse ten blocks from his office. As the blocks dropped off, the neighborhood grew seedier. Travis paid a homeless man twenty dollars to watch his Jag and rang the bell.

Janica called down through the voice box. "Who's there?"

"Travis." She didn't buzz him in, so even though he'd known her since she was in pigtails, he said, "Travis Carson."

"You're kidding me," she said, and he would have grinned at her reaction if he weren't so stupefied by what he was doing. "What are you doing here?"

"Let me in, Janica," he growled.

The buzzer sounded, and he opened the thick metal gate. It slammed shut behind him as he made his way up the concrete steps to the second level.

Janica leaned against the door, scowling at him. "What do you want?"

Travis had always admired Janica for sticking up for her older sister. Even though she was a perfect size two, Travis had the sense that Janica wasn't the kind of woman who disrespected women larger than she. On the contrary, she seemed to go out of her way to make them look beautiful, as was evidenced by the line of plus-sized clothes Travis saw hanging from a rack by the window.

"What are those?" he asked, ignoring her biting question.

She gave him a triumphant look. "Lily was such a hit at my show that I've been asked by a local boutique to design an entire line of clothes for plus-sized women. Real women, like Lily. Not like those plastic *uber*idiots you always date."

Her stance was tense. She looked ready to spring and strangle him at any moment, the bear cub who would do anything to protect its mother.

"Relax," he said, "I'm not here to malign your precious big sister."

"Watch who you're calling big," she said as she approached him, a menacing look in her eyes.

Travis held his hands up and took a step back. "I didn't mean big as in big," he said. "I meant big as in older."

"Whatever," she said, not looking the least bit appeased by his explanation. "Tell me what you want, then get out."

"I need an entire wardrobe for Lily."

"What?"

"By tonight."

"Excuse me?"

"For Tuscany."

Janica sat down heavily on a dusty windowsill. "You've completely lost me. When did Lily make plans to go to Tuscany?" Her eyes narrowed with suspicion. "And what do you have to do with the trip?"

"I've hired her to furnish one of my clients' houses. We're going on a quick buying trip."

"You're kidding me," Janica exclaimed, before her doubts returned full force. "Then again, I shouldn't be so excited. I'm sure you have a perfectly nefarious reason for asking her to do this. You always do. Just like that time you showed up at Luke's house with some total slut and completely ruined her birthday dinner. I know you did it on purpose, just to hurt her, shoving some skinny bitch in her face like that."

Travis tried to shake off a sense of guilt that he felt at Janica's words. Sure, he might have accidentally crashed Lily's birthday party a year ago, and he might be taking Lily to Italy out of some self-serving need to get her out of his system, to teach her what happened to women who dared to say that he wasn't a good lover; but in his own defense, hadn't he just given her the professional opportunity of a lifetime?

The fact that it was one he knew she couldn't say no to, one that included rights to her body whenever he so desired, didn't make it any more unfair than business as usual, did it?

So what if all the balls happened to be in his court? It happened to be where he liked all of the balls to be. Which only made him think of the way she had caressed his balls earlier by the pool. . . .

Forcing himself to turn off his libido, Travis deftly switched the facts around to suit his needs. "She quit her job at Barker's yesterday." It was the truth, or nearly, even though he was leaving off some pertinent details, like the fact that he was the one who convinced Lily to quit. Hopefully, if he presented it right, he could get Janica off the scent of his actual nefariousness. "I found out about it and wanted to help her out."

"You wanted to help her out?" Janica's disbelief rang out loud and clear. "I never would have expected this in a million, billion years," she muttered. Staring at him, no, staring straight through him with those damn all-seeing Ellis eyes—so much like Lily's, Travis saw the first hint of smile and wondered where it was coming from.

"Tell me what you need," she said, her demeanor changing from black to bright white. "If I have anything to do with it, Lily is going to look like a goddess in Italy, you can count on that."

JANICA PICKED UP her phone the minute Travis left the office. "Luke," she said, calling her sister's best friend. "It's Janica."

"Is Lily all right?"

Janica had always appreciated how well Luke looked after her sister. She used to wonder why they weren't boyfriend-girlfriend, but over the years, Janica had decided it was a good thing. Maybe one day she could convince Luke to see her as a woman instead of Lily's kid sister.

"She's fine, at least I think she is." Getting straight to the point, she said, "I heard that Lily went home with you after the fashion show. Is that true?"

The line was silent for several long moments. "Not exactly," he finally said.

Her suspicions about Travis's impromptu visit grew. "Were you even at my show?"

Luke cleared his throat. "No. I got called into the ER. It was really bad timing on my part, and I wish I had it to do over."

Janica pieced two and two together and, unfortunately, it was exactly what she had already deduced. "You sent Travis in your place, didn't you?"

Luke sighed. "I'm afraid so."

"How could you?" she exploded, forgetting for the moment that she lusted after Luke. It was one thing for Travis to treat her sister like she wasn't good enough for him—at least you knew a self-important snake when you saw him slithering around—but it was worlds worse for a nice guy like Luke to turn on the person she loved most in the world.

"How could you have done something so . . . so awful? You of all people know how he ignores her. He acts like she doesn't even matter." Luke was silent as she fumed, which pissed Janica off more. "Don't you have anything to say for yourself?"

He let out a long breath. "I blew it. Trust me, I've been beating myself up for it ever since."

Janica hmmphed. That was more like it. *He should feel bad,* she thought. Luke's thoughtlessness had caused Lily no end of problems. In the back of Janica's mind, it occurred to her that maybe she had been the start of Lily's problems: After all, if she hadn't forced Lily to be in the fashion show, then Travis wouldn't have come in Luke's place.

No, she thought, *I won't blame myself. Why should I when it's clearly Luke's fault?* Forcing any traces of guilt from her mind, she worked to get the rest of the facts straight. "So Lily went home with Travis?"

"Janica," he said, not bothering to hide his growing impatience, "maybe you should be asking Lily these questions."

Janica snorted. "Yeah right. Like she'd tell me anything. She would never talk to me about her sex life in a million years. She still thinks I'm twelve or something." *Just like you do,* she almost said before she caught herself. Pausing to think things through, Janica said, "So she went home with Travis. But there's no way they, you know . . ." She blushed furiously in the privacy of her design studio, glad that Luke couldn't see how embarrassed she was. "So why is he taking her to Italy?" she added, speaking more to herself than to Luke.

"He's what?"

"He just came by to pick up a complete wardrobe for her for their trip. For tomorrow."

Fury bursting from every word, Luke said, "Janica, if you would excuse me, I need to go have a word with my brother to make sure that he treats Lily with the respect she deserves."

The line went dead, and Janica hung up the phone, confused, but, for the first time, hopeful that her sister might actually be living life instead of hiding behind a wall of responsibility and fear. There were so many times that Janica had wanted to tell Lily to go out and get a life. To dress up and get her hair cut in a sassy new style. To stay out all night with a totally inappropriate guy. To look in the mirror and actually see how beautiful she really was. But Janica knew Lily would never do any of those things.

For some crazy reason, Janica mused, Lily thought that she wasn't a stunning woman because she wasn't stick-thin. Janica had watched Lily suffer through one diet after another until she wanted to scream with it.

But then again, Janica marveled at how Lily was, all of a sudden, getting all the guys. Not that Travis was any kind of super prize, of course; he was way too much like a typical macho guy for her.

But Luke, on the other hand, had definite possibilities. Big, throbbing possibilities. Smiling again as she got to work on her latest men's suit design, Janica couldn't help but envision how Luke's broad shoulders and trim waist would look in her clothes.

Or better yet, without them.

∽∞∾ ∽∞∾ ∽∞∾

LILY STOOD IN THE MIDDLE of the huge, busy warehouse and ran her hands over the beautiful imported upholstery fabrics, feeling as if she were a fairly-tale princess in a perfect dream. How else could she possibly be standing amid all of this multi-colored, richly textured beauty, able, for the first time, to let her imagination roam freely?

After the most pleasant five minutes she had ever spent with Albert All in Barker's that morning, where she picked up the sweater she had forgotten and watched him sputtering and spitting all over himself at her resignation, even though she hadn't had the nerve to tell him exactly what she thought of him, she hopped in her car and headed straight for the San Francisco Design Center.

When she had first graduated from design school she loved to walk through the cluttered building, letting all of the beautiful furnishings fill her soul to the brim. But then, when she finally accepted that she didn't have the guts to start her own design firm—not with so many other talented, driven designers out there all vying for the same jobs—she stopped coming to her favorite place. All it did was make her feel even more like a loser. Especially when she saw somebody from her graduating class walking around with a cell phone making purchases for a client. She knew she had to accept that she worked at a subpar furniture store, selling pressboard armoires and faux-leather couches. Hundred-thousand-dollar rugs and cut-crystal chandeliers had no place in her world.

Today, she almost felt like she belonged in the showroom, and it was wonderful. Lily felt freer than she had since she was a child, safe in her mother's arms, before her parents had died in the car crash on Highway One. Overnight, Lily had become a mother to Janica, giving all of herself up to make sure that her baby sister's life was as good as it could possibly be under the circumstances. Grandma Ellen had done the best she could with them, but Lily knew she was the only one who could even come close to loving, supporting, and taking care of Janica the way their mother and father had. Lily didn't regret one single moment with Janica. She wouldn't take back any sacrifices in the name of her sister's happiness. Lily was the sensible, grounded one, happy to let Janica fly free into the world.

But, somehow, amazingly, Travis had given Lily the gift of flying free herself.

Not that she trusted him, though. Not one bit. He had clearly brought her out to the pool to seduce her, and although she definitely didn't mind his incredible lovemaking—oh, who was she kidding, there was no love about it, it was sex, pure and simple—she minded the fact that Travis thought all he had to do was crook his finger in her direction, and she'd come running.

She ran her fingers through the soft weave of a plush rug sample and thought about the sensual pleasure of running her hands through Travis's hair. Regardless of what happened with him, even if he reverted to his usual superior behavior with her and never looked at her with lust in his eyes again, she didn't regret one single second in his arms. The memories of his loving would be the perfect antidote to lonely nights in her apartment with only cable TV as her companion.

At the same time, Lily wasn't naive enough to think that this job didn't come with strings attached. But right then, lost in her own creative heaven, she decided she wasn't going to care.

Lily could hardly believe that she was going to furnish the beautiful Tuscan-style villa. This was her chance to make her mark in the design community. Regardless of how her private life was going, she wasn't going to blow her one big professional opportunity. Under no circumstances was she going to go crawling back to Albert at Barker's.

Her cell phone rang. She reached into her purse and looked at the number on her caller-ID screen. "Janica?"

"Lils, why didn't you tell me you were going to Tuscany?"

Lily blinked in confusion. "Tuscany? I'm not going to Tuscany. Who told you that?" Her call waiting beeped. "Hold on a sec, honey, I'm going to get the other line."

"Lily, it's Luke. I wanted to congratulate you. Whatever you did with Travis, it worked like a charm."

Glad that her best friend couldn't see her blushing through the phone as the clear vision of riding Travis's cock in a stranger's swimming pool popped into her head, Lily said, carefully, "You mean because he hired me to decorate one of his clients' houses?"

"So that's why you're going to Italy?"

Lily held the phone away from her ear and looked at it like it was speaking in foreign tongues. "Why is everyone talking about my going to Italy?"

Travis emerged from behind a tall stack of rugs, looking darkly dangerous and handsome as sin. He took the phone from her ear, closing it with a quick snap. Lily gulped for air and put a hand out to steady herself.

"Because we're leaving for Rome tomorrow. That's why."

A thrill shot through Lily at Travis's words. Travis wanted to take her to Italy? Just the two of them? Visions of walking with him hand in hand through olive groves, on ancient streets danced in her head.

Don't be silly, she reprimanded herself as she worked to tamp down her fanciful imagination. She composed her face into a mask of professional politeness, wanting to show him she wasn't a complete fool who fell for his every line.

"Travis," she said through tight lips, "while I greatly appreciate you handing me this incredible decorating job, I'm afraid it doesn't give you license to mock me at every available opportunity."

Travis took a step closer, and she backed into the pile of rug samples. "I'm not making fun of you, Lily," he said, his voice quiet, his tone intense.

Willing herself to be strong in the face of such undeniable maleness, she burst out with, "Yes you are. You have been either making fun of me or just flat out ignoring me since we were kids, and I am sick to death of it!" She pointed a finger at him and took a step in his direction, deciding not to run from him for once. "Either you respect me as a business partner or I'm going to have to walk."

Lily thought she saw a flicker of admiration in Travis's eyes as he studied her for a long moment. *All I needed to do was stick up for myself all these years?* she thought, with no small measure of surprise. Lily was unable to believe that it could have possibly been as simple as that.

But when Travis grabbed her outstretched finger and pulled her close to him, she knew that it wasn't going to be quite so simple at all.

"Nobody is going to walk," he growled. "I'm taking you to Italy on a buying trip. It's business," he added, but even he didn't look one hundred percent convinced.

"Oh," she said, upset that she couldn't come up with a more interesting response. She felt herself melting into Travis's gaze, and she knew his lips would be coming down on hers any second. But before she let herself fall under Travis's spell again, Luke's words sounded loudly inside her skull.

"Women make it too easy for Travis to have them. And dump them. Whatever you do, Lily, you need to make him work to be

with you. But first you'd better decide if that's even what you want."

Travis had pulled her close enough that she could feel his erection straining toward her. She had certainly proved that she could make his penis hard. But, she mused, perhaps that was the easy part? The only problem was, she could only think of one way to make life difficult for Travis.

And while she knew it was exactly what Travis needed to knock him down a peg or two, Lily hated the impact it was going to have on her on sexual satisfaction.

Deciding she either had to bite the bullet, or she'd lose her nerve, Lily pressed the full length of her body against Travis. She smiled at his swift intake of breath, working hard to ignore the tremors of lust that filled her. Leaning into him, she whispered into his ear, "On second thought, Travis, the trip sounds *fine.*"

She felt his spine stiffen at the word "fine" and fought back a giggle. Were men really and truly so easy to control?

"I do have one condition, however."

Travis's hand came around to caress the curve of her hips. "Anything," he said, and she knew he was never going to see the blow coming.

Pulling back to stare deeply into his incredible sea-green eyes, she said, "I want our relationship to be purely . . . " She let her words drift off and licked her lips.

Travis leaned in to kiss her.

"Professional."

He leaped back as if she were on fire.

"Excuse me?"

"If you have a problem with my stipulation, I'd be happy to forgo the trip," she bluffed.

Travis looked at her as if she'd lost her mind. "Fine with me," he said, clearly disgruntled by the turn of events. "If you want purely professional, you'll get purely professional. The airport limo will be picking you up at 2:00 P.M. tomorrow. Don't be late."

He threw her cell phone to her, and she barely caught it as he turned and walked out of the showroom without another word. Lily wasn't stupid. She knew there would be hell to pay for her making Travis feel like a fool. She was shaking after their showdown, but the truth was, after besting Travis like that she felt so good she wanted to scream with joy.

Italy. With Travis. It was incredible how every one of her dreams was coming true.

TRAVIS DROVE to his loft in a blaze of frustration. He hadn't felt this out of control since he was a kid, and he didn't like it. Not one bit.

He let himself into his sparsely decorated living quarters and went into the kitchen to pour himself a drink. Lord knew he badly needed one. But for some reason he was drawn to the framed pictures resting atop the grand piano. He picked up his favorite and blew off a patch of dust that the housekeeper had missed during her weekly cleaning.

In it, he and his brother were standing in the shade of a large oak tree with their mother, who was kneeling to hold onto both of them. They were in their Little League outfits, streaked with dirt from a game. His mother was wearing a billowy dress, as she usually did, and she looked just like a mother should: round and comforting. He could still remember their conversation that day by the tree.

"Mom, did you see my home run?"

"Oh, honey," she rubbed his back, "you were wonderful out there."

Luke butted in, "Did you see me get the guy out on first?"

"Sure did. I was the proudest mom in the whole world up there in the stands."

Travis rubbed his eyes and put the picture down. His father must have snapped the picture right before they ran off to celebrate with the other kids. They didn't know it then, but the cancer was already growing inside of her. Travis wished, for the millionth time, that he had known how little time they had left with her. He would have curled up with her warm, soft body more often, instead of spending hour upon hour playing video games with his friends.

She had been gone a long time, nearly twenty years, and he didn't know why he was being so maudlin out of the blue.

She would have loved Lily.

The voice in his head shocked him. So what if it was true? What did it matter what his mother would have thought about the grown-up Lily? It was his life. And she wasn't his type at all.

He was glad she had clarified what they were to each other. Purely professional was exactly what he wanted. He must have been crazy to even consider touching Lily again. But now that he'd given in to his idiotic impulse, he was going to be stuck with her for five days in Italy. He consoled himself with the thought of ditching her as soon as they landed. He'd find plenty of lusty Italian women to take to bed.

A knock sounded at the door. He yelled, "It's open," and Luke came strolling in with a six-pack. "What are you doing here?"

"Twin ESP. Thought you could use a drink," Luke said as he plopped the beer on the kitchen island and handed a cold one over. Travis scowled at Luke, but tilted his head back and drank.

"So, I hear you're taking Lily to Italy tomorrow," Luke said as he plopped his large frame onto Travis's black leather sofa.

Travis nodded and just as negligently unfurled onto a facing chair. "That's right."

"She said you gave her a big decorating job."

"Also right," Travis said. "What's your point, little brother?"

In a heartbeat, Luke was on Travis, and his shirt was bunched up in Luke's hands. "If you do one single thing to hurt Lily, I will personally see to it that you pay." He let go of Travis and stood up. "Well, I gotta go. Have a nice trip," Luke said, then walked out of the loft, closing the door behind him with a click.

6

LILY BUCKLED HER SEAT BELT and accepted the glass of champagne from the pretty, reed-slim flight attendant. "Thank you so much," she said as the attendant moved on to serve a well-to-do couple behind her. Lily surveyed her first-class surroundings with wonderment. *I could get used to this kind of life*, she thought with a smile. *From now on, it's first-class or nothing.*

Lily laughed out loud at such a ridiculous thought. She still couldn't believe that she was sitting in the lap of luxury on a Virgin Atlantic flight. They were going to change planes in London, then it was straight to Rome. There was even a neon-striped bar in the compartment back behind the seats. It was so decadent. So lavish. So stimulating. Just like Travis's hands had been on her breasts. Just like his mouth had been between her legs. Just like his cock had been . . .

Stop it, she ordered herself sternly. With a shake of her head, Lily forced herself to concentrate on the various goodies that had been waiting for her at her seat. She was rubbing a free sample of tea tree oil on her hands when Travis walked into the aisle.

Her smile went. He was so big he seemed to suck all of the oxygen from the cabin. She had to resist a crazy urge to pull her emergency oxygen mask from above her seat. But God forbid she give Travis the satisfaction of knowing how badly he affected her. In the aftermath of their sex-in-the-pool play, she had greatly enjoyed having the upper hand with Travis.

His bright green eyes sizzled for a brief moment, going clear so quickly Lily was sure she must have imagined the heat. Closing her eyes, figuring that she'd been about as brave as she could be, she replayed her talk with Luke.

"I can't do this," she had said, giving in and calling her best friend at midnight even though she knew she should be packing her pathetic, dumpy clothes for Italy.

"You're doing great," he had replied, a virtual thumbs-up across the wireless lines.

"No, you don't understand." Feeling like a bigger idiot than ever before, she had whispered, "He's flying me to Tuscany, and I told him that I want our relationship to be strictly platonic."

Luke whooped and Lily had held the phone back from her ear. "That's perfect, Lily. A stroke of genius."

"But what if it's not genius?" Lily blushed fiercely, thankful that Luke couldn't see her face. "What if he's happy about it and never wants to, well, you know . . . ever again?"

Luke had laughed. "Travis hasn't done anything this spontaneous since we were kids. I have a feeling that you are getting to him, and good." Oblivious to Lily's inner shame at lusting helplessly after Travis, Luke added, "All the better that you're making him beg for it. Just stay strong and keep up the good work."

Lily had hung up and given up on her clothes—they all were so ugly she really should burn them. Instead, she had settled in to spend the rest of the night worrying instead of sleeping. What if she didn't let him touch her again, and he left her untouched for good and was glad? What if she let him touch her, and he got bored? What if she let him touch her, and he didn't want to out of disgust? What if he *did* want to touch her, for whatever strange reason that she still couldn't figure out, and she wasn't strong enough to resist him, then he left her high and dry and even more pathetic and needy than before? What if he could feel the heat between her legs that he always caused simply by breathing and knew without a shadow of a doubt that she wasn't strong enough to resist him? Hour after hour passed in an endless wheel of doubts and self-recriminations.

In the clear light of day that was streaming in through the oval window at her left shoulder, Lily reopened her eyes and watched with trepidation as Travis stalked her in her oversized leather seat. His eyes roved over her outfit, and Lily couldn't help hoping he liked what he saw. She had dressed in one of her few nice outfits, a flirty red dress that Janica had made for her several years back. Lily hadn't had the courage to wear it before, but as she got dressed after a long, scalding shower she realized she was going to need all the confidence she could get. Evidently Travis had liked her red suit enough to have sex with her in the swimming pool, so she figured red was a good bet. Now, seeing the heat rise in his eyes—*Thank God he wasn't totally immune to her,* she thought with a rush of pleasure mixed with relief—Lily wished that she owned a few other sexier outfits.

"Hello," he said, his voice husky and warm.

Lily shivered under his gaze, and he bared his white teeth in a smile so beastly, she almost pushed past him to go lock herself in the bathroom for the duration of the flight.

"Hello," she replied in a remarkably steady, light voice, even as she wished that she could be so lucky as to wake up to a naked and warm "Hello" in his bed in the near future.

But that, of course, was out of the question given her brilliant plan. Although it was looking less and less likely that she would be able to hold out during their trip, not if she was wet and wanting him in the first five seconds of their flight. That is, she reminded herself with harsh reality, if he even wanted to be with her again.

Five days in romantic Tuscany with Travis was going to be impossible.

The familiar taste of the fear of rejection hit Lily like a brush of cold air, and she shivered, picturing the scene too clearly: Travis hitting on a lovely dark-haired, olive-skinned lady in a bar, while she nursed a glass of wine in a dark corner and tried not to feel ugly and out of place. Travis making passionate love to the lithe, vibrant woman, while she made do with the dildo she had packed and gallons of chocolate gelato. It was all too real. All too possible. All too much like her life had been up to that point.

Travis cut into her negative visions. "Are you cold?" he asked, making no disguise of staring straight at her rapidly hardening nipples. "Should I get a blanket from the stewardess for you?"

Fighting the urge to cover her breasts with her arms, Lily shook her head and shot Travis a brilliant smile, pulling her one and only ace out of the hole. "Thanks for your concern, but I'm *fine*." She accented the word "fine," knowing how much it bothered him ever since their mind-blowing sexual interlude in the pool.

Her taunting seemed to do the trick, since he immediately stowed his briefcase in the overhead bin and sat down next to her without another word.

The stewardess leaned a little too close to Travis in a blatant display of youth and sexual confidence. "Would you like a glass of champagne, sir?"

Travis nodded and took the glass as the woman said, "Let me know if you and your wife need anything else before takeoff," then turned back toward the cockpit.

Lily blinked stupidly. *You and your wife?* Someone actually thought that she could get a guy like Travis to marry her?

As if sensing her thoughts, he leaned toward her. "I wonder what gave the stewardess the impression that you and I were married?" he said, his words slightly mocking, implying that Lily was the obvious responsible party.

All of her stuffed-down embarrassment bubbled up inside her, mixing with something that tasted remarkably like rage. "I certainly didn't."

The plane taxied and soared over San Francisco Bay, up beyond the clouds. Lily tried to focus her attention on the bright blue sky, on the clouds, on anything but Travis's thigh and arm only inches away from her. Briskly, she opened the thick romance novel she had bought at the airport newsstand and tried to lose herself in the story, but she could hardly make sense of the words that swam before her. It was no use, not with Travis in the seat next to her at thirty thousand feet, so she pretended to sleep, all the while horribly aware that she wanted him more than she ever had before.

Overwhelmed by Travis-induced claustrophobia, Lily realized that if she didn't get up out of her seat and away from Travis in the next second, she was going to lose it completely. And since she didn't want to leave the rest of the first-class passengers with the memory of some big girl breathing into a barf bag to stop hyperventilating, she kicked off the soft blanket across her legs and stood up, trying to figure out how to slide past Travis without touching him.

"Excuse me," she muttered to his knee.

Travis shifted barely an inch. "Getting up to stretch your legs?"

Lily stopped staring at his knee and glared into his pupils. There was a threat implied somewhere in his seemingly innocuous words, she knew there was, even if she didn't know exactly where. And the smug way that he stayed buckled into his seat really bugged her. He knew perfectly well that he was making getting into the aisle virtually impossible for her. Why, she wondered furiously, couldn't he be a gentleman and stand up so that she could get into the aisle without rubbing every inch of her heated flesh against him?

"Yes," she hissed. "Now will you please move?"

Travis smiled placidly, but Lily didn't miss the devil in his eyes. "You can get past me, can't you?"

"No problem," she said, her voice flat with suppressed anger. "I'd hate to disturb you when you look so comfortable," she said with disgust. Travis merely nodded and raised an eyebrow while waiting for her to slide on by.

What had she ever seen in him? Why had she pined after such an out-and-out jerk all these years? So what if he had a huge cock and knew just what to do with it? So what if the things he did with his tongue made her want to slip into a coma? Big deal if his hands on her nipples was as close to heaven as she'd ever get. Phenomenal sex was no excuse for the way he treated her.

I hate you, she thought and it was so good to feel something other than lust for Travis, that she thought it again. *I hate you, so there.*

Now that she had decided she hated Travis Carson, once and for all, all that remained was to figure out how to get past him into the aisle without bringing herself to orgasm on some part of his body. She looked at his thigh and remembered her wetness on him, then cursed herself for being lily-livered again.

"Maybe I should change my name to Jennifer," she muttered.

"What was that?" Travis asked, all innocence.

"I wasn't speaking to you," she said, and licked her lips, trying not to notice that Travis closely followed the progress of her tongue, then shifted in his seat, looking suddenly uncomfortable.

Back to her plan for making it out to the aisle in one piece. No matter how she looked at it, there was no way to win. Either she was going to smash her boobs into Travis's mouth or she was going to suffocate him with her butt. And then she wouldn't be able to keep an eye on him. Who knew where his hands might go if she wasn't looking? She caught the amusement and blatant sexual challenge in his eyes at her quandary and knew that she had no choice but to slide out with her eyes fixed on the blackguard.

Sucking her stomach into her rib cage as far as it would go, Lily pressed her spine into the back of the seat in front of them and slid to the left. Right then, Travis's book fell off his lap onto the floor and he bent forward to pick it up. Silky black hair brushed against Lily's nipples, and she sucked in a breath.

"Stop that!" she whispered, her face hot with need and annoyance.

Travis straightened up and put the book safely on her empty seat. As if he didn't realize she was caught between the seat in front of him and his thighs, he brushed a red curl away from her cheek. "My book fell."

His gaze fell to her hard nipples, and Lily wanted to scream with frustration. Suddenly her rash decision to put on something enticing seemed like the stupidest thing she'd ever done.

How could she have thought that wearing something so revealing with virtually no support was a good idea?

Closing her eyes, she pushed past Travis, ignoring the warm hand that somehow found its way to her thigh. Finally, she was in the aisle, and freedom had never felt so good.

Or so cold now that Travis's heat was gone.

I'm finally free of him, she told herself, planning on spending the rest of the flight at the bar, but instead of feeling happy, she couldn't help but feel a little let down.

Shaking her curls out, she straightened her shoulders and smiled at the cute young bartender, who was making no bones about his appreciation for her dress. "Can I get you something to drink?" he asked.

Pleased by his appreciative smile after all of Travis's barely disguised mockery, Lily slid onto the round barstool with a sigh of relief. "I'd love a gin and tonic," she said, feeling naughty and giddy. "And I love your accent," she added, wanting desperately to have a normal conversation with someone after the stilted repartee that she and Travis were so good at it. "Where are you from?"

The young man grinned as he mixed her drink. "London."

Lily rested her chin on her hands. "I'd love to go to England one day for more than just a layover." The bartender set her drink in front of her, and she took a sip. "Delicious," she said, enjoying the buzz that crept into her skull. She took another sip, and said, "I've never been anywhere before. I can't believe I'm going to Italy."

The bartender leaned onto the counter, his brown eyes soulful and not-a-little lustful, about to reply when his eyes shifted over Lily's shoulder.

"I'll have whatever she's having," Travis drawled as he slid onto the barstool next to Lily, trapping her hips between his thighs, making his possession of her perfectly clear to the bartender.

Instantly the young man stood and was once again a consummate professional. Lily put the gin and tonic to her lips and gulped the rest down. "I'm done," she said. Getting up as fast as she could, she had to steady herself on the gleaming wood bar. "Got to work on upping my tolerance," she muttered as she hoisted herself back onto her heels. She walked briskly down the aisle past her seat, past the curtains where the flight attendants gossiped, into a private compartment with one bathroom door. She prayed that it was unoccupied as she reached for the handle.

It turned easily and she raised her eyes to the plastic paneling on the low ceiling of the aircraft. "I owe you one," she said, and stepped into the rather large bathroom. The wind was all but knocked out of her as something large pushed in behind her and locked the door.

She spun around, or tried to, in the space that was definitely not big enough for two. "Are you crazy?" she said. "Get out of here."

Travis looked sickeningly at ease in the bathroom with her, and she wanted to poke his eyes out. Or wrap her legs around him to ride him into submission. She couldn't decide which until he said, "I wanted to make sure you were okay. You seemed a little unsteady there at the bar when you stood up."

Definitely poke his eyes out, *then* ride him.

I hate him, she reminded herself, then said, "I don't like you very much right now," which seemed a bit harsh to her ears.

But Travis wasn't scared off by her declaration. "Why not?" he asked, his voice silky and hot. "I like you Lily. A lot," he said as he deftly turned them around and pressed Lily back against the door.

"Remember what happened last time?" he said, the devil tempting her with memories of one of the best orgasms of her life, of his tongue slipping in and out of her wetness, of his teeth closing in gently on her clit.

Lily shook her head and closed her eyes. "Please go," she begged, hating herself for being weak, hating herself for not being the kind of woman who could kick Travis out. Hating herself for wanting him so bad she was going insane with it.

"Ever heard of the mile-high club?" Travis's voice wrapped around her like cashmere, and she found herself looking into a mouth made for cunnilingus. His lips found hers, and she could have sworn the plane dipped a thousand feet as she fell into him, desperate for more of his taste, for the pleasure that only he could give her.

From somewhere deep in her subconscious, Luke's voice was fuzzy in her brain. *Women make it too easy for Travis. Make him beg, Lily.*

With sudden clarity she knew that wrapping her legs around Travis's thighs and riding him in an airplane bathroom was definitely not making him beg. Mustering up every ounce of control she possessed, and then some, she slid her hands from behind his neck around to his chest and pushed with all her might.

Travis fell back against the toilet with a loud thud and a stewardess knocked on the door. "Is everything all right in there?"

Lily stared at Travis, shocked by what she'd done, but obviously not as shocked as Travis, judging by his confused and bewildered expression. Smiling, Lily called out, "I'm fine, thank you. I lost my footing for a moment."

She heard the click of the attendant's heels as she moved away from the door. "Strictly professional, Travis," she said as she slipped out the door and walked back to the bar, a new spring in her step.

"Another gin and tonic," she said as she savored her victory. God it felt good to best Travis, she thought with a giggle. No doubt he was going to kill her for embarrassing him like that, but right then, with a cool fizzy drink in her hand, and Italy awaiting, for the first time in her life Lily really didn't give a damn.

Unfortunately, the rest of the trip seemed to go on forever. Especially when Travis blatantly flirted with the pretty stewardess after making it clear that he and Lily were only business partners. She had watched them as surreptitiously as possible through barely open eyes, a blanket tucked up around most of her body and face to hide her spying. It didn't help that Travis kept "accidentally" brushing up against her to reach for the window shade, or to pick up his pen, which he dropped a dozen times throughout the flight. Every time his body came in contact with hers, goose bumps covered her skin, and her traitorous nipples went hard.

Landing in London, picking up luggage, going through customs, boarding a small plane to Rome, the limo ride to their hotel: Everything was a blur for Lily. She couldn't remember ever being so tired. Or horny, a niggling little voice whispered to her. All she wanted was to stand under a hot shower and crawl under cool sheets to sleep away the nightmare of being so painfully close to Travis and yet so far because of her *own* stupid rule. But even grumpy and sleepy, the magic of Tuscany started seeping in the minute they began to wind through the ancient streets in the long black limousine that picked them up at the airport.

She had pressed herself all the way against the corner of the limousine's backseat in an effort to stay as far away from Travis as she possibly could, but the light playing off the cypress trees and golden hills drew her like a moth to a flame. She rolled down her window with the touch of a button and let the sweet smells rush across her face.

"It's beautiful," she murmured to herself, having, for the moment, completely forgotten about Travis.

"Yes," he said, that low hoarse voice of his thrumming straight through her. "It is, isn't it?"

Lily couldn't help turning to look at him, such was the pull he had over her. "Simply beautiful," he said, staring straight into her eyes.

Lily bit down on the inside of her lip to keep from either yelling at him for teasing her, or, worse yet, kissing him. There was no way he could be talking about her being beautiful, she knew that with every fiber of her heart. Especially not after her little performance in the airplane bathroom. Why did he have to kiss her like he needed her to breathe one minute, then mock her the next?

Clamping her mouth shut, she turned back to the window, the beautiful sights around her blurring behind an image of Travis's face above hers, watching her intently as she came, his green eyes black as a moonless night.

7

Travis gritted his teeth as Lily turned away from him again to look out the window. He wasn't particularly interested in getting the silent treatment for the next five days. Maybe after she got a few hours of sleep Lily would be her normal self. The only problem was that Travis hardly knew what "normal" Lily was anymore. Normal Lily was supposed to be a wallflower who didn't have an ounce of guts. But from the first moment she had stepped onto the fashion runway on Saturday night, Lily had become a new woman to him.

Travis cursed himself for his rash decision to hire Lily to decorate his clients' house. If he hadn't been so wrapped up in the need to sink into her again, if he hadn't had to prove to himself that he could make her come—he could make anyone come until they went blind with pleasure, how could he have possibly doubted himself?—he could have thought straight and done the smart thing by dropping Lily back out of his life. As it was, he had definitely been thinking with the wrong head.

When he had decided to take Lily to Italy, he had planned to screw her brains out for five days straight. He'd intended to keep her mouth filled with his cock, his hands full of her incredible breasts, and both of them so exhausted that they would never even leave the hotel. He could have cared less whether or not they found rugs or tables or couches. His clients' house could be a barren wasteland at this point, he was so focused on doing Lily.

He still couldn't believe that she had actually shoved him onto the toilet in the airplane. He could tell by the way she had responded to his kiss that she wanted it as much as he did. The things he was planning to do to her in that small cubicle . . . But then she had to ruin everything by growing a spine. Or, he thought with a rueful smile, at least a small part of a spine.

How could one woman—Lily, no less—be messing so badly with his mind?

Travis searched the rolling hills and pink-tinged buildings for clarity, but no answers were forthcoming. All he knew was that as soon as they got to the hotel he was going to take a quick shower and head straight to the nearest bar. If he was lucky, he would meet some pretty young Italian girl who could clear his mind with a few hours of meaningless sex.

It wouldn't be meaningless with Lily, a voice in his head said, and Travis started in his seat. He shot a glance at Lily to see if she noticed his sudden movement; but, thankfully, she was leaning back into the seat, her eyes closed, her breathing soft and even.

Of course sex with Lily had been meaningless, he told himself.

Just because he wanted to watch her eyes change color as she exploded beneath him, just because he wanted to hear her say how much he had pleasured her didn't mean that sex with her was any more important than his last affair with . . . whatever her name had been.

Just because he'd never felt so complete with any other person, not even his brother Luke, didn't mean that he needed her. It didn't mean that he suddenly wanted to be her friend. And it definitely didn't mean that he was going to keep his dick in his pants for five days. If not Lily, someone. Although, he asked himself, *Why not both?*

The limo pulled up outside their hotel, the sumptuous Villa Rossi. Their driver opened the door and reached for Lily's hand to help her out, but when he saw that she was fast asleep he turned to Travis with a smile.

"The signora is beautiful when she sleeps, no?"

Travis narrowed his eyes at the driver, making it perfectly clear that the sleeping beauty was all his, staring him down until the driver stepped away from the door and went to the trunk to remove their luggage.

Travis slid close to Lily's soft, sleeping form and he brushed a red curl away from her face, unable to keep from touching her.

"We're here," he said quietly, not wanting to startle her, not when she looked so peaceful, and yes, beautiful, too.

Sleepy blue eyes opened, and Travis couldn't resist bending forward to steal a kiss. His lips touched hers, and something warm spread through him. Her tongue slipped into his mouth, and the pit of his belly hurt with lust and something else. Something he didn't want to examine. Ever. More thrown off by this warm feeling than he wanted to admit, he pulled away just as Lily's arms wrapped around his waist.

"Travis," she whispered against his lips and reached for him, but he moved out of the way just in time, before she could weave her magic spell around him again, before he stopped being able to think clearly. Before he did something stupid like beg her to make love to him again like only she could.

Scooting out the door, schooling his face into a mask of impartial politeness, he held out a hand for her. Lily looked confused by his abrupt change of demeanor for a moment, but as she became fully awake her confusion was replaced by a swift burst of anger.

"I can get out of the limo all by myself, thanks," she spat at him as she lowered one round leg, then the other, to the golden gravel outside the villa. Without waiting for him, she pushed open the heavy carved wood door and walked into the gleaming tiled entryway, her hips swaying provocatively.

When did she learn to do that? Travis was angry at everything and nothing at the same time. She wasn't supposed to be so sexy.

Travis saw the driver admiring Lily again and shot a well-aimed scowl at him. He tipped the man an amount barely enough to be courteous after all of that ogling, then grabbed their bags himself, brushing past a whey-faced bellboy. By the time he reached the counter, Lily was checking in.

"I believe you have a reservation for Lily Ellis," she said, gracing the good-looking older man behind the counter with a sexy smile.

"*Buono*," he said, giving Lily a slow perusal, stopping at her breasts for much too long.

She smiled back, all innocence. Travis snorted. She was so naive she didn't even know that she was being hit on. These Italian men would have her on her back with her legs spread wide so fast she wouldn't even see it coming. The image of her beneath some foreigner sent fire shooting through his gut.

She flicked her hair over her shoulder, and Travis watched as the Italian's eyes refocused again on her incredible breasts. One thing was clear: He had no choice but to protect Lily from these prowling, skirt-chasing Italians.

And the only way he could do that was if they thought that

she belonged to him. Travis was mulling over how he was going to pull off the necessary protective measures without angering Lily even more, when fate stepped in. Looking slightly embarrassed, the man behind the counter shook his head. "Signora Ellis, I am afraid I do not have any reservation under that name."

Lily looked momentarily flustered and then shot an accusing glance at Travis. "You did have your secretary book two rooms, didn't you?"

Travis leaned against the counter. He couldn't have hidden his smug grin if he'd wanted to. He scratched his chin, as if giving it some deep thought. "You know," he said finally, "I very well might have forgotten to mention that one small detail."

Giving him a look that spoke volumes about how much she despised him, Lily turned back to the Italian. "I'll take any room you've got. No," she said with increased venom, "I'll take the most expensive room in the hotel. I'm sure my business associate would be happy to pay for it."

Travis crossed his fingers and smiled as the man said the very words he hoped to hear. "I'm sorry, signora, but we are completely full. There are no available rooms."

"No available rooms?" she repeated in a hollow voice.

The man bowed his head. "I'm sorry, but there is only the one room for Signor Carson."

"With two double beds?" she asked, a final shred of hope lingering in her tone.

He shook his head. "I'm afraid not, signora. One large bed, perfect for two lovers."

Travis watched Lily clench and unclench her hands. He wouldn't have been surprised if steam started coming out of her ears at any minute. Nonetheless, he couldn't help but admire her poise in the face of adversity. Who would have thought that Lily Ellis had an ounce of poise to her name?

"Fine," she said as she snapped, looking like a glorious goddess in her anger. She grabbed her suitcase and dragged it behind her. "I'll go stay somewhere else."

"Signora," the man called out after her, "you will not find another room for miles. The *Festivale di Matrimonio* will be this weekend."

Travis did a quick translation and felt the sucker punch in his gut again. The Festival of Weddings? This whole thing with Lily had turned into some kind of sick joke.

First, he couldn't keep his hands off her. Then she wouldn't sleep with him again. And now, they were going to be surrounded by dozens of happy couples who were pledging their undying love to each other. Travis was certain that the man upstairs was having a good laugh right about then.

Making a clear effort to keep hold of her good manners, Lily turned back around, and calmly said, "Excuse me, the town is hosting the festival of what?"

The man smiled placatingly, but Travis didn't miss the wicked gleam in his eyes as he glanced at Lily, then Travis. "In your language, signora, it is the Festival of Weddings."

Lily looked ill. "The Festival of Weddings?" She glared at Travis, who shrugged. Turning on the innocent man behind the counter, her poise clearly in shreds, she repeated in a hollow voice, "The Festival of Weddings. You've got to be kidding me."

"No, signora, it is for real. The Festival of Weddings takes place in Saturnia once every twenty-five years. It is the most wonderful of all nights." He placed one hand over his heart. "Love is everywhere during the festival. No one can resist it."

Travis shifted uncomfortably, sensing something ominous and murky in his future, but Lily simply gave a quick sidelong glance in Travis's direction and snorted.

"I can sure as hell resist it," she muttered none too quietly.

"We have been preparing for the festival for many months, and now it is nearly upon us."

Glad that the ball was firmly back in his own court, Travis said, "Looks like we're going to be sharing a room after all," not bothering to keep the sound of victory hidden from his voice.

Lily grabbed the key off the counter and spun around to face Travis. "Fine," she said, "but if you think this changes one single thing about the strictly professional terms of our trip, you are dead wrong." Poking a finger into his chest, she repeated, "Dead wrong."

With that she grabbed the key off the counter and stalked up the granite stairs toward their room.

Travis smiled. "Women always get so cranky after long flights. Send up a bottle of your best champagne."

The man looked at Travis with a mixture of commiseration and envy before switching back to a professionally bland manner. "You are in Room 305, signor. Top of the stairs to the right. I will send the champagne right up."

LILY FUMED all the way up the stairs. So much for her long hot shower. So much for her perfect nap. So much for making it through the trip in one piece. She wouldn't be able to get away from Travis for one minute, not even to hide out in her room.

Because it was *his* room, the stinking pig! She sincerely doubted that he would have made the "mistake" of booking only one room if she were a middle-aged gay male interior decorator. She laughed at the image of Travis being chased around a hotel room by another man who couldn't wait to have his way with him.

But her smile quickly fell away as she wondered why she was even the least bit surprised by Travis's dastardly behavior. One room with one bed "made for lovers" for both of them for five whole days.

Travis was the most infuriating man she had ever known, she thought, as she fought with the ancient key in the old wood door. "Stupid door," she said, but when it finally swung open the only thing Lily could do was gape in wonderment.

She and Travis were going to be sharing the most romantic hotel room in the entire world. Not to mention the biggest. The suite had to be twice the size of her Noe Valley apartment. She was standing in an enormous sitting room, the bathroom and bedroom a long way off. White marble gleamed as late afternoon sun came pouring in through the floor-to-ceiling windows. The sofas were covered in beautiful muted blue-and-green fabric so plush she wanted to take off all her clothes and rub herself against them like a kitten. A balcony outside the windows beckoned her as views of rolling hills captured her imagination.

Forgetting all about her anger, she moved toward the balcony as if in a dream. The vista before her was more beautiful than any picture could be.

She tried to describe it in her head, tried to put words to the view before her so that she could call Janica and explain the wonder of Tuscany, but undulating hills covered in vineyards, old cobblestone streets, a sky so blue it seemed to have invented the color, none of that even scratched at the surface.

A sound from inside the room startled her, and suddenly she remembered: She was in Tuscany with Travis, and she was going to have to share a king-size bed with him while holding firm to her no-sex rule for five days. Scratch that. Since she was utterly certain that Travis wouldn't agree to sleep on the couch, Lily decided that she would have to be the one to suffer, even though she was desperate for a real bed. She groaned and turned around, surprised to see that the sitting room was empty.

Leaving the balcony, she saw that Travis had opened his suitcase on one of the couches in the sitting room then disappeared, probably taking his medicine bag into the bathroom to clean up. Still craving a long, hot bath, she decided she would treat herself after she kicked Travis out for a while to give her some privacy.

His bag cried out for her to snoop through it, and Lily couldn't resist. To her surprise, it looked like he had women's clothes in it. Feeling a little bad about snooping, but not that bad after the way he had tricked her into sharing a room and a bed, she realized his bag was full of one neatly folded, gorgeous dress after another. There were no tags on the dresses, nothing to indicate size, or designer, or where they had come from. The fabric on the dresses was so soft, so colorful, she was tempted to try one of them on, even though she was certain they would be too small for her. Besides, he'd know that she'd been snooping through his bag if she pulled the clothes out of their neat pile. And the last thing Lily wanted was for Travis to think that she actually cared if he had plans to meet another woman while they were in Tuscany.

Oh God. It was so obvious. Why wouldn't he have a lover in every town he visited, Lily asked herself. He was gorgeous and rich, and when he touched a woman she melted with need.

She couldn't fight back the jealousy when it reared its ugly head, laughing at her and taunting her for thinking Travis would ever choose to spend time with her when he could get a pretty, thin, perfect woman in his bed inside of thirty seconds.

Lily had seen the kind of skinny twits that Travis liked hanging off his arm, and she doubted their IQs were much higher than their dress sizes. Feeling nasty and spiteful, she picked up her suitcase and stomped into the bedroom, angry at Travis for being such a womanizer but even angrier at herself for caring.

He could have a hundred Italian lovers for all she cared.

Besides, she thought with a devious smile, she had brought The Dress with her. Travis wouldn't be the only one with beautiful foreigners falling at his feet. Lily *knew* the power of The Dress could transcend anything.

On Saturday night hadn't The Dress single-handedly gotten the lust-of-her-life into bed with her? No reason it couldn't work its potent magic again. On anyone but Travis, she reminded herself.

She reached into her suitcase and unfolded the precious dress, smoothing out a few small wrinkles with her hands. She wasn't going to be quiet, pathetic Lily for another minute longer. She was going to wear The Dress to find her own Italian lover. And any chance she got, she was going to torture Travis. She was going to make him so hot for her he was going to need an extinguisher by the time their stay was over.

And no matter what, she wasn't going to let him make love to her. Even if she had to lock herself in the bathroom with a dildo all night long to deal with the way he made her feel, she was going to hold out on him.

"Go away," Lily said to the loud and insistent voice of doubt that told her she was crazy, that said she had no hope of torturing Travis, not when she rated a negative number on the "how sexy are you?" scale compared to Travis's off-the-charts score. Grasping at strings she searched her travel-muddled brain for the positive affirmations she had read in the book at the back of her bookshelf. Looking around the suite to make sure that Travis wasn't going to witness her talking to herself like a lunatic, she said, "I am a strong, beautiful woman. I love myself, and others love me, too."

The sound of running water made her jump halfway out of her skin. Travis hadn't heard her, had he? She could only imagine the kind of ridicule he would heap upon her for repeating her stupid, never-gonna-happen mantras.

Hoping she looked calm and composed, she turned to look through the door of the bedroom into the living room. Travis was leaning against the bathroom door on the far side of the gracious suite, wearing nothing but a towel. His chest was tanned with a light dusting of dark hair in the vee between his pecs, and Lily couldn't help but think that he should have an infomercial on TV selling some sort of abdominal exercise products with a six-pack like his. It took Lily every ounce of willpower not to give away her intense and immediate arousal from just looking at him.

"Like the room?" he drawled.

Even as she breathed a sigh of relief that he hadn't overheard her doing those stupid affirmations, Lily wanted to smack him for being so supremely confident. So deliciously male. So perfect. Why did he have to be so flawless? It wasn't fair that she had been given a laundry list of shortcomings, while Travis had been showered with brains, beauty, and unflagging confidence.

Travis was still staring at her from across the room. The challenge was clear in the heat of his gaze, the indolence of his stance. Lily knew it was time to make some decisions, and quick.

I'll never get what I want out of life if I don't go for it.

Reaching for her new feminine wiles, she said, "This room is amazing," letting her voice drop to a husky burr. She kicked off her heels and moved past him into the exquisite bathroom. A huge sunken whirlpool tub in the middle of the room was filling with steaming water. Glancing at Travis over her shoulder, Lily purred, "Thanks so much for running a bath for me. I really needed one after such an exhausting flight."

Trying not to worry about cellulite, reminding herself that she had been completely naked and in control with Travis at his client's pool just days ago, Lily dropped one strap of her red dress from her shoulder, then the other, pushing the stretchy red fabric of the dress down. The bodice had an inner support built in and wasn't meant to be worn with a bra, so her nipples popped up above the fabric. Lily stilled, unable to continue.

What am I doing? She looked up into the mirror and saw herself half-naked, with Travis standing mere feet behind her in nothing but a towel.

Almost afraid of what she might see, she forced herself to look into Travis's eyes. The unbridled lust in them infused Lily with a new shot of confidence. She stripped the rest of her dress off along with her panties and stepped into the tub, sliding down the slick porcelain into the safety of the hot water.

Feeling much more confident with her lumps and bumps at least partially hidden beneath the bubbles of the jets, she whispered, "Ahh, it feels so good," and had to bite down on the inside of her lip to fight back her smile of victory at Travis's instantaneous reaction to her erotic teasing.

The towel around his waist did nothing to conceal his enormous erection. Patting the tile surrounding the tub, not knowing whether she was being foolish or brave, Lily said, "There's enough room for both of us in here. Besides," she said, dropping her eyes to hide her lie, "I trust you to honor our agreement."

Travis ripped the towel from around his waist and Lily got an eyeful of his glorious cock before he climbed into the opposite end of the whirlpool tub, the hair on his legs tickling the skin on the outsides of her thighs as he stretched his legs out around her hips. Lily pulled in her legs just enough that her knees crested at the top of the water, anything to get away from Travis's heat.

Every nerve ending in Lily's body was on fire. Every part of her begged to touch him. She wanted to feel the hot length of his shaft in her hands. Against her lips. In her pussy.

It took every ounce of strength not to straddle him in the tub. She was already so wet, so ready for him, that she knew how easily he would slide deep, so deep, into her slickness. Her muscles contracted at the thought. Too tired to fight her arousal any longer, and knowing that she'd never be able to relax or sleep again until she relieved her intense arousal, Lily let her hand drift under the bubbles.

Gently, she touched herself between her legs, pushing one finger inside. Slick fluid coated her finger, and her vagina clenched, disappointed that the slim digit wasn't nine hot inches.

Lily could hear Travis's breath coming out in short, loud puffs, and it excited her even more. *I'm getting to him,* she thought with satisfaction. *I'm driving him crazy.*

Not only did she desperately want to make him suffer, but God almighty did she need to come, or she was going to go crazy herself. Feeling deliciously naughty, instead of pulling her hand away from her mons and putting it back on the tile rim of the large tub, she allowed her hips to settle firmly against Travis's calves and rubbed small, firm circles against her clit. From beneath her half-closed eyes she could see Travis watching her breasts as they floated on the surface of the water, her nipples appearing above the water, then moving below again.

"What the hell are you doing?" Travis growled.

Not stopping the movement of her hand on her clit, Lily

opened her eyes wide, giving Travis her most innocent look. "Taking a bath," she replied, knowing that he had begun to watch her hand under the bubbles as she swirled the moist and swollen nub between her legs.

Feeling incredibly bold, she turned the question on him. "What are you doing?"

Travis pierced her with his green eyes. "Watching you masturbate, I think."

Lily's hand stilled at his audacious words. How could she continue like this? Lily Ellis wasn't a bad girl! She was a good girl who masturbated in the privacy of her own bathroom, not in front of a virile man sharing a tub.

But the hunger in Travis's eyes told her she was doing everything just right, and somehow, Lily managed to stay the course, never forgetting for a moment that it was imperative to make herself come like a rocket while leaving Travis high and dry.

Lily shifted to let her breasts surface again. "If you had gotten me my own room, we wouldn't have this problem. I would have been able to masturbate in the privacy of my own bath, as often as I felt like it."

A choking sound emerged from deep in Travis's chest.

"You can leave if it's making you uncomfortable," she offered, knowing that a thousand horses couldn't drag Travis from the tub.

"I don't think so," he said with a grin, which seemed a tad forced. She wondered what it cost him to stay on his side of the tub, when she knew he desperately wanted to suck on her nipples.

"I'm happy to sit back and enjoy the show," he added. "Unless, of course, you need some help."

Lily smiled a purely feminine smile, even as she admired his bravado. "Now, Travis, you know that would be a strict breach of our agreement. Besides," she added, "I can take perfectly good care of myself."

With that she closed her eyes and spread her legs farther. She heard Travis switch off the jets. Knowing that he would be able to see everything she did to herself only made her wetter. She brought one hand up to fondle her breasts while the other swirled her increasingly sensitive clit.

She had dreamed of Travis watching her touch herself, but knowing that he was in the room with her, smelling his essence was driving her positively insane. *I'm in a bathtub with Travis,* she marveled and the thought was so wicked, so delicious, that a wide smile curved across her lips.

Her womb felt heavy and thick, as if all the blood in her body was pooling between her legs. Spreading her legs even wider, she slid down another inch in the tub to give her fingers better access. She slipped them between her slick folds, past the tight entrance. She was incredibly aroused by Travis's eyes on her, the pressure of his thighs and calves against her hips.

Her finger swirled in tighter and tighter circles, and she was about to open her eyes, to watch Travis's face while she came just inches from him, when the water rippled across her breasts and her eyes shot open. Travis was moving toward her, one hand reaching for her, the other pumping up and down on his shaft.

"Oh God, Lily, you've got to let me . . ."

Lily desperately wanted Travis to touch her, to run his tongue over her nipples, to slip a finger into her. But, much to her surprise, in that crucial moment, even more than she wanted him to give her sweet release, she wanted to see him beg.

Lily needed to see Travis suffer for wanting her like she had suffered for wanting him all these years.

Mustering up the courage of her own no-longer-latent sex goddess within, she put her foot in the middle of his belly, directly above the throbbing head of his glorious cock. "Stay over there," she said as she pushed him back into the water with a splash.

His face was a picture of surprise, much like it had been in the airplane bathroom, and Lily had to swallow a giggle. It was time to finish what she started. Settling back against the edge of the tub, she stretched one leg out until the arch of her foot was pressed against the long, thick length of Travis's cock. Pulling up the knee of her other leg, opening herself wide to Travis's astonished glance, she rubbed herself while gently rubbing her toes against the head of his shaft.

The heavy silence in the room was broken only by the sound of the water lapping against porcelain and their heavy breathing. Lily looked away from Travis's mesmerizing eyes and focused on his penis, so glorious even underwater, velvety soft against the sensitive skin on the bottom of her foot.

She bit her lip and, on the edge of coming, moved her foot away and cried out at the thought of Travis ramming into her. He reached for himself, and she was undone.

Her head fell back against the thick tile rim. "Travis," she moaned, as her hips bucked up in the water against her maniacally moving fingers. Her orgasm, while not as good as anything Travis had made her feel with his tongue and cock, was so much better than any orgasm she had ever had solo. She didn't simply contract between her legs, she convulsed.

Travis panted, "Jesus," and when she opened her eyes, Lily watched him come in thick spurts, the cords of his neck taut, his biceps flexed, his abs tensed into a perfect six-pack.

Get out of the tub, Lily, she advised herself silently. *Get out of the tub, and it will be Lily, one, Travis, zero.* But the combination of warm water with a huge orgasm was a powerful relaxation formula. She so badly wanted to close her eyes and go to sleep.

Get up before he convinces you to go for round two. She couldn't help it, she smiled at the thought of round two. And three. And four.

Get up before he punishes you for pushing him away.

Her eyes grew wide at that thought. In a flash, she was up and reaching for a cream-colored plush bath towel.

"Lily," Travis growled in a menacing tone from behind her. She instinctively scurried to the door before she remembered that she was in control of this situation. Conjuring up a playful, unconcerned glance, she peeked at Travis over her shoulder, and said, "I'm starved, aren't you?"

Travis's eyes ran from her head to her toes, then back up. Lily's blood rushed hot, but she pointedly ignored her arousal. "I'm going to get dressed and find a restaurant," she said, heading into the bedroom without waiting for an answer, hoping that Travis hadn't noticed the towel shaking in her trembling hands.

Why, oh why, did the first thing to come out of her mouth when she was stark naked in front of Travis be about food?

Lily sighed and dried herself off. Somehow she was going to make it through the trip. Either that or throw herself off the balcony, where she would surely crush a lovely rosemary plant when she fell.

8

TRAVIS TOWELED OFF his hair with quick, angry strokes. He couldn't remember the last time he had been left so unsatisfied by a sexual encounter. Lily was turning out to be one mean cock-teaser.

Either that or she's just not that into you, buddy.

Travis stood up too fast and bumped his head on the marble counter around the sinks. He scowled at his reflection in the mirror. "Bull," he said, before wrapping the towel around his waist. "She's into me," he stated, trying for a cocky grin, but it fell flat, and he knew it.

Travis had never had to work so hard with a woman. He beckoned, they came. He wanted, they gave. He left, well . . . he didn't know exactly what they did when he left. But the one thing he did know was that there was no way that Lily was going to mess up his sexual self-esteem.

Travis turned and walked out of the bathroom, colliding with Lily as she headed for the main door of their suite.

He grabbed her arm roughly, hoping it looked like he was

trying to steady her, when really all he wanted was to finally touch her. He repressed a groan of desire as his fingers wrapped around her upper arm, lightly brushing against her incredible breasts.

"What are you doing in that dress?" he said, regretting his sneer and tone the minute the words flew from his lips. Dealing with Lily was difficult enough right then—he was so horny he wanted to drag her by her hair into the bedroom and take her again and again and again—but seeing her in that dress, the incredible sheath from the fashion show, was enough to send all of the remaining blood away from his brain.

Lily wrenched her arm from his grasp and took a step away from him. Licking her delicious red lips, she narrowed her eyes. When did her eyelashes grow so long? Travis wondered inanely as he watched her pupils dilate.

"Not that it's any of your business, Travis," she said, his name sounding like a curse, "but I'm going out to eat dinner."

Travis took another step closer to her. "Everything you do in this country is my business," he said, unable to stop the rush of words even though he knew he sounded like an idiot. "I brought you here, and whatever you do you're going to be doing with me." *If only that were true,* he thought.

Lily's eyes widened. "Oh." Her mouth formed a pretty little circle. Sweet as sugar, she said, "I didn't know you were so proprietary with your colleagues. I wonder why you even brought me along if you were planning to make all of the decisions anyway?"

Travis didn't trust himself at all standing so close to Lily, particularly when she was wearing *that* dress. If she were any other woman, he would have kissed the smirk off her face; but for the first time, he wasn't sure if a woman wanted him to kiss her. Yet again, Travis regretted his impulsive decision to bring Lily to Italy. He had been blinded by the need to bury himself between her breasts, to sink into her wet heat.

Angry at her, but even angrier at himself, Travis ground out, "Wait here for me. I'm coming with you." Lily sighed dramatically but had the good sense to head back into the living room to sit down. If she had tried to bolt, he would have had to spank her until she knew who was boss.

His cock surged beneath the towel at the thought of bringing his hands down onto her round butt cheeks. He grabbed his suitcase off the living room couch and walked into the bedroom. God forbid Lily knew that he couldn't keep from getting a hard-on around her, even after he'd beat off like a schoolboy in the tub minutes before. Then she'd think that she actually had some sort of control over him.

No matter how cool he had to play it from that point forward, he was going to make sure that she never found out how badly she affected him. *Lose the hard-on and get dressed, moron,* he instructed himself with cold practicality.

Five minutes later he emerged in faded jeans and a Red Sox T-shirt. Lily, who was lounging on one of the plush sofas, had the nerve to raise an eyebrow when she saw him, and say, "Nice T-shirt."

Travis had hoped to shame her into changing her outfit by dressing like a slob—her dress messed with his brain waves in a big way—but the opposite had happened: He felt like a schmuck for underdressing.

The only thing left to do was to get out of this godforsaken hotel room—the bathtub would never look quite the same again—and into the crisp, clear Tuscan air. After a quick dinner he'd drop Lily back off at the hotel and prowl the bars in town.

If a festival of weddings was going on, there were bound to be plenty of single, desperate women dying for an American businessman to show them a good time.

Travis held open the door. "Let's go."

Lily ignored his brusque manner and as he followed her down the stairs, he felt like a double-sized schmuck. At the bottom of the stairs, the man behind the counter inquired, "Is the room okay, Signora Lily?"

Lily graced him with a wide smile. "Oh, Giuseppe, it's absolutely perfect."

Jealousy bubbled up inside Travis at their easy informality. "Giuseppe?"

Lily shrugged one pretty shoulder. "I called him to ask about restaurants while you were getting dressed."

"I told the bella signora"—Lily blushed and Travis wanted to punch Giuseppe in the mouth—"that she would find much, how do you say, romance, at Diletto."

At the mention of romance, Travis grunted and stalked out onto the sidewalk, making a mental note to give Lily a much overdo lecture on the dangers of flirting with strange men, especially strange men named Giuseppe.

Lily's tinkling laugh spilled onto the narrow street. Holding her arms out wide, she spun in a circle. "I'm in love . . . whee!"

Her hair flowed around her shoulders, and her delight was more potent than the twilight. Travis hated how he was holding his breath, waiting to find out who she was in love with. If she said Giuseppe, he was going to lock her in the hotel room for the next five days. Or better yet, he'd put her back on the airplane and send her home. Now why hadn't he thought of that before?

"Who are you in love with?" he grumbled, when she didn't finish her sentence.

Giving him an impish grin, she moved down the lane. "With Saturnia, of course," she called out.

Travis admired the sway of her hips, thinking how impossibly *right* she looked in Italy. But it wasn't a case of the country making the woman.

Tonight, Lily's presence made Italy come to life.

He tugged at the front of his jeans, which were suddenly tight and uncomfortable, and ran his fingers through his hair. What was happening to him? If he didn't know better he'd think Janica had cursed the dress with some sort of lust potion that was messing up the normal lines of communication between his brain and his dick.

He followed after Lily, down the curving streets, down into the valley below. A wide smile lit her face as she turned and pointed to the restaurant. "This is it! Diletto. Giuseppe said it means 'delight' in English. Isn't that the perfect word to describe this restaurant?"

Travis raised an eyebrow, but said nothing. Obviously, Lily didn't know that many people thought that the word "dildo" derived its origin from the Italian word. He decided to keep the knowledge to himself. For the time being.

He did have to admit, however, that the interior of the restaurant was a cut above. The walls were stucco, tinted with a golden yellow; the floor tiles looked perfectly ancient, seemingly worn with the soles of millions of Italian feet.

She glided inside and the maître d' immediately approached her, kissing her hand and touching her far too much for Travis's liking. None too gently, he shoved the man aside, taking his place at Lily's side. She was just opening her mouth to say something, but Travis was sure that whatever she said would be misconstrued by this lusty Italian as, "Please come back to my hotel room."

"We would like a table for two," he said, placing a possessive hand around Lily's shoulders. She shot him an irritated glance and tried to shrug his arm off, so Travis held her tighter.

I'm only doing this to protect her from depraved foreigners, he told himself. Not that he minded the feel of her breasts pressing up against his chest, however.

The maître d' eyed Travis with laughter in his eyes, and for what seemed like the hundredth time since landing in Italy, Travis had to restrain from decking a guy. What he wouldn't give to be back in the United States, where no one looked twice at Lily.

Or did they?

Lily's round warmth was pressing into him, and it felt good. Really good. She was shapely, without being too round. Voluptuous, but not surgically enhanced, like so many of the women he had bedded. And he knew for a fact that the curves of her body fit his better than anyone else's ever had. No, he thought with some dismay, it wasn't impossible that men back home would find Lily attractive. After all, he had impossibly high standards, and he couldn't keep his hands off her.

Confused by his wayward thoughts, Travis let Lily escape his grasp as they were led to a small round table in the center of the room, where the scene was obviously set for romance. He had been hoping for a private table in the corner. Instead, they were center stage.

But instead of being embarrassed by being seen with Lily, Travis was jealous of every man in the room who dared ogle her. Something they all were currently doing.

"This table is perfect," she said, and in her glee she bestowed a kiss on the maître d's cheek.

Didn't she see how the man was leering down the front of her dress? Didn't she have any sense of personal boundaries?

Travis was furious at Lily for being so free with her sexuality, for kissing another man while she was out with *him*. Travis vowed that from this point forward, he was going to be so charming that she wasn't going to look at anyone else.

He pulled out her chair and roughly shoved her into it, ignoring her cry of, "Hey!"

So much for charming, he thought with a grimace. He'd obviously have to try a little harder.

"You wanted to eat, so let's eat," he said, picking up a menu and opening it with a thwap on the table.

His incredibly unwitty banter wasn't going to win him any points either.

Lily glared at Travis across the table, her bountiful breasts heaving with anger. "I won't let you do it," she said, her words stiff and cold as she shoved back the chair to stand up.

The maître d' hurried over to help her up, but Travis shot him a look that said, "I'll cut your balls off if you come over here again," and the man stopped dead halfway across the room.

Travis slammed the menu shut. "You won't let me do what?" he asked, his voice as sharp-edged as hers, even as he cursed himself for losing grip of every smooth move he had in his arsenal.

"I won't let you ruin Tuscany," she replied, dripping ice with every word.

He opened his mouth to protest, but he knew he was going to make the situation even worse if he said another word, so he shut it.

"I don't know what you have against me, Travis," she said, standing across from him, her hands pressed hard into the table, her breasts swaying provocatively toward him. He forced himself to concentrate on her face and not her incredible nipples as she said, "I don't know what you've always had against me, why you feel you have to treat me like I'm beneath you."

Her accusation snapped his mind back to attention, mostly because the validity of what she was saying made him feel like the smelliest piece of garbage in the gutter. The room spun, as she said, "I wasn't kidding when I told you I was through with your attitude. I may have agreed to share a room with you for the next five days, but I absolutely refuse to let you stomp all over the most glorious—"

"I'm sorry."

The words were out of his mouth before he knew they were coming. Lily's mouth opened and closed several times, but at least she stopped saying all of those things that were wrenching at his gut. It was easier to apologize to her than to deal with her accusations.

I've always treated her like she's beneath me?

"I'm sorry, Lily," he said again, fumbling over himself to get her to sit back down. "I promise I'll stop being such a jerk. It's just . . ." He gestured around the room. "It's just that all of these men are staring at you in that dress, and I can't stand it because I know that they want to—"

"They are?"

Lily looked around the room in surprise, her anger replaced with surprise.

Travis breathed a sigh of relief that he had turned her attention away from what a raging jerk he was. He said, "Every single one of them, Lily," and she sat back down while biting her lip in a show of disbelief.

"Like who? Show me who."

Thank God she's not leaving, he thought, as the fist unclenched in his gut. He pointed a thumb over his shoulder at the maître d', then the waiter beside him, then gave up, and said, "The whole lot of 'em, Lily. Every last man in here wants to strip you out of that dress. The minute you walked in the door they started wondering what your breasts would feel like in their palms, how it would feel to have your legs wrapped around them while they—"

"Okay, Travis," she interrupted, her face pink, her eyes bright. "I get it. You don't have to say anything more. Let's try to have a nice dinner, then get some sleep so that we can get some work done tomorrow."

She opened her menu, and Travis wondered at her sudden change in demeanor. Any other woman would have eaten up the attention she was getting, but Lily seemed unsure of how to deal with it. He should have kept his mouth shut, but he leaned across the table and reached for her hand.

"Attention isn't a bad thing, you know," he said, not quite sure why he was trying to make Lily feel better but all the same certain that he had to try.

Lily stared at her hand in his and blinked uncertainly. "All my life I've wanted to be invisible," she said softly. "No," she corrected, pain radiating from her, through his hand, with her words. "I have been invisible. Who wants to look at the fat girl unless they have something mean to say?"

"Lily, you're not fat," Travis said, realizing that he wasn't just saying it to appease her. He actually meant it.

She pulled her hand away. "I told you to stop making fun of me. Why won't you stop?" she pleaded.

Travis shook his head. "I'm serious, Lily. You look beautiful."

"Yeah right, whatever," she said, and he could tell she was trying to be strong, but the break in her voice gave her away.

A band started playing, and Travis decided there was only one way to break the tension. Getting up, he held out his hand. "Dance with me."

After a moment's uncertainty, Lily let him help her up and walk her over to the dance floor. He pulled her into his arms, feeling her tense and stiff against him. He let his fingers play in her curls, thrilling at the soft, silken strands. As he had hoped, the lulling music worked its spell on Lily, and he felt her muscles soften. Her body eased against him, the dress flowing against his legs, and he had to work to keep himself from growing any harder than he already was, sure that he would scare her away if she could feel the thick bulge in his jeans. Thank God they weren't relaxed fit; otherwise, his cock would be liable to attack Lily right there on the dance floor. After the way she had teased him in the bathtub he had wanted to tie her to the bedposts in their hotel room and do every possible thing he could think of to her lush, responsive body.

Trying to shake the incredible image of bondage games with Lily from his mind's eye, Travis made himself focus on how well they moved together, he and Lily. Her curves were the perfect foil for his taut strength. Over her shoulder he saw lust in the eyes of the other men. He wanted to wear a badge, something to declare, "She's all mine."

The song ended, but he didn't want to let her go. He again started to wonder what was wrong with him, but then he realized he just didn't care anymore.

If this was how right wrong felt, he couldn't believe how much time he had wasted fighting it.

He smoothed back a lock of Lily's hair, brushing it past her ear, watching it flow over her shoulder. Every part of him wanted to kiss her, to take her earlobe between his teeth, to taste the soft, sweet-smelling skin on her neck, to go lower, to caress the top of her breasts with his tongue . . .

Lily's stomach growled and broke the spell. She pulled back

and giggled self-consciously. "I guess my stomach knows when it's time for dinner, no matter where I am in the world."

Travis's midsection grumbled loudly, and he grinned. "Did you hear that?" Lily nodded and bit her lip in that sexy way again. "Look what you've started."

Lily led the way back to the table. "Everything looks so delicious," she said, as they opened their menus, "and I don't even know what the words mean."

Travis laughed and it felt good. And long overdue. He motioned for the waiter to come over. "We'll have what they're having," he said, pointing to the couple sitting behind them. "And a bottle of Chianti."

Lily smiled at him, and Travis's stomach flipped over. Probably just hunger pangs, he told himself, but suddenly he wasn't so sure.

THEIR FOOD WAS SERVED, and it looked and smelled better than any meal Lily had ever had. She wanted to dig in and devour the gnocchi in front of her, but her usual insecurities reared yet again. What if he thought she was a pig? Even though he had said she wasn't fat—like she'd believe that in a million years—the last thing she wanted to do was remind Travis of how big she was, not when she had The Dress on, anyway. So instead of digging into the gnocchi, she took one dainty bite of the pasta and had to stifle the groan of ecstasy when it melted on her tongue. She put her fork down and dabbed at her lips with the napkin.

"Something wrong with your food?" Travis asked, his brow furrowed with concern.

"Oh no," she said, "it's incredible. I'm, um . . ."

"What? You're starved, right? Eat up."

Travis slurped in a bite of angel-hair pasta, and some sauce landed on his chin. Before she realized what she was doing, Lily reached over, wiped the sauce off with her middle finger, and licked it off.

Travis groaned. "There's only so much a man can be expected to take. Do that again, and I won't be responsible for my actions."

Lily looked at her licked-clean finger and started. "I didn't . . . I wasn't . . ."

Travis grinned. "I really wish you would, you know," he said, then returned to his pasta with gusto.

What is that supposed to mean? Lily thought as she looked at him, confused by absolutely everything that Travis had said to her since he had apologized for his surly behavior when they sat down.

The smell of pasta and fresh-baked bread and sweet red wine wafted beneath her nose, and her stomach grumbled again, even more insistently this time. Watching Travis enjoy his food while she was using every ounce of will to ignore hers, she couldn't help but think, *Why can men eat as much as they want? Why do I always worry about eating in public? Who am I trying to impress? Travis? He'll never be impressed by me, so why am I depriving myself of the best food I've ever seen?*

Lily looked around the restaurant at the other diners, who were very much enjoying their dinners, and made up her mind. She was in Italy, and she was going to make the most of it. Reaching for her fork she took a bite of gnocchi, then another. A soft moan of delight escaped her lips, and when she looked up from her plate, she saw Travis watching her intently, his green eyes glittering in the candlelight.

Forcing the fearful fluttering in her belly to stop, she said, "Do you want some?"

Travis nodded, so she scooped up a forkful of pasta and held it out across the table. He wrapped his long, tanned fingers around her hand, sending a jolt of awareness up and down her spine. His eyes burning into hers, he put his mouth around the tongs of the fork and pulled the pasta onto his tongue. Lily could practically feel his warm lips suckling at her nipples.

But no matter how swept away Travis's touch made her feel, she had to remember that Travis had many lovers. Lily couldn't fool herself into believing she was special. And judging by the beautiful clothes in his luggage, he had one stashed away nearby.

Abruptly, she pulled her hand away and set it down on the plate with a clank. "I'm tired," she said. "If you don't mind, I'm going to call it a—" But before she could bid Travis a good night and get away from the hot promise she read in his eyes, a gorgeous young Italian stallion approached the table.

"Bella signora, will you honor me with a dance?"

"Me?" She fought the urge to look over her shoulder to see if the young man was talking to a woman behind her. And then she remembered. *I'm wearing The Dress.* Evidently its magic powers hadn't worn off quite yet.

Gracing the stud with a wide smile, she held out her hand to him, glad for the excuse to get away from Travis.

"The bella signora," Travis interrupted with a sneer, "is otherwise occupied right now."

If Lily hadn't been so confused by the show of masculine rites going on between the two men, she might have been able to laugh at how Travis was obviously flexing his biceps.

It was just her luck, she cursed, that Travis had picked that particular night to become possessive of her. Especially when she had already decided that she was not, under any circumstances, going to give in to her body's demands, no matter how much she wanted to feel his heavy weight pressing her down into the mattress. Besides, since she was nearly positive that he had an Italian lover stashed away, Lily wasn't about to miss out on her one chance to dance with a sexy foreigner. Sure, his shoulders weren't as broad as Travis's, his brown eyes didn't have the smoldering heat that Travis's green eyes did; but all that aside, he was definitely the second-cutest guy who had ever asked her to dance.

Ignoring Travis, Lily let the young man lead her to the dance floor. The stud held her close, pressing the firm lines of his body against hers, but Lily was hardly able to pay attention to him; not when Travis was staring holes into her back, not when she would rather have been in Travis's strong, warm arms.

As if from a distance, she saw herself dancing with the gorgeous foreigner, his hands moving down her back, and knew, without a doubt, how proud Luke would be of her. *Travis has never had a woman taken away from him,* Luke had said. At the time, Lily hadn't thought that she would be the first one, but now she hoped that when Travis saw how interested this guy was in her, he would begin to want her even one-tenth as much as she wanted him.

The warm chords of the classical guitar reminded her of that fateful night at the fashion show. It seemed like a lifetime away, a life where she was the invisible girl hiding in the corner, and Travis was the larger-than-life pirate who could ransack an entire ship and never once notice her for all the gold and silver blinding him. There in Italy, in The Dress, Lily felt that girl slipping away. It was frightening to lose the person she had always been; but the joy she felt at emerging from her cocoon, even if it had taken thirty years, was so great she wanted to sing it out to the whole world.

Caught up in a sudden rush of joy at the new colors that she saw before her, she pulled the Italian closer and relished the sensations of hard male muscle against her soft curves. He wasn't Travis, but he was life, and right then, that was the most important thing.

The song changed from soft and slow, to pulsing and intense. Lily followed the lead of her partner, melting into him. He moved so well and she was feeling so alive, so brand-new. She was in beautiful Tuscany, in the arms of a well-built Italian man at least five years her junior.

Suddenly, all her senses came alive. *Travis isn't at our table anymore*, she realized. He stole her from the Italian without a word and pulled her into his arms. She pressed her hips against his, rubbing herself against the thick bulge in the front of his jeans.

Lily didn't have any idea where her previous dance partner had disappeared to. All she knew was that she was finally where she belonged. In Travis's arms.

In a replay of the night at the fashion show, Travis pulled her off the dance floor and out onto the street. But, instead of being in San Francisco, instead of going back to his loft to attack each other greedily, they were a part of the mysteries of Tuscany.

Travis seemed to know exactly where he wanted to take her as he led them down the street away from their hotel, then through a crack in an ancient rock wall. They crossed a narrow dirt road to a field of wild olive trees. Travis was moving so fast, Lily stumbled in her heels.

In an instant he spun around and caught her. A thin patch of moonlight gleamed through the olive branches, illuminating the lust in Travis's eyes, full and undisguised. Lily shivered as he backed her up into the trunk of the tree. He pressed into her, and several olives shook from the branch to the ground.

"You're mine," he growled, then his mouth was coming down over hers. His warm breath fanned against her lips, and her heart stopped beating. The sensual friction of his thighs pressed against the vee between her legs was unbearably wonderful. She was moist, so slick and ready for him. Just one kiss, and she'd explode.

But he didn't lean forward to kiss her. Instead he waited for her to make the first move, saying, "Tell me what you want, Lily," and she didn't know whether to laugh or cry. After all, this whole "professional boundaries" thing was her stupid idea.

For one night, in an olive grove in Saturnia, couldn't she forget Luke's admonishments not to give in to Travis? Wasn't it fair for her to steal a few hours of carnal pleasure with the most incredible man on any continent?

Travis shifted his leg ever so slightly against her, and her body practically wept through the thin fabric of the dress, through the almost nonexistent lace of her thong. New life surged through her again, and with it came a new power. He wanted her, she knew he did.

The old Lily would have hidden from these feelings, sure that giving in to Travis's need, giving in to her needs, was wrong.

The new Lily was going to take as much pleasure, as much joy, as much of Travis as she could get. She had thirty years of drudgery to make up for, and by God, making love with Travis in a grove of olive trees under a Tuscan moon was the perfect place to start.

Pressing up on her tippy toes, she licked at Travis's full lower lip. She groaned as his taste exploded on her tongue—an all-male essence mixed with Chianti and need. His lips turned up with pleasure, but still, he pulled away ever so slightly.

"Tell me, Lily."

Lily found herself unable to look him in the eye. All of her shyness hit her like a brick, but she realized, with a force akin to anger, how much she hated feeling shy.

Boldly turning her gaze to his, she brushed her thumb across the dark, sexy stubble on Travis's chin. "I want you, Travis," she said, and he groaned and came forward to kiss her. Lily stilled him with a finger across his lips, soft and yet strong at the same time. "I want you to be my business partner this week," she said, and his face fell. Feeling wicked, she added, "And I want you to be my lover, too."

Her words registered, then his lips were on hers and his hands everywhere. In her hair, on her breasts, running up her thighs. She untucked his soft T-shirt and ran her fingers up his taut abdomen, loving the hills and valleys of his muscles. Unable to get as much of him as she wanted, she tugged his T-shirt up over his head. He let go of her long enough so that she could strip him. She threw his shirt up in the air and it landed on a branch in the olive tree they were leaning against.

She couldn't help it, she was so incredibly happy, and her laugh rang out through the grove of trees into the glorious night. Travis cupped her face in his hands and tilted her mouth toward his to get better access to her. He sucked and licked and bit and tasted, and she mirrored his every move.

Her fingers were trembling with excitement, and she fumbled with the snap on his jeans, wanting to feel the velvety hot softness of his cock in her hands. "Help," she said between love bites, but all he did was chuckle softly and shake his head no.

"Too busy with your perfect breasts," he murmured, and it was true, he was palming and cupping her globes, taking her nipples between his thumb and forefinger and rubbing them in such a delicious way she really couldn't argue with him.

Finally, the snap popped open on his jeans, and she hurriedly unzipped the fly. "Yes," she said in victory, having won the battle with his stupid pants. If it were up to her, he would walk around naked, or maybe, in a Roman toga. Surely the Romans hadn't worn anything under their togas, so she would have easy access to his cock whenever she needed it.

Like right then. God how she needed to touch him.

She shoved the jeans down his lean hips as he pulled the dress up to her waist.

"Nice thong," he said as he admired the wispy black lace with red kisses on it. "Gives me some ideas." He began to kneel down, but as much as Lily wanted him to tongue her clit, she needed to take him in her mouth more.

"No, me first," she said as she dropped to her knees, barely wincing as a hard olive crunched under her kneecap. What was a little pain when she was face to cock with the most incredible penis ever created?

He was so hard his veins were visibly pulsing. A thick dollop of clear precome rested on the tip, waiting for her to lick it off. "Yummy," she said as she leaned forward and swiped her tongue across the head.

Travis groaned and threaded his hands in her hair, pushing the tip against her plump, puckered lips. She turned her head sideways and licked and sucked at the length of him, purposefully staying away from his sensitive head. Her fingers toyed with his balls, the soft skin of his anus. He bucked into her mouth, finally managing to slip the head between her lips.

Lily sucked at the tip, so big and round and deliciously swollen, letting her tongue tease the tiny hole. And then he pushed into her mouth, and she was taking him into her throat as deep as she could, wanting to suck all of the life out of him. All the while, she felt herself growing impossibly wet, her juices beading down her thigh, knowing that she was mere seconds away from feeling his tongue lapping at her clit.

"Oh God, Lily," he roared, as his penis pulsed once then twice then three times in her mouth, his hot come shooting down her throat. Lily wanted to suck down every last drop of his sweet essence and instinctively she tightened her lips around his shaft and squeezed his balls as he came.

His legs grew limp and she smiled around his cock, still rockhard in her mouth. His fingers loosened in her hair, then he was kicking his feet out of his shoes, stepping out of his jeans to be naked on his knees in front of her, kissing her deeply, passionately.

"You're incredible," he said.

"I love the way you taste, Travis."

"Let me taste you now," he said, repositioning them so that she was lying on her back, cradled by the old roots of the olive tree. He pushed her dress up over her breasts. "Raise your arms, sweetheart." He pulled the dress off and gently laid it down before turning to look at her in the moonlight, with only her wispy lace thong and bra covering her naked skin from his gaze.

"Bella Lily," he whispered reverently and her heart swelled up with something she was afraid to name. He thrust his thumbs beneath the edges of her thong and slid it down her thighs, inflaming every inch of skin that he touched, following his fingers with love bites and kisses.

His fingers found her swollen nub, and he absently began to press and swirl at it. She raised her hips into his fingers and he looked at her, a naughty gleam in his eyes. "Did you know that some people think the Italian word 'diletto' is where we get 'dildo' from?"

As he said dildo, he slipped two fingers into her. Lily's muscles contracted with delight. She was so close.

She shook her head, more from dizzy delight than in answer to his question. "No," she panted, "I didn't know that."

"Ah," he said, sliding his fingers in and out of her, each fraction of an inch more perfect than the next against her fevered skin, "you like dildos don't you, Lily?"

She would have blushed if she hadn't already been so flushed with longing. How could he know about her collection of mail-order dildos? How could he know how much she loved to play with them late at night after seeing him at one of Luke's parties, after watching him longingly from across the room?

"Have you ever used a dildo?" he asked, and when Lily groaned, "Yes," he bent over and tongued her clit in the same rhythm that he pumped his fingers in and out. "Tell me about your favorite one," he demanded when he took his mouth away from her.

"I . . ." she gasped, "I can't. Please Travis," she begged, but he had slowed his fingers down, and she knew she had to obey him.

"How big is it?" he asked, his voice a husky syrup.

Lily could hardly breathe, so she wasn't sure how she could answer him. Why was he torturing her like this? But she knew why, because every second that passed felt better than the next.

"For every answer," he promised, "I will lick some part of your body."

"Nine inches," she said, and he raised an eyebrow in question. "My clit, Travis. Lick my clit now."

"Just like my cock," he said as he bowed his head and replaced his fingers with his tongue, slipping it deep into her canal. Again and again he thrust, then pulled out and laved her clit before raising his head.

"Does it vibrate?"

Again, she could hardly breathe, she needed to come so badly. His twenty questions were sweet torture. "Yes, it vibrates," she said through shaking teeth. "My nipples," she cried.

His fingers slipped back into her, his thumb gently pressing against her clitoris, then his hot breath was on the plump underside of her breast. He sucked at her flesh and moved his mouth, repeating himself until only her nipple remained dry and stiff with longing. He settled his lips around the rosy peak, and she arched into his mouth. His tongue played with the puckered flesh, then, finally, he sucked hard while plunging his fingers into her cunt hard and fast and deep.

The orgasm hit Lily like a bullet, exploding through every cell in her body. Travis alternated from one nipple to the other, rubbing his stubbly cheeks against her soft mounds, finally rearing up over Lily to take her mouth with his.

Roughly, he jammed on a condom from his back pocket, and, midexplosion, he plunged into her. Her orgasm started all over from the beginning. He was all man, and she was all woman: Adam and Eve in the olive grove where life was bursting from the soil below.

Lily rubbed herself against Travis, matching each thrust of his tongue with her own. Matching the pounding of his hips with her own frantic pulsing. No dildo could have ever prepared her for his hot, hard length inside of her, and she milked him, pulsing against his throbbing shaft.

The fire raged, then, sated for the moment, they lay panting on foreign ground. Lily rubbed Travis's back, happier in this moment than she had ever been before, safe within the cocoon of newfound femininity, her first taste of a life sweeter than anything she had ever imagined.

Throwing caution to the wind, Lily decided that for the rest of the trip she was going to be free and wild. An American woman learning about true passion in Italy.

Regardless of the consequences.

9

GIGGLING LIKE KIDS as they pulled Travis's T-shirt down from the olive tree, they got their clothes back into some semblance of order and walked, arm in arm, back up the winding street to the hotel. Travis felt looser than he had in years, as if a huge weight had been taken away from him. He was tempted to fight the feeling—he had always kept firm control over any emotions that threatened to jumble his well-ordered life—but he decided this once to go with the flow. After all, this was Tuscany.

Living a little wouldn't kill him.

The only blip in the perfect evening was upon their return to the hotel. He had been dreaming of tying Lily to the bedposts, but as soon as they walked into the room, she pulled her hand from his.

"What's wrong?" he asked, more afraid than he wanted to admit about what she was about to say. *This is a mistake* or *I take back what I said about us wanting to be lovers.*

Instead she pointed to his suitcase. "I can't believe I forgot all about that."

Travis looked at his bag and then back at her. "Forgot about what?"

Anger flashing in her incredible blue orbs, Lily moved toward his bag and dumped the contents on the floor. "About these clothes! How dare you make love to me when you're planning to meet another woman here. How could I forget for a single second that you're a man with a lover on every street corner? I'm such an idiot."

Lily's voice broke, and Travis was shocked by her emotional volatility. She'd always been such a mouse, and now she was making him come on a regular basis and freaking out about everything. Why couldn't things go right for once? Where Lily was concerned it was one explosion after another. And the worst part of it all was that Travis knew he was responsible for laying all the bombs in their path.

He could see how strong she was trying to be, but her lower lip was on the verge of trembling. He dragged her into his arms.

"I brought them for you," Travis said, feeling more than a tad guilty about leaving off the fact that he only went to go pick up the clothes for Lily because he didn't want her to walk around Italy with him in shapeless, colorless sacks.

Abruptly she stopped struggling in his arms, and he could see her weighing the truth of his words. "I stopped in at Janica's studio before we left."

Lily surprised the heck out of Travis by bursting into laughter. "You and Janica in the same room together? I can't believe you don't have scars all over your body. I mean," Lily rambled on in a fit of giggles, "Janica really hates you."

Travis forced a grin even though he was stung by Lily's words. "No kidding. She was on the verge of cutting me into pieces with her massive scissors." Forcing the words past the lump of guilt in his throat, he said, "You looked so incredible in her dress at the fashion show I wanted you to have some more just like it."

Lily rubbed the tears of laughter from her eyes. "You were willing to brave Janica's claws for me?"

Travis didn't trust himself to speak. If he did, he might accidentally come clean with Lily about his real reasons for picking up the clothes, then she'd hate him all over again. He simply reached out for Lily's hands and nodded, hoping that she wouldn't probe any deeper.

Lily pulled him closer and wrapped her arms around him. "Travis," she breathed into his ear, "you can be so amazing. Thank you."

Surprised, he said, "Do you really think so?"

Lily's eyes shimmered with appreciation as she gazed at him. "I really do." With a wicked glint, she said, "Now it's my turn to show you how amazing I can be," and planted a kiss on his pulse point. His heart raced to triple speed and his cock begged for release from within the confines of his jeans.

As his body responded to her like it never had with any of the bean-pole, fleshless women he'd been with since puberty, Travis had some small insight into the fact that he was, to put it bluntly, an idiot. How could he have ever thought that Lily would embarrass him? In fact it was exactly the opposite—he needed to bat away men with a large, pointy stick.

He closed his eyes, relaxing into Lily's caresses. One of her hands was roving over the thick bulge of his sex, the other was squeezing his butt. Travis wondered how he could have been so blind to Lily's innate sexuality. Had he actually been in the same room with her hundreds of times and never noticed the way she made his libido shoot straight up into the stratosphere?

"Let's get you naked," she said as she undid the snap on his jeans. All of the remaining blood in his body shot straight to his penis as she made quick work of his clothes. Taking his hand in hers, she grabbed a handful of silk ties from his open luggage on the floor. Bolder than he had ever seen her before, she said, "Follow me into the bedroom. All this silk has given me an idea that I'm dying to try out. Anyone willing to volunteer?"

Travis pointed to his penis. "I'm pretty sure he is."

Lily tried to keep a straight face, but her grin won the battle. "Yes, he certainly seems, shall we say, up for the challenge."

She pushed Travis down onto the bed, and he said, "What the heck. I might as well volunteer too." He grabbed her wrist and planted a hot kiss on the soft inner skin. "But only if you're gentle with me. After all, this is my first time."

Lily muttered, "I seriously doubt that," but then she was kissing him, and he forgot all about the smart retort he was about to make.

In bed, Travis had always been the aggressor. He instigated every sexual escapade. But every time he had sex with Lily, she surprised him. First, that night when she had masturbated in front of him on his bed, then in the swimming pool when she had been unafraid to make love in broad daylight, and again in the hotel bathtub, when she had unself-consciously pleasured herself just inches away from him. And now she was tying him up. Taking his brilliant idea and running with it.

Lily said, "I love looking in your eyes when you come inside me," which got Travis so hot and hard that he hardly heard her say, "but right now, I think it'd be much more fun, *so much more fun,*" she repeated in a husky whisper, "if you were my slave."

The word "slave" had Travis nearly bucking off the bed with need. Oh God, how did this woman know about every man's fantasy, to be tied up and captive beneath a woman who wanted him for sex?

She picked a red-and-blue pin-striped tie from the pile on the bed. "My blind slave," she said, gently and firmly wrapping the tie around his eyes.

While his hands were still free—and he had a feeling they wouldn't stay that way for long—Travis cupped Lily's breasts through her dress. She moaned as he kneaded the flesh and buried his face in the soft valley between them. He rubbed the stubble of his cheeks against her hard nipples even as he pulled down the mesh fabric that kept her luscious skin from him.

Lily pushed into him one final time with a moan of pleasure, then deftly captured his hands in hers and pulled them away from her tits. "Uh-uh-uh," she said, "you're my slave now, Travis. You'll do what I want when I want."

Shaking her breasts the rest of the way out of her dress, she rubbed the very slightest bit of skin against Travis's face. He wanted desperately to suck her nipples, but she wouldn't let him. In a daze of wanting, he hardly realized when Lily slipped another tie around his right wrist and secured him to the iron bedpost. After fastening the knot, she ran kisses down his arm, from his wrist to the inside of his elbow to his shoulder.

This was the first time Travis had ever been in a subservient position in bed, but if it felt this good, it was certainly not going to be his last. "Lily, you're killing me," he said with appreciation, glad to hear her tinkle of laughter in response.

"I sure hope so," she murmured as she got to work on his left wrist. Travis ached for her to kiss the inside of his left arm and couldn't suppress the groan of pleasure when she did. But when, seconds later, her soft mouth was on his cock, he did more than groan.

He begged.

"Suck me, Lily," he urged.

At which point his dick was left cool and bereft as her mouth lifted away. "Am I going to have to put a gag on you, too?" she threatened.

Travis shook his head, loving how in control she was of this game. "No, Lily. I'll be good," he said, trying to keep the smile off his face. "I swear."

"Hmm," Lily said, running one finger lightly up the inside of his thigh, stopping at the undersides of his balls. "How can I be sure?" she said as she repeated the sweet torture that set every inch of his body on fire. "Who is your mistress?" she asked in a hard voice.

Travis's cock grew another impossible inch at her tone. "You," he said when he was able to catch his breath.

She curled her fist around his cock, hard. "And who is my slave?"

Travis bucked up into her hand, unable to find words.

Lily licked his aching head. "I asked who my slave is, Travis."

"Me," he groaned. "I am. I'll do anything you want. Anything."

He could feel her smile, even if he couldn't see it. Lily liked being in charge. What a surprise. And was she ever good at it.

A moment later she straddled Travis's chest, and he desperately wished that he had a free hand to caress her wet pussy. He could smell her essence, and it was the most powerful turn-on in the world.

"I'm going to untie your hand, but you have to promise me that you'll do exactly what I tell you to do."

Travis nodded. "I promise, Lily." Anything to touch her. To taste her on his lips.

She untied his right hand and wrapped his fingers around something that felt oddly like a penis. "It's my dildo," she whispered in his ear, letting her tits brush against his chest.

Travis groaned. "Oh God Lily, please tell me you're going to let me . . ."

"Be quiet!" she said, and Travis shut up and tried to wait patiently for what was definitely going to be the highlight of his life up until now. "I'm going to spread my legs wide above you, then I'm going to let you guide the dildo into me, one inch at a time."

Travis's hand shook with the need to get to work on Lily's cunt, but Lily was clearly enjoying the torture of making him wait for it. Lord knew he greatly enjoyed her enjoyment.

"I'm so wet, Travis," she said, and as she spread her legs wider above his chest her sweet scent became more potent. And then her finger was on his lips. "Taste me, Travis," she said.

Greedily, he sucked her finger into his mouth, and as he did so she guided his free hand toward her thighs. "Right here, Travis," she said. His finger searched for a button at the base of the dildo, something that would bring it to vibrating life, and finally he found it.

The whirring sound joined their heavy breathing, and Travis felt the tip of his cock grow wet. He couldn't believe it, he was practically about to come into thin air, he was so turned on.

He pressed the length of the dildo against her slick lips and barely slid it against her clit. "I'm coming, Travis," she said, her voice no longer a harsh command, but a plea for release. "Don't stop!"

He couldn't have stopped for the world. Increasing the pressure of the dildo by degrees, he continued to slide the length against her wetness. God how he wanted to be the dildo. She bucked into the plastic sex toy, and as her moans turned into a scream of pleasure, he slid it in to the hilt.

When her tremors slowed, he slid the sex toy out and threw it to the bed. Before she could regain control he simply had to taste her, so he wrapped his palm around her backside and slid her cunt up to his mouth. She settled in with a sigh of pleasure, and he greedily licked and sucked her juices, slipping his tongue into her tight vagina.

He slid two fingers into her, and Lily's muscles held him firm as she began to ride his hand. "Travis, yes, there, again," she cried, as her second orgasm ripped through her.

Travis sucked at her clit even as he rammed his palm against her. He wanted her pleasure as much as he wanted his own. He had no time, however, to dissect this thought because Lily was sliding off his face and retying his bindings.

"Good slave," she said, then she bent down and took his mouth in a savage kiss that shot all the way to his soul. "You taste like come," she murmured as she nipped at his lower lip. "My come." She captured his mouth again and stole the rest of his breath away. When had she learned to kiss like a goddess? he wondered, then he forgot everything but the throbbing of his cock as she wound her hand around it. Her mouth trailed a path of destruction down his chest, stopping to suck his nipples, finally finding his shaft, hard and throbbing and about to blow at any second.

"Lily," he said, "I can't take any—"

"Yes, you can," she said, sucking him into her sweet mouth, laving her tongue around his head, caressing his balls in time to the circles her tongue was making.

Just as Travis reared up into her mouth, about to blow, Lily's mouth was gone, a condom was rolled on, and his cock was in the hot, wet pussy of his dreams. She bent forward and dropped first one nipple, then the other into his mouth as she rode him straight into oblivion.

He shouted her name and everything went black in his mind and he couldn't concentrate on anything other than the vagina that was squeezing every ounce of come out of his dick. He barely heard her scream her pleasure, he barely noticed that he was sucking at her nipples like a hungry babe. He barely knew his own name as he exploded inside of Lily.

Black turned to blue, and everything went dark for a minute as Travis tried to remember how to breathe. Lily must have untied his wrists, because she was in his arms, and he was holding her tightly to him.

Janica hadn't been kidding when she said Lily was going to be a goddess in Italy. Lily was, no question about it, a goddess through and through.

And she was all his.

HIS TAN LOOKS NICE ON ME, Lily thought as she woke up, tucked under Travis's arm. His head was nuzzled into her neck, and she loved the way his soft, warm breath tickled the hair at the base of her head. And to think she had been planning to sleep on the couch. What a waste that would have been.

He stirred, and his hard, hot penis pressed against her thigh. "Morning," he said, rolling her over on top of him.

Even filled to the brim with the glow of Travis's incredible loving, Lily couldn't bat her deep-seated insecurities away. She was too big to be sprawled atop anyone, even if he had been the one to position her there. She had been able to let go and enjoy their little bondage game once she blindfolded Travis. But now, in the bright light of morning, he would see everything she so desperately wanted to hide from him. Lily started to wiggle off him, but Travis stilled her with a firm hand on her rear.

"Where do you think you're going? Don't you think it's only fair if I get to be the master today?" he teased.

Sure she was turning a hundred shades of pink, Lily made a

joke out of her discomfort. "I don't want to crush you," she said, faking a carefree, sexy laugh.

Travis's green eyes flashed with regret. "You're not crushing me," he said, but just like that, the spell was broken, and he went soft against her. Stifling her groan of discontent, she feigned happiness.

"Let's not waste another minute," she said brightly. "I can't wait to comb through every antique shop in town. Give me a minute, and I'll be out of the shower."

She fairly ran out of the bedroom into the bathroom, locking the door safely behind her. *Face facts*, she told herself, *last night was an anomaly.* The spell of Tuscany, combined with jet lag and Chianti had wrapped around them both, and they'd done some crazy, albeit wonderful, things together.

But something inside of her, some irrationally hopeful part of Lily's heart, wished that she was wrong. Maybe the first night, at the fashion show, had been an anomaly, maybe even the day by the pool was an accident, but last night . . . wasn't last night special?

No, not special. Amazing was more like it.

Last night he wanted me like a man wants a woman, she thought, remembering the way they'd ripped at each other's clothes in the olive grove, the moment she'd dropped to her knees beneath the moon and taken his hot length into her mouth, the incredible sensations that rippled through her as Travis had slid the dildo into her, the wholeness of joining together as lovers, the safety of waking up with his arms wrapped tightly around her.

Lily turned on the shower—she couldn't use the bathtub again, not after the memories she and Travis had created there together—and stepped under the hot spray. No matter what, no matter how worried she was about their great sex being a fluke, she was going to have a good time in Italy. She was in a fairy-tale land, after all, with a fairy-tale budget to buy furnishings for a home more beautiful than anything beyond her wildest dreams.

Except for Travis, of course. No question about it, he was the most beautiful thing she had ever seen.

WHEN LILY RAN OUT of the bedroom and locked herself into the marble bathroom, Travis wished he could claim to be confused. Unfortunately, he wasn't. He knew exactly what had happened.

His own past behavior was coming back to haunt him. In a big way.

How many years had he purposefully ignored Lily? He could teach a course in looking right through her. At doing exactly what she had accused him of: acting like she was beneath him.

It had never occurred to Travis to ask himself why he was such a prick before, but today as sunlight streamed through the enormous windows, the rays of light brought uncomfortable clarity with them.

You can't hide anymore, a voice from deep inside told him.

Oddly enough, it was almost a relief. Another small chunk of that invisible burden he had been carrying around with him for so many years was falling away. First last night in the olive grove and now, alone in the bed that bore the marks of their frantic, wicked lovemaking, Travis could feel something inside of him stretching and pulling at its bindings.

He got out of bed and, naked, paced the room. He wasn't going to be able to fit the puzzle pieces together today, because before he could do so, he had to collect them all. Instead of turning his back on what he felt, rather than drown in nameless, faceless sex with some girl who meant nothing to him,

Travis searched for the courage not only to acknowledge his feelings for Lily, but to find out what these feelings actually meant.

More than that, he needed to find out what these feelings cost him.

Lily hadn't leapt from out of nowhere onto his radar screen in the past three days. The fashion show had been a major catalyst, certainly, but it wasn't the beginning of Lily's importance in his life.

No. The truth, likely long obvious to anyone but him, was that Lily had always been important to him.

And maybe it was the magnitude of just how much Lily mattered that had been his problem all along.

Lily emerged from the shower, wrapped from head to toe in fluffy cream towels. "Your turn," she said.

Travis caught Lily as she tried to skirt past him. Her eyes were downcast, her movements jerky and awkward. He knew she was afraid of his rejection, that he'd start acting like she wasn't good enough for him again, but they were in Tuscany, just the two of them, where what went on between him and Lily was for their eyes only.

Travis wouldn't think beyond the end of their visit. Even though he'd always been a planner, he hadn't planned on the effect Lily would have on him once she'd touched him. Once he'd touched her.

But first things first, he needed to put a smile back on Lily's lips, and the sparkle back into her big blue eyes.

"I know you're excited to get cracking," he said in a voice filled with sensual promise, "but I'm expecting a rain check for this morning."

He was rewarded with a surprised grin from Lily, and followed it with a smacking kiss on her shower-flushed lips.

"When am I going to have to pay?" she asked, her voice coy, her eyes flashing mischievously.

Travis reached for her towel, pretending to tug it down. "Any more talk like this," he growled, "and you're going to be paying right now." The pulse in Lily's throat leaped to attention, and he couldn't help but add, "I can't think of anything sweeter than tasting your skin, clean and sweet from the shower."

And it was true. Travis had never appreciated a woman's natural beauty so much. He had always liked his women made up and well dressed, not scrubbed clean and smelling of lavender soap.

Lily stilled against him, and he pulled her closer, running his lips down her cheek, to cover the wild pulse in her neck. In an instant, he had her on the edge of the bed, her legs wrapped around him, a condom on, and his cock thrusting hard and sure inside of her. As he shuddered within her, Travis could have stayed inside Lily forever.

This time, instead of pushing the thought away, instead of making an excuse about how Lily's cunt was as good as any other woman's, Travis let the word resonate in his skull.

Forever.

From five days to forever in a heartbeat, it was crazy. But crazier still was the smile that eased across his face and through his whole body.

One puzzle piece was firmly in place. He wondered how many more he would discover throughout the day.

BACK HOME IN SAN FRANCISCO, Janica and Luke were holding a summit at her design studio. Thinking how good Luke looked in her domain, how nicely he filled up the empty spaces with his broad shoulders, Janica turned and fiddled with her espresso machine to hide her ridiculously lustful thoughts. He was her sister's best friend, for God's sake, and had known her since she was still putting bugs in her mouth. For all she knew, Luke had a crush on Lily. And why wouldn't he? Lily was sweet, comforting, the best friend anyone could have. Janica's heart sank even as she hated her petty jealousy. Resolutely, she made sure her fingers were still and calm as she poured Luke's drink and brought it over to the café table in the corner.

"You probably know why I asked you to stop by," she said.

Luke nodded and absently picked up his cup and blew on the hot drink to cool it off. "I'm worried about her, too," he said.

Janica paused, not sure how to say what she needed to say without hurting Luke's feelings. After all, Travis was his brother. "Um, the thing is that your brother is, well . . ."

Luke looked up at her and deftly finished her sentence. "A complete jerk when it comes to women?"

Color crept into Janica's cheeks. "Exactly," she said crisply, wondering where the outspoken version of herself had disappeared to. "And I wasn't sure if you had noticed that . . ." She let her words fall away. She didn't want to make Lily look bad by saying that she had a crush on Luke's unworthy brother if Luke didn't already know.

Again, Luke came to her rescue. "Lily has a crush on Travis?"

"Bingo," she said, and inwardly cringed. Bingo? What kind of moron said "bingo" when sitting so close to a truly hot guy? "I'm really worried about her. I don't know how she's going to make it through an entire week with Travis treating her like she's not good enough to shine his shoes. Maybe," Janica said, watching Luke carefully, "we should go to Italy."

Luke's face lit up. "Why didn't I think of that? You're a genius, Janica."

Janica's heart grew at least a full size bigger at Luke's compliment. He had never really noticed her before. Sure, he had always been nice enough, but it was the kind of nice that you'd be to a puppy. Still thrilling from the genius comment, Janica grinned widely, and said, "Great! I'll get online and make some plane reservations for tonight." Too late, she realized that she was acting way too excited about going to Italy to save her sister. She couldn't bite back a small bit of guilt over her other reason for wanting to go to Italy with Luke: Some alone time with a hottie like Luke would be sheer heaven.

Luke pulled out his Palm Pilot to check his calendar. "Tonight won't work. I'm on call for the next forty-eight hours."

"Can't you switch with someone?"

He looked morose. "No, unfortunately I can't. Everyone has already been on for forty-eight." He rubbed his eyes and looked bleak. "My hours are crazy lately, which is exactly how I got Lily into this mess in the first place. Some best friend I am."

Janica wanted to stroke his broad shoulders and tell him that he shouldn't be so hard on himself, but somehow she kept the urge in check. God forbid Luke find out she had a crush on him. She'd never been a pathetic girl, and she wasn't about to start.

"But I've got some time off coming to me. I could probably take a few days without it becoming too much of a train wreck at the hospital."

"So I'll book the flight for Saturday and we'll get into Rome early Sunday night?"

"Sounds good. Call me with the flight info and I'll meet you at the airport."

Janica nodded, tense with anticipation. Funny how all of a sudden saving Lily from Travis's evil clutches placed a very distant second to being close to Luke for several days.

10

ILY AND TRAVIS'S FIERY LOVEMAKING was the perfect jolt of
caffeine for their first morning in Italy. After gulping down
scalding espressos at a corner café, they hopped in the rental car
that Giuseppe had hired for them and took joyfully to the
streets of Saturnia. Travis had been to the region on buying
trips in previous years, but the sun had never seemed so bright,
the sky so blue, the espresso so perfectly bitter. He wanted to
show Lily the finest leather shop in the world, the ancient rug
factory, the famous gelato stand outside the piazza. Beauty was
a gift from him to her. At every turn she surprised him, her decorator's eye finding the little touches that would make his
client's house a delight to everyone who entered. Any lingering
doubts about Lily's ability to decorate the entire house vanished
as she found hand-painted tiles for the kitchen, a whimsical
fountain for the courtyard, and soft, sheer silks for the bedroom walls.

All day, Travis couldn't resist playing a dangerous game with
Lily's hand soft and warm in his. His imagination overflowed

with visions of their naked bodies slipping and sliding against the silks that hung around their very own master-carved four-poster bed.

Quietly, as he watched her run her talented hands over an ancient statue at his favorite wholesale landscape store, another puzzle piece slipped into place. What if he gave in to the way Lily made him feel?

Leo, the proprietor, said something that made Lily throw her head back and laugh. Her laughter washed over Travis, and he snapped back to attention, feeling left out of the joke and wishing he was the only person who could make Lily look so happy.

He slid his arm around her waist, and as Lily leaned her head on his shoulder, the proprietor conveniently left them alone with each other. "I swear," she said with a sigh, "I'm going to move here."

Travis smiled. "I've thought of that a time or two myself." He mock frowned. "Don't tell me Leo asked you to marry him."

Lily giggled again. "Well . . . now that you've come right out and asked . . ." She kissed Travis on the cheek. "Actually, he said I should be a model for one of these." She gestured to a statue and blushed. "I know he's a big ol' flirt, but still . . ." Her voice drifted away, and she looked unsure of herself.

Not wanting anything to ruin her good mood, especially not her insecurities about the very body that he found himself having an ever-growing appreciation for, Travis made a show of inspecting the life-sized female statue in front of them. He ran his hands over the breasts and grinned wolfishly.

"First of all, your breasts are much more impressive than hers."

Lily smacked him on the shoulder. "Shh. Not so loud! You're embarrassing me."

Travis raised an eyebrow. "What? Don't you think that Leo has already noticed and admired them?"

Lily crossed her arms across her chest, but not quickly enough to hide her rapidly hardening nipples. "No, I hadn't thought that, thank you very much," she said, but she couldn't hide her grin.

"In that case, young lady," he teased, "you have quite a lot to learn when it comes to men. Particularly any man with Italian blood in his veins." Travis turned back to the statue and ran his hands down past her waist. "Yup, I'd have to say you are a lusher, much more intriguing package than this broad. No question about it."

"Lush?" Lily snorted. "When did you introduce that word into your vocabulary?"

Travis took Lily in his arms. "When I made love to you for the first time."

Lily blushed, but she didn't pull away when he bent down and gently kissed her lips. The kiss wasn't so much about passion as it was about comfort. And just as he had all day whenever things felt too right, too good, whenever his new feelings for Lily threatened to overwhelm him, Travis had to fight the urge to let go of her. To run as far away from her as he could.

Somehow, the thought of going back to the life he had always loved so much—the freedom of being with a different woman every weekend, someone who looked pretty on his arm, but rarely was witty enough to make him laugh—didn't seem all that great anymore.

As if she could read his mind, Lily gazed at him, turning shy and anxious as he grew quiet and pensive. Amazingly, it was Lily's uncertainty that made Travis snap out of his mood.

I don't want to go back to how things were before, Travis thought with sudden clarity. *This is so much better.*

He grabbed Lily's hand, called out to Leo that they'd telephone later to arrange for shipping, and said, "Let's go have some fun."

Lily followed him out to their little rental car and climbed into the passenger seat. "I'm already having such a good time, Travis. This whole day has been a dream come true for me."

Travis threaded his hands into her hair and kissed her once, hard and possessive. He turned on the radio and drove past fields of olives and grapes, whistling to the pop songs on the radio. He pulled Lily's hand onto his lap and was happy when she left it there, drumming her fingers on his thigh in time to the music. He tried not to think dirty thoughts, but with her fingers inching closer and closer to his growing erection, he was having a hard time working the stick shift.

He pulled the car into a small gravel lot outside an old stucco farmhouse. He hoped Nonna was home. The grandmother of one of his previous clients. Travis had met Nonna five years ago on a buying trip, each time he was in town, and visiting her was like coming home. And he was certain that she would adore Lily. The gate opened, and she spoke in rapid-fire Italian. Lily emerged from the car, and the woman approached and kissed both her cheeks.

Travis explained, "Nonna makes the best picnic basket lunch in town." He squeezed Nonna's hand. *"Cestino per il picnic?"*

She nodded with glee. *"Certo!"* Nonna looked slyly at Lily. *"È una bella donna, vero?"*

"Yes," he said as Lily blinked uncertainly at the both of them. "She is a very beautiful woman."

Lily blushed and began to protest, but Travis cut her off. "You don't want to insult Nonna's ancient wisdom when she's about to put together the best lunch of your life, do you?"

"No," Lily said, as a radiant smile took hold. "I wouldn't want to insult this lovely woman. Oh, how I wish I could understand Italian."

Travis and Lily followed Nonna into her kitchen-cum-store. "Next time, we'll come stay for a month. You'll pick it up in no time."

Lily stopped dead in her tracks. "Next time?"

Travis was at a loss for what to say. He had been stunned when the words came out of his mouth, but they felt so right he had let them fall. And since he couldn't think of a response, he did the only thing left in his repertoire: He kissed her.

Nonna cackled with glee behind them. Lily pushed him away. "We're embarrassing her," she insisted.

Travis, relieved to have sidestepped the awkward moment, said, "On the contrary, she's loving it. I think you're the one who's embarrassed."

Rising up to his challenge, Lily grabbed him, said "Is that so, wise guy?" and thoroughly French-kissed him. When she finally released him, he had to concentrate on breathing for a full five seconds.

Travis hid his smile of victory. "Nope. I guess you've proved me wrong."

Lily kept proving him wrong again and again. From mousy to magnificent in a matter of days—what could possibly be next?

He pulled out a chair for Lily, and they sat at a worm-eaten wood table sipping the glasses of grappa that Nonna poured from a short, round bottle with dried red wax along its throat. The three of them fell into a companionable silence as Nonna cut thick slices of homemade brown bread stuffed with black olives and capers. She pulled a large wicker basket from the hooks on the ceiling and loaded the bread in along with fresh pâté, a handful of cheeses, salami, prosciutto, olives, pickles, and a bottle of Chianti.

Lily's stomach grumbled, and Travis chuckled as her cheeks turned pink. "Every time I get near Nonna I become a ravenous beast," he said, to try and ease Lily's hang-ups about food. He leaned close to her and said, in a soft voice full of promise, "Actually, the same thing happens every time I get near you, too."

Lily smiled, but it wasn't a big, true smile. It was a trembly little smile that made Travis want to stroke her hair. "I'll bet you've been here with a lot of girls. I wonder how Nonna thinks I compare."

Travis stifled a groan but couldn't completely suppress his irritation. "Lily, do we have to keep doing this?"

Lily reddened and faced him. "I'm not the one who's had dozens, no silly me that's not nearly enough, more like hundreds of girlfriends! Why is it so wrong for me to assume that you have been here before with at least one other woman?"

Nonna stopped filling the picnic basket. *"Ha un'accelerazione da zero a sessanta in dieci secondi."*

Travis nodded. *"Sì,* Nonna."

"What?" Lily slapped her open palm onto the table, jumping with surprise when she looked down at her hand and realized what she'd done. Somewhat sheepishly, she said, "How do I say sorry in Italian?"

"Scusi."

"Scusi, Nonna," she said, her big blue eyes filled with repentance, then narrowed them and turned back to face Travis down. "Go ahead, I'm waiting. What'd she say?"

Travis cleared his throat and tried not to laugh. Now was not the time for humor, not when Lily looked mad enough to castrate him. "She said you go from zero to sixty in ten seconds."

Lily's mouth dropped open. "Me?"

Travis nodded.

"She must be mistaken," Lily said, dropping her hands to her lap and clasping them together primly. "I'm very even-keeled."

Travis pried opened her hands and squeezed them between his own. "Trust me, Nonna means it as a great compliment. In her day I'll bet she was a real firecracker."

As if Nonna understood his words, she winked at them over her bony shoulder. "And by the way," he added, "since you were wondering, you are the only woman I have ever brought to see Nonna."

Lily raised her blue eyes, a small flicker of hope shining through. "Do you swear?" she whispered.

He placed her hands on his heart. "Cross my heart, Lily."

Nonna sighed and handed Travis the picnic basket. *"Divertirsi!"*

Lily thanked Nonna with the only Italian words she knew so far, but her *"Tante grazie"* was cut off by the woman's spontaneous hug.

Travis pulled Nonna into a hug next and made a mental note to send a generous gift to the wonderful woman. Then he picked up the picnic basket with one hand and Lily's hand with the other. He was still smarting from her attack in Nonna's kitchen, but at the same time, he wasn't clueless enough to think he hadn't brought it on himself. He couldn't think of a single time in the past twenty years that he had done anything that would have captured Lily's trust.

So then why was he suddenly so desperate to have it?

"Got anywhere special in mind for the picnic?" she asked, as they drove back down the hill from Nonna's farmhouse. "Or should I be keeping my eyes open for a rock wall in a patch of shade?

Travis took his eyes off the narrow road to grin at Lily. He was glad her good mood was back. "I think you'll like the place I have in mind." He took a sharp left at a crumbling shed.

As the road became bumpier and less maintained, Lily said, "If I didn't know better, I'd think you were trying to kidnap me."

"No one will ever find you out here, my pretty." Travis faked a maniacal laugh.

Lily giggled as they crested the final hill. Travis stopped the car in front of a wide, tall cypress bush next to several other beat-up cars. He grabbed the basket and motioned for Lily to follow him down a narrow footpath. "It's through here." Although Lily looked doubtful, she followed him.

Moments later, they were standing on the banks of a small, stunning lake. Several couples and families were spread out along the grass while their babies threw sand up into the air with miniature shovels. "It's so beautiful," Lily said softly.

She caught sight of the large wooden swing on an ancient oak tree and ran over to it. She slid onto the wooden seat and swung herself off the ground.

Travis gave her a firm push. She gasped, "Not so high, Travis!" as she flew up into the air, but when she came back down he pushed her hard again and again, until her hair was flying free behind her and her skirts were up over her knees and she was laughing.

Travis couldn't resist her laughter, so he let her come back down to earth and, when she landed, he caught her in his arms and kissed her.

Travis's stomach grumbled loudly. "Guess it's time to eat," Lily said, her breath warm against his ear before she pulled away and reached for the woolen blanket that Nonna had given them to sit on. Lily spread it out on the soft grass and unloaded the food.

"My God," she said as more and more wrapped packages emerged at the bottom of the basket. "I guess I wasn't paying attention to what Nonna put in here. There's enough food to feed an army."

"Nonna knows I've got a big appetite," Travis said with a wink, trying to step carefully around the food minefield by turning the focus to himself.

"Well," Lily said with a laugh, "I've certainly noticed that you have a big appetite for something."

Travis made a show as if to pounce on her, but she just laughed and stuffed a piece of bread in his mouth. "Eat," she said, so he relaxed back into the blanket and watched the sunshine play off the calm lake as he munched on the crust.

They ate companionably in the dappled shade beneath the huge shelter of the oak tree, and Travis couldn't remember ever feeling quite so content. Sated, he stood up and drew Lily into his arms.

"Dance with me, Lily."

"Travis," she said, her laughter coming out in warm puffs against his neck, "everyone will think we're crazy."

He pulled her close, then dipped her until her red locks nearly brushed the ground. Gently curving her back toward him, he said, "They're too busy thinking I'm the luckiest guy in the world."

Lily stiffened in his arms. Travis wondered why his compliments had such an adverse effect with her. Most women lapped them up like cream. How could she doubt that what he said was true when he had been fighting men away from her left and right?

Travis surveyed the flowing layers of red-and-lavender silk that caressed her curves. Her dress dipped low to expose the creamy flesh of her breasts. The hem twirled sexily around her slim ankles, which were encased in strappy sandals, and her brightly painted toes peeked out with every step.

"Have I told you how beautiful you look today?"

Lily kissed his cheek softly. "Thank you," she whispered into his ear, sending chills through him, straight to the rapidly growing bulge between his legs.

He ran his hand down her back. "I can't keep my eyes, or hands," he said, with a mischievous smile, "off you today."

Lily shook her head and tried to pull away. "It's not me that's beautiful," she protested. "It's Janica's dress. She's so talented, she could even make a hippo look good."

Travis scanned the park. "Funny, I don't see any hippos anywhere." He lowered his voice to an intimate hush. "I see you, Lily, and you are incredibly beautiful to me."

This time, Lily let herself be held by him. A soft wind blew over them as time stood still.

LILY DIDN'T GET IT. The Travis she had been with all day was straight from her fantasies. Even when she'd had her little hissy fit at Nonna's, which she was still awfully embarrassed about, Travis had been gallant, charming, and, amazingly enough, impressed with her creative ideas for his client's house.

He had been, simply, the perfect man to share Tuscany with.

Which meant, of course, that all day Lily was waiting for the other shoe to drop. She couldn't help but wonder at his abrupt transformation. After so many years of being treated like a second-class citizen—none of which had stopped her lustful dreams about him, sadly enough—the new-and-improved Travis was almost too much to take in.

Lily needed some time alone to process things. It was all happening so fast. She felt perilously close to overload. They parked their rental car at the hotel and walked into the square.

When Travis got engrossed in a conversation with a master woodcarver, Lily took it as her chance to escape for a little while.

"Travis, I'm going to go down to the corner café to jot down some notes." He made a move to wrap up his conversation, but she insisted, "Please don't rush on my account. Take all the time you need."

His eyes flashed something unreadable. Lily actually thought that she might have hurt his feelings for a minute, but that was laughable. How could she, Lily Ellis, actually make the king of all players upset?

Her head spinning with an odd mixture of hope and confusion, Lily made her way down the sun-filled lane to the café they had passed a few minutes ago. She stopped at a postcard display on the sidewalk and thumbed through them, wishing that Janica could be there. How her sister would love the natural, overwhelming beauty of Italy.

Lily could only imagine the kind of designs Janica would come up with after seeing the way the locals dressed. Tuscan women had a natural sexuality to them, whether they were big or small, and Lily noticed that they made a special point to show off their breasts and hips. Lily wished she had the guts to dress like that on more than just special occasions. But she would feel so naked without her layers of clothes to cover her flaws. Maybe Americans didn't have that special brand of European confidence, she mused. But Janica did, and Lily was certain that her sister would understand how to tap into the Italian flair for sensuality and beauty.

But then again, Lily thought with a naughty grin, if Janica had been there, everything would have been different. No shared baths with Travis, no trysts in an olive grove.

Lily clasped the postcards tighter as the realization hit her that this was the first time she'd ever been on her own without someone to take care of.

Taking care of Travis? That was laughable. He could be thrown into a fast-moving stream with no paddle, and he'd somehow manage to not only come out of the ordeal alive, but with the white water wrapped around his little finger, obeying his every command.

But Lily had always taken care of Janica. Even before their parents died Lily had felt responsible for her baby sister and her happiness. This really was the first week she could ever remember truly being on her own. Until the trip to Italy there had been no time for pampering herself.

Had she given too much of herself away in the raising of her baby sister?

No, that was crazy. Everything she had done for her sister she had done for love. And that made it all worthwhile. Not to mention the fact that Janica had grown up to be a brilliant designer and Lily's best girlfriend in the whole world.

She was so lost in her thoughts that when a gorgeous Italian man slipped the postcards from her fingers, and said, "I will buy these for you," she nearly jumped out of her skin.

"Oh my," she said, her hand clutching her rapidly beating pulse, "I didn't see you standing there."

The tall, dark man smiled, and something warm fluttered through her. He wasn't Travis, nonetheless, he was very yummy-looking. He placed some coins on the counter and took her arm, leading her down the sidewalk.

"Oh no," she said, looking over her shoulder at the storefront. "I can't let you pay for my postcards."

"I am Raffaele," he said, ignoring her protests, "but my friends call me Rafe."

Lily blushed under the heat of his gaze and the special meaning he had attached to the word "friends." She wished she had more practice at this sort of thing. What did one say to a gorgeous man when he was picking you up in a foreign country?

"And your name?"

Ah yes. Her name. Too bad she was too flustered to think of the simple things. "Lily," she said. "My name is Lily."

Rafe gave her another penetratingly beautiful smile and guided her into one of the outdoor wicker seats at the café. He snapped his fingers in the waiter's direction. Seconds later, two steaming cups of espresso were placed in front of them.

"American?"

Lily nodded.

"Beautiful," he said.

Rafe's accent licked around Lily like a warm blanket on a cold night. It seemed that being with Travis had opened her up on so many levels. While she didn't want to go to bed with Rafe—as gorgeous as he was, there was only one man she had eyes for—she didn't mind the impromptu flirting lesson.

Conjuring up her latent inner-flirt, she pretended to misinterpret his compliment. "Yes, America is beautiful. But Italy is stunning."

"No," he said, as he boldly ran one finger down her cheekbone, "you are beautiful, Lily."

Trying not to flinch from his overly forward touch, Lily raised an eyebrow, and said, "Tell me, Rafe, do you hit on every American woman who comes through town?"

It took her new friend a long moment to answer her question. His gaze barely wavering from her breasts, he said, "You are special, Lily."

Had she not been interested in learning the finer points of flirting to use on Travis later that night, Lily would have snorted her disbelief.

She might have been inexperienced, but even so it was perfectly clear to Lily that Rafe was playing the part of an obviously well endowed Italian (she would have been blind not to have noticed the huge bulge between his legs) who rescued lonely American female tourists. Which wasn't that bad a thing, really, considering how potent and sensual Rafe looked to be fully clothed. For the briefest of moments Lily let herself indulge in a little daydream about what it would be like to sleep with this anonymous Italian, trying not to feel guilty about Travis as she indulged her imagination.

"Who the hell are you?"

Lily's daydream was cut short by Travis's appearance. His anger was palpable. It was bad of her, but Lily couldn't resist the chance to see how much Travis truly wanted her.

"Rafe, this is Travis. Travis, this is Rafe."

She gave the introduction as if she were introducing the two men over tea in the garden, which only seemed to piss Travis off more.

Rafe looked from Lily to Travis with amusement. "Is this man your lover?" he said to Lily. From the tone of Rafe's voice, it was clear that he thought Travis to be a subpar American.

A giggle gurgled up in Lily's throat. She couldn't believe these two magnificent men were fighting over her.

Over little old me! she thought with glee.

Travis reached for her arm to drag her up out of her chair. "We're going to be late for our next meeting."

Lily made a show of fighting his presumptuous maneuver, but inwardly she was thrilled by his possessive actions. "Meeting? What meeting?"

Travis glared at her. "Forget it. I'll go by myself," he said. "I'd hate to interrupt you and your new friend when you're looking so cozy together."

He turned away and walked briskly up the street. Lily panicked. So much for testing her new feminine wiles and making Travis jealous. Instead, all she was succeeding in doing was driving him away. Lily felt like a nasty, terrible person. Travis had treated her to an incredible day, and she had repaid him by being a wanton flirt with the first guy who smiled at her.

Without so much as a backward glance at Rafe, Lily shot away from the table to run after Travis.

"Travis!" she yelled, hating the desperation in her voice. She fumbled for a way to smooth things over, saying, "Travis I—" but the look he shot her was so full of disgust that the words got stuck in her throat.

Her heart grew even heavier when Travis didn't speak to her during their walk back to the hotel. At the lobby entrance Travis's eyes were cold steel. "Don't ever play games with me."

He turned away from her and headed back into town.

Lily's heart stopped beating as she tasted the fear of losing Travis in her mouth. His sharp words were a cruel reminder that she would never be in his league.

What had she done? Her fantasy had quickly turned into a nightmare. Instead of a perfect evening to end their perfect day, Lily had screwed the whole thing up with her little game. Why had she felt the need to tease Travis with Rafe? How would she have felt if Travis had dangled a lithe, Italian beauty in front of her face?

Well, she would have expected it, thinking that her time was up and he was moving on to greener pastures. Even so, she would have let him try to explain.

Or would she? Lily thought about her outburst in Nonna's kitchen when she had attacked Travis for his "other women." And now she had flirted with a strange man in a café to try and get a rise out of Travis.

Lily cringed. She had thought that the quiet and insecure Lily was giving way to a sexually confident and adventurous woman. But now she wasn't so sure. Maybe she was just plain turning into a bitch on wheels. Seeing herself in this light wasn't pretty. Maybe she should go back to the old Lily. It wasn't nearly as much fun, and she would never experience such mind-blowing sex again, but all in all it was so much safer.

"Ah, Lily," Giuseppe said, pleased to see her. "How was your day? What do you think of our little town?"

Lily gulped back her unshed tears. She didn't want Giuseppe to think she didn't love Saturnia. Because she did with all her heart. "It's wonderful, Giuseppe," she said, forcing a wide smile that never made it to her eyes.

He nodded slowly, sensing something was wrong. "Good, good," he said, scratching his chin. "And where is Signor Carson? Getting a bottle of wine for a romantic evening, perhaps?"

Lily's bottom lip trembled, and she knew she had to get up to the room or she would embarrass herself in front of the kind man. "Yes, probably," she said, then added, "I think I'll go up to our room to take a nap now," before hurrying up the stairs to the room she and Travis shared. She closed the door behind her with a soft click.

That's when the tears started falling.

And didn't stop.

TRAVIS HEADED FOR THE NEAREST BAR. His chest had a gaping hole in it, one that only alcohol could cure.

He ordered a shot of whisky. It burned a path down his throat, but Travis welcomed the pain. One more, then two. But drinking wasn't making anything better. It wasn't even making him drunk. A waste of perfectly good whisky.

A dark-eyed girl at the end of the bar kept trying to get his attention by shaking her breasts farther and farther out of her low-cut top. Several times he'd almost gotten out of his chair to make his move. *That would show Lily,* he thought.

Who was he kidding? Booze didn't have a chance in hell of curing what ailed him. Big breasts on some Italian stranger weren't gonna do it either.

He wanted Lily.

And Lily wanted to screw some stranger.

Travis lifted a finger in the bartender's direction for shot number four and swiveled around on his stool to stare at the stranger's breasts again.

Which only made him think about Lily's breasts, worlds plumper and softer than any he had ever touched, ever tasted.

He slammed his fist down on the thick wooden bar. That scum bag at the café had been about to fondle Lily's breasts right there at the table. Travis had nearly jumped across the nearby tables to pummel the man into bloody pulp.

His pride was ground deep into the mud. It was a strange, awful sensation. They all were.

Losing control.

Being jealous.

Wanting Lily again and again, never feeling like he had enough of her.

The shot glass at the edge of his lips, Travis realized he had a hard choice to make. Was Lily worth it?

The answer hit him square across the chest, knocking the breath right out of him: Of course she was worth it. Only a complete idiot would turn his back on this kind of happiness, this kind of pleasure, this kind of unbelievable sex. And if he wanted to claim more of the incredible joy that being with Lily had granted him, he'd have to face his demons head-on, not sit hunched over a bar downing whisky shots.

Throwing several euros on the counter, Travis left the bar. He had one quick side trip to make before he went back to the hotel room. If he played his cards right, maybe he could convince Lily that he was worth another chance after all.

1 1
✣

LILY FELT LIKE AN IMPOSTER in her pretty silk dress. Not to mention the fact that the delicate material was splattered with tears. She rummaged through her suitcase and pulled out a crumpled heap of linen at the very bottom of her bag. Throwing her silk dress into a corner, she put on the dumpy linen shift that Janica referred to as her Mrs. Potato Man dress.

The awful dress worked its frumpy magic immediately. Lily felt completely invisible.

She tried not to think about where Travis was. Or, rather, whom he was with.

Hoping a good book would take her mind away from her pain, she grabbed the novel she had been unable to read on the airplane from her suitcase. Padding into the living room, she curled up into a ball under a soft blanket. But not even the steamy sex scenes held her attention.

Dropping the book onto the coffee table, she stared out at the rolling hills beyond the window of her hotel room and tried not to cry. This would teach her for thinking she could overstep her boundaries in life.

Thin, pretty girls got to have all the fun. Big women got to watch with envy.

The sound of the heavy wood door opening startled her and she looked up, wide-eyed, from beneath the blanket and heaps of pillows. Travis stood in the doorway. When his eyes locked with hers, Lily couldn't fight the burst of hope that swelled within her chest.

He was so beautiful. That was the problem. It had always been the problem, even when they were kids, and he deliberately didn't choose her for his soccer team at recess. Even then she had gazed at him with wonder.

His dark hair looked windswept, not unlike they way it looked in the aftermath of their lovemaking. His lips were full, yet incredibly masculine. Where they curved up ever so slightly at the corners, Lily wanted to lick with the tip of her tongue. His green eyes gleamed with promise, and Lily shivered, even wrapped in the heavy throw.

He looked uncertain as he asked, "Can I come in?"

Mute, unable to believe he had returned to her instead of going off with some Italian hottie, Lily nodded. She backed up farther into the pillows as he joined her in the living room.

Travis sat down on the edge of the couch, and Lily finally noticed the brown paper bag he clutched in his hand. He set it down next to her novel.

"Lily," he said, then cleared his throat, looking up toward the frescoed ceiling as if searching for the words there.

Finally, Travis turned to face her and her breath went. The truth of her feelings smacked her across the face like a wet towel, and she visibly flinched in response.

She would never be able to look at him without loving him. No matter how awful he was to her, she would always love Travis. It was her cross to bear.

"Lily," he began again, "I know I'm not very good at this, but . . . " He paused again and half grinned. The smile didn't last long, though. When it fell away, Travis looked more beaten down than ever.

Lily's heart broke. If only there were a drug that could cure heartache.

Two a day for life and she might be able to manage.

"I acted like a complete jerk this afternoon, and I'm sorry." His words came out in a rush.

Lily detected a hint of self-loathing behind his apology. Surely she was mistaken? She had never known anyone more confident than Travis.

At her continued silence, Travis shifted uncomfortably on the couch. "I brought a peace offering," he said, gesturing to the brown paper bag.

Lily eyed the bag. "Let's see it," she croaked out of her tear-ridden throat. She sniffled once, and Travis's eyes roved over her face.

"I made you cry."

He reached out for her, but Lily cringed even deeper into the cushions. It was a vicious cycle: She wanted Travis to comfort her, but he was the reason she needed to be comforted in the first place.

Sick, sick, sick, she thought, vowing to be strong in the face of temptation, no matter what from then on.

He got up off the couch. "My stupid peace offering sucks. I don't know what I was thinking. I'm a jealous bastard who can't control—"

Lily sat up. "You're what?"

Travis sat back down. "A jealous bastard?" he repeated, searching her eyes.

The first hint of a smile crept across Lily's face. "And?"

"And . . . I can't help it, Lily."

"You can't?" The smile won.

Travis shook his head and sighed. "No. I can't. Another guy so much as looks at you, and I want to beat him senseless. Being in Italy with you has been killing me. I'm going to have to get a machine gun to deal with all of the scum I want to take down from the way they look at you."

"Wow," she said, hardly able to believe what Travis was saying. "You're actually jealous." Travis looked distinctly uncomfortable, and Lily couldn't resist letting him live with it for a while. But not for too long.

"So how were you planning on making it up to me?"

So much for being strong in the face of temptation, she thought. But how could she resist him? Not only had she gotten an apology, but Travis had admitted that he was jealous, and he'd brought a peace offering.

Maybe everything would work out okay after all.

Travis pulled a container out of the plastic bag.

Lily shot up off the couch and grabbed the carton from him. "Chocolate gelato?" Her voice was shrill and distinctly unpleasant. Sometimes, she realized, the only thing a woman could be was a grade-A bitch. Particularly when a man was responsible for pushing her too far.

She threw the gelato at Travis with all her might. The container split open and splattered all over him. His hair, his face, his shirt, his pants. All covered with sticky sweet, dark brown Italian ice cream.

Travis wiped away the glob of gelato above his left eye. "Lily," he said in a placating tone, but Lily wasn't going to listen to one more minute of his lies.

"Is this some kind of sick and twisted joke? Tell the fat girl you're sorry, and then ply her with sugar and cream? You bastard!"

Her fists were coming at him. She wanted to hurt him as bad as he kept hurting her. She didn't want to remember, but she couldn't help it.

"Lily, Lily two-by-four. She can hardly fit through the door."

It was the day before Christmas break, and the teacher had thrown the kids a party. Cakes and cookies were strewn across the back table, and even though all of the other kids had eagerly gobbled them up, Lily was too self-conscious to eat anything in front of her classmates. But the lure of chocolate ice cream was too much for any twelve-year-old to bear. She scooped out a small portion of ice cream, telling herself that no one would notice. They were too busy playing games and eating their own bowls of ice cream.

But she had been wrong.

"Lily, Lily two-by-four. She can hardly fit through the door." She had looked up at Travis, begging him with her eyes to defend her. To tell the other kids to be quiet. But instead he just looked away and kept eating his cake.

Tears had filled her eyes as she ran into the girls' bathroom to hide. Travis hadn't even tried to stop them from making fun of her. He used to be her friend, but now he wasn't anymore. And that was the worst thing of all, worse even than some kid in class calling her fat.

The memory combined with the here and now, and Lily lost control. She threw her whole body behind her attack. She was going to tear the beautiful bastard from limb to limb.

"Lily! Stop hitting me." Travis imprisoned her wrists in his large hands. His mouth fell open, and he stopped apologizing when he saw her outfit. "What the hell do you have on?" he said, his surprise evident.

"What do you care?" she spat. "What does it matter? You can dress a cow up in fancy clothes, but she's still a cow. Isn't she?"

Lily dared him to disagree with her.

But instead of being intimidated by her fury, Travis's mouth set into a dangerous line. "How many times am I going to have to say this to you, Lily?" Each word hit her like a bullet.

"You. Are. Not. Fat."

Two tears ran down her cheeks, and the will to fight left her body. "I am. I always have been. I always will be. Lily, Lily two-by-four."

"No, sweetheart." His voice was more gentle than she'd ever thought it could be. "That was just a stupid kid who said those things."

"Why didn't you defend me?"

"I was scared."

"Of what?"

"Of you. I thought you were perfect."

"No."

"Beautiful."

"No."

"I loved you, Lily, even then."

Both Travis and Lily looked at each other in shock.

Travis took a deep breath, then smiled. "I love you." He swallowed, as if testing the words on his tongue, in his mouth. "I love you, Lily."

Lily's arms went limp as she leaned into Travis's warmth. Everything was instantly forgiven, and even though she wished she knew better, she didn't.

Travis had just said the words she had been longing to hear her whole life.

"You love me?"

Softer than a feather, Travis kissed her lips, and moved his hands past her wrists to intertwine with her hands. Lily was afraid to say anything that would break the spell. She was afraid Travis would start laughing, that he'd say, "Just kidding."

But then he whispered the words, "I always have," against her lips, and she was lost to anything but him.

With a groan that spoke volumes of desire, Travis threaded Lily's red locks between his sticky fingers. He tilted her head to get better access to her mouth. Lily opened wide for his invasion, meeting his passion with her own. Whisky merged with Travis's signature essence. He tasted like magic.

He pulled her tightly to him, cupping the huge bulge between his legs in the soft valley of her thighs. Lily wanted to sink into him, to be naked and filled all the way to the brim with his raw heat.

Her unspoken prayer was heard. Travis laid her down on the floor. "This dress has got to go," he said. Before she realized it, his fists were curled around the collar at her neck and he was ripping the dress clean down the middle.

Underneath the linen atrocity, Lily was stark naked. She had stripped off her sexy underwear along with her sexy dress.

"On second thought," Travis said, "you can wear that dress as often as you like, as long as you promise to be smooth and naked beneath it."

"I hate that dress," she said as she reached for Travis to pull him down to her.

"Me too. Ugliest thing I've ever seen."

They laughed together, but when he laid his heavy weight on

her, their laughter faded away. Lily sucked in her breath as sticky cream smeared onto her breasts from his shirt.

Travis ran his hands between their bodies. "Uh-oh," he said, "looks like someone has gelato all over her."

"Do you like gelato?" Lily murmured huskily.

Travis smeared the chocolate around her puckering areola. "That depends."

"On what?" Lily held her breath as Travis bent his mouth over her breast.

"On how it's served."

His words were hot against her flushed skin. Lily arched up into his mouth, but instead of sucking her nipple into his mouth, he gently pushed her back into the soft carpet and lapped chocolate off the undersides of her breasts.

"Mmm," he said, rearing up over her. "You should taste this."

He swept his tongue inside her mouth. Lily sucked the chocolate off his tongue and he groaned.

"More?"

Lily nodded, her heart beating so hard she was afraid it might leap out of her chest altogether. *I love you.* The words pulled at her insides and sat on the tip of her lips unsaid.

Travis licked ever-narrowing circles on the soft flesh of her breasts, until her tight nipples were the final bit of chocolate surprise. "I always save the cherry on top for last," he said with a wicked grin.

Nearly incoherent with need, Lily watched Travis's lips surround her nipple. She closed her eyes as his teeth lightly raked over the sensitive tips. He sucked one peak hard into his mouth.

"More," she moaned.

Cupping her breasts between his palms, Travis showered loving attention on both nipples at the same time. He ran his tongue through the deep valley between them. Light stubble raked Lily's inflamed skin.

Having never felt so safe before, Lily reached for his hand and tried to put it between her legs. Travis looked up from her breasts, his pupils dilated, his breath coming hard. "Is that sweet pussy of yours feeling neglected?"

Unable to form words, she nodded.

Barely above a whisper, he said, "Let me see."

Lily spread her legs so that he could see how wet she was. Travis leaned down over her cunt, so close that his breath teased her something terrible.

"Oh my," he said, running his index finger down the length of her lips, "you are wet, aren't you?" Travis brought his finger to his mouth and sucked her juice in. Tilting his head to one side, he raised an eyebrow. "Hmm. Needs a little something."

Lily gasped as he spread her legs wider and spread cold gelato onto her vagina.

"Now that looks like the kind of dessert I like. I'd better eat you up before it melts."

Lily closed her eyes and held her breath as she waited for Travis to lick the chocolate cream from her cunt. None of her fantasies could have ever prepared her for this kind of loving. Somehow she had found a lover who knew what she wanted before she knew herself.

His tongue, warm and broad, curved into her, then up and over her swollen clitoris. Again and again he stroked her cunt with his tongue. His face was buried firmly between her thighs, his hands cupped and squeezed her ass.

The orgasm hit her full force, and Travis responded to her spasms by plunging two fingers in and out of her while sucking her clit into his mouth.

"Your mouth, oh God . . ." Lily never wanted it to end.

Travis's fingers continued to work their magic as he reared up over her, biting and sucking her breasts, tonguing her nipples. His mouth worked up to the pulse point in her neck and shivers ran though her. The tail end of her first orgasm merged into another.

"Good girl," Travis said, as her muscles squeezed his fingers with renewed vigor. In an instant his head was between her legs again, and he was licking and sucking everywhere at once. Lily grabbed his head with her hands. She wrapped her legs around his neck and ground his mouth and teeth and tongue into her pussy.

Finally, she fell limp. Travis rained kisses on the inside of her thighs, wet with her arousal and his saliva and chocolate gelato. He ran kisses down her legs, behind her knees, down her calves. His warm hands massaged the soles of her feet. She was too exhausted from her two incredible explosions to do much more than groan with pleasure.

Lily relaxed and enjoyed the sensuous magic of Travis's massaging hands. At long last, she opened her eyes. He was kneeling between her legs, his gaze roving over her large breasts, her pink, wet pussy lips.

Somehow, when he looked at her like that she forgot to be embarrassed. She felt like the most beautiful woman in the world.

And he loved her.

Her heart had been in his hands for so many years. And now he had offered her *his* heart. She reeled from it all. The only way she was going to make it through the night in one piece was if she concentrated on all the things she wanted to do to Travis.

"Too many clothes," she murmured, her voice coming from somewhere far away. Travis smiled at her, his heart in his eyes. Something new and wonderful burst to life inside her.

"Come here, big boy," she said, ready for her turn to play with a hard cock and some chocolate gelato.

On all fours, Travis came up over her. While Lily undid the buttons of his shirt, they loved each other with their mouths. She tugged his shirt down his arms, then ran her hands over the hard planes of his chest.

"You are so beautiful." She would never get enough of him.

How could a man this perfect love her?

The thought assaulted her, backhanded. Her hands stilled on his chest.

Travis picked up on her emotional shift right away. "Sweetheart?"

The sound of his voice brought her back to the present. Hoping to cover her tracks, she teased, "I can't wait to taste my first chocolate-dipped cock."

Her words mobilized Travis, who took matters into his own hands by stripping off his pants. Naked, he stretched out on his back. Lily wrapped her hand around his penis, marveling at how beautiful every inch of Travis was.

Travis urged her to go ahead with her culinary plan. "If you're gonna dip me, Lily, you'd better do it fast."

A thick bead of precome emerged from the head of his shaft, backing up his statement. Lily eagerly licked him clean.

Her eyes crinkling, she reached for the carton of gelato. "Delicious, as always, but you were right. Tonight definitely calls for a special Italian touch."

Lily smeared gelato up and down Travis's shaft. His hips tightened beneath her hand. "You like that, don't you?"

Travis squeezed his eyes shut and nodded.

"Well, then, how about this?"

Starting at the dark, springy hair at the base of his shaft, Lily licked Travis up. He was the best chocolate ice cream pop she had ever tasted. She tortured him with her tongue, cleaning up every square inch of his cock. For her final touch, she opened her mouth wide and took him all the way.

"I can't stop—" he cried, as hot come shot down her throat.

Lily readily gulped him down, thrilling in such intimacy with the man she had always and would always love. She continued to suck, even after his strong spurts had stopped.

His muscles went lax, and Lily levered herself up onto her elbows, putting her chin in her palms.

"Delicious," she said, smacking her lips together.

Weakly, Travis said, "Need. To. Shower."

Lily got to her feet and helped Travis up. He pulled her to him and kissed her softly on the lips. "You blow me away." he whispered.

"Ha-ha," she said, but Travis refused to go along with the pun.

"I'm serious, sweetheart. I've never felt like this before."

His eyes were deep green and so full of love that tears sprang to Lily's eyes. "Me either."

1 2
ॐॐॐ

*A*FTER AN INCREDIBLE SHOWER they fell, exhausted, into the soft down bedding. Within seconds, Lily was asleep. Lucky girl.

Sweet girl.

His girl.

He kissed her forehead, and she snuggled closer to him. He wrapped his arms even tighter around her.

Now that everything was so clear, Travis almost had to laugh at what a fool he had been for so many years. Everything pointed, so obviously, in the same direction.

Straight toward love.

Love.

It was the most incredible sensation, one that he never thought he would feel again. The last time Travis remembered feeling so safe, so complete, was when he was ten running around with Luke and Lily on the playground playing pirate ship. His mother hadn't gotten sick yet. That little boy hadn't had any idea of the depths of pain that he would go through.

Travis didn't want to deal with twenty years of pain, but as Lily slept in his arms, he knew it was long past due. He had wasted so much of his life hiding from anything that made him yearn for happiness, safety, comfort.

And most of all, love.

Travis had vague memories of his childhood, memories that he wished he had been able to hold on to. Wrestling with Luke. Staying out at the playground so late that their mom had to come hunt them down with the threat of no dessert if they didn't get into the kitchen and wash up immediately for dinner. Having his first crush in the first grade on a cute little girl named Lily. Trying to convince her to play doctor with him behind the bushes in second grade.

And then, out of the blue, his worst nightmare had come true and his mother had left them forever. At ten years old, Travis hadn't understood what breast cancer was. But he understood too well that his mother had deserted them.

Forever.

He remembered listening to Luke cry in the middle of the night on the bottom bunk in their bedroom. He remembered his dad coming home late from work and having too much to drink. But apart from that, Travis couldn't remember feeling anything at all.

Nothing, that is, apart from an emptiness that hadn't gone away until he'd kissed Lily for the first time at the fashion show.

The other kids at school had left him alone, everyone except for Lily, who kept trying to invade his space, who kept trying to get him to admit his feelings, his hurt to her. She was his friend, she'd said, and she knew he was sad. Having already lost both her parents by then, he supposed she felt it was her duty to reach out to him and Luke. She offered comfort and understanding, and with Luke, it had made the two of them closer, like brother and sister, even after all these years.

But Travis had thought that Lily was trying to expose him as weak, as a coward. Couldn't she see that he had to stay strong? If he hadn't been there to hold his brother and father together, what would have happened to his family?

So from that day forward, he shut her out in any way he could. He ignored her. He turned away from her when she needed him. He let her down again and again until one day she stopped trying to talk to him. Of course, the fact that she was bigger and more insecure than everyone else made his job all too easy. But still, she was always on his radar screen. He even knew that she had watched him tongue the cheerleader beneath the bleachers and knew that her adoration of him *had* been a turn-on, even as he tried to convince himself that she meant nothing to him.

Lily snuggled in tighter to him and sighed softly. Travis smiled into her hair and stroked one soft shoulder. He hated to admit how awful he had been to Lily all these years, but by God he was finally going to own up to it. Could he ever make it up to her?

By a sheer stroke of fate—some magic, maybe, that was sewn into the seams of the dress Lily wore at the fashion show—he had finally been able to see past his own idiocy, and he and Lily had finally come together.

Lust had broken down the door, letting love saunter right on in.

I'm finally doing something right, Travis told himself as he lay with Lily in his arms, looking out the large window at the Tuscan moon. Sure, he was still scared. Who wouldn't be?

But he'd just take it one day at a time. With Lily by his side.

Travis smiled and closed his eyes. Lily's soft, even breathing lulled him to sleep.

EVERYTHING ABOUT the next two days was perfect. They found endless treasures for his client's house, and as Lily grew more confident in her decorating skills she began to lead the buying trip. Tips from vendors led them to little towns and old farmhouses. Between meetings with unique craftsmen, they pulled the car off into deserted valleys and made sweet love.

On Sunday night they drove their rental car back into the village and found the streets blocked off at the bottom of the hill. Travis parked the car. He and Lily got out, and she pointed to the large banner strung between buildings.

"Festivale di Matrimonio." She clapped her hands. "Oh, Travis, it's the Festival of Weddings that Giuseppe told us about! Do you think anyone will actually be getting married?"

Travis shrugged and grabbed her hand. "Let's go find out."

Beautiful music streamed down the streets of Saturnia. There were musicians on every corner. Locals were dancing in the street, so Travis and Lily joined them, spinning and twirling and laughing. The sun was beginning to set, turning the hills and the stucco buildings to gold.

Travis felt utterly content. "We should stay here forever."

Lily sighed with longing. "Wouldn't that be heaven? I'd miss Luke and Janica way too much, though."

Travis's heart skipped a beat. Luke. Janica. What were they going to think about him and Lily? He twirled Lily again to hide his conflict from her. In the past three days he had almost started to believe that he and Lily were in a safe cocoon where the rest of the world didn't matter. But if the mere mention of their siblings' names made him panic, what was going to happen when he introduced Lily to his friends and colleagues as his girlfriend?

She's my girlfriend, he thought, startled by the revelation. A hundred bells rang out, and Travis let the music of the bells carry his doubts away. Together, they ran up the narrow streets toward the festival, eager to witness whatever magic the Saturnians had for them on this beautiful night.

Colorful lanterns hung between buildings and from every window. The effect was dazzling, a thousand fireflies twinkling. Travis kissed Lily again and again as they made their ascent to the top of the street.

Their giggles fell away when they spotted the festival. White paper wedding bells mixed with the lanterns. Women in incredible wedding gowns held on to the arms of their men, dapper in dark suits and tuxedos with bright, colorful sashes.

Everyone was drunk on love, and the many stalls selling grappa and fruity pinot grigios didn't hurt any.

The bells sounded their final chime, and a band began to play. As couples took the floor, one after the other, Lily and Travis were swept up into the music. Together they twirled and laughed and kissed.

"I've never been this happy in my entire life." Lily nestled her cheek against Travis's lightly stubbled jaw. "I love Tuscany," she breathed.

"I love you," he replied, his breath blowing softly across Lily's ear.

Neither one of them noticed when the music stopped. They held tight to each other and swayed to the beating of their hearts. Travis looked up and realized that everyone was clapping and hooting and looking at him and Lily.

"Um, Lily," he said.

"Yes," she said, looking up at him with stars in her eyes.

"I think the locals are trying to get our attention."

Lily peeked over Travis's shoulder and blushed. "Why are they all looking at us?" But before he could reply, several women grabbed her hands and pulled her from his arms. They herded her off toward a grove of olive trees with a white canopy between them. She looked over her shoulder and saw that Travis was getting the same treatment from the men.

"Now would be a good time to know some Italian," she muttered, as the women fussed and cooed over her. But she was willing to go along with their fun until they started to undress her.

"What are you doing?"

She didn't want to slap their hands away, but she had no idea what was going on, and it unnerved her. The days with Travis had showed her that she had a bold side, but that boldness didn't include getting naked with a bunch of strange women in the middle of a crowded piazza.

An old woman motioned for the others to cease their ministrations for a few moments. In her arms she held a white dress. Lily looked closer. "Of course," she murmured with a smile, "a wedding dress."

All of the women except her were wearing wedding dresses. She must have looked out of place. Smiling at the women, she hoped to make up for her earlier behavior. "*Grazie*." She pointed at the dress. "*Bella*."

New smiles on their faces, the women converged on her again. Her dress was removed, and the wedding dress was slipped over her head. It fit beautifully, layers of antique lace with corset strings in the back to mold it to her figure. Her hair was brushed and primped, her face was made up, satin shoes were slipped on her feet.

"I feel like Cinderella," she said and several women nodded their heads vigorously.

"*Sì*," they said, "Cinderella!"

The final touch was a thin lace veil. It lent a soft, shadowed, extraspecial glow to the entire evening for Lily.

The elder whistled, and the band began to play. Everyone in the piazza stomped their feet and clapped in time to the music. Lily was led out from the olive trees with pride by the women who had dressed her. She held her head high. She knew she looked beautiful, and she couldn't wait for Travis to see her.

She hoped he had his camera with him. She wanted to show Janica and Luke pictures when they got home. Otherwise, they would never believe her story of getting handpicked to be a part of the Festival of Weddings in the heart of Tuscany.

She felt a light buzzing across her skin. She knew Travis was watching her. She searched the crowd, but she couldn't find him. She hadn't thought to look at the stage in front of the church, however. Which was precisely where Travis was standing.

With a man who looked remarkably like a priest.

And Travis seemed to be playing the groom.

Which made sense, she supposed after a moment's confusion, since she was clearly playing the bride.

He blew her a kiss, and Lily beamed and blew him one back. He reached out with his right hand and caught it, then pressed his hand to his heart. The elder presented her to Travis, and when Travis took her hand, the crowd cheered again, the noise level rising tenfold.

"They don't mess around with their festivals, do they?" Lily said with a grin. "This looks just like the real thing, doesn't it?"

Travis looked stunned, and Lily was pleased that she had surprised him in the beautiful gown. Finally, he managed, "You look beautiful, Lily. The most beautiful bride in the world."

"You say the sweetest things," she teased. "What a fun game this is. I love your sash."

She let the bright red, orange, and yellow striped silk tied around Travis's waist slide through her fingers. "Were you worried when they started to undress you?" she asked, but right then the man playing the priest raised a flag, and the crowd silenced.

The man began speaking. Lily couldn't understand a word he said, so she let herself relax into the perfect evening with the man she loved. She squeezed Travis's hand, and he squeezed hers back. Shivers ran up and down her spine at the look in his eyes, like he wanted to eat her up and worship her for the rest of time. Marriage was the furthest thing from her mind. She might have been in love with Travis most of her life, but they had spent less than a week together. Still it was fun to play make-believe.

The lyrical foreign language washed over Lily like the warm breeze that held essences of olives and sweet sunflower petals. With Travis's hands holding hers she knew the deep contentment she had been searching for her whole life. She closed her eyes and breathed deeply of love, of life.

The crowd cheered again, and Lily opened her eyes. She wanted to sing out her pleasure for the whole world to hear. Giving in to a spontaneous urge, Lily unthreaded her hands from Travis's, lifted her veil, and pulled his mouth closer, her hands wrapped into his thick, soft black hair.

She felt his grin without even seeing it. Their lips touched, and flames exploded. She tasted his lips with the tip of her tongue, and he groaned. In an instant, he was devouring her, and she was sinking into him, body and soul.

Gasping for breath, Lily murmured against Travis's lips, "Let's get out of here."

Travis looked into her eyes with such intensity it seared her soul.

She licked her lips suggestively. "I'm not sure they were exactly looking for a live sex show up here, do you?"

Travis grinned. "Is that what we're doing?"

Lily ran a finger down his cheek. "Kiss me like that again, and I'm pretty sure that's what they're going to get."

Travis threw his head back and laughed, the beautiful sound echoing off the centuries-old stone buildings. The priest took a step forward and took each of their hands in his. The crowd silenced to a hush.

Lily's breath caught in her throat at the power that coursed through the mock-priest's hand into hers. Suddenly, everything seemed so serious. Several of the men who had dressed Travis joined them on the stage, holding violins. Three men played a haunting melody while the fourth sang the poignant lyrics. Even without being able to understand the language, Lily knew the song was about the truest kind of love.

"What a beautiful song," she said to Travis, hardly able to believe that they were getting such a wonderful serenade on the spot like this. Travis didn't reply, but stared holes into the men, and Lily's pulse raced a bit faster.

"Are you okay?" she whispered.

Travis blinked hard and seemed to surface again. "Fine," he said, and Lily didn't want to ruin their perfect evening by probing too hard, so she turned her attention back to the mesmerizing music.

The elder who had dressed her stepped out from behind the

priest and handed Lily a thin green glass vase. Lily looked at the vase with surprise.

"Is this our door prize?" Lily asked Travis.

Travis shook his head. "I think we're supposed to smash it to the ground."

Lily gasped and held it to her chest. "No! I don't want to. How else will I remember this day?"

Looking serious again, Travis said, "I doubt that's going to be a problem."

Lily tilted her head at him in puzzlement, but before she could get a good answer out of him the priest placed Travis's hand over Lily's on the vase, raised their arms high into the air, then let go.

"I think this is our cue," Travis said with an air of foreboding that made Lily shiver with sudden unease. Looking Lily in the eye, he said, "On three. One, two, three."

The pretty vase smashed onto the stage before them into a million pieces, and the cheers were deafening. Lily stood frozen, like a statue. The townspeople lifted her and Travis off the stage while throwing brightly colored confetti everywhere. When her feet touched solid ground again, she reached for Travis.

"What just happened up there?" she asked in a shaky voice.

Travis's voice was a low rumble. "I'm not sure you want to know."

Fire shot into Lily's eyes. "Tell me what happened, Travis."

With a sigh, he said, "My Italian is pretty rough."

"Stop stalling."

"You and I were just . . . " His words fell away again, but Lily was pretty sure she could finish the sentence for him.

"Married."

She expected him to pull away from her, to go running off

down the hill. The Travis she had always known would have
been on the next plane to the farthest place he could get to.
Away from her. Even if it was just a pretend marriage for one
night in Italy, she knew he had to feel caged. Trapped.

Lily stiffened every part of her body to try and steady herself
for his rejection. So when Travis pulled her into his arms and
kissed her like a man kisses a woman he's in love with, it took a
few seconds for it to sink in.

"I love you, Lily."

Lily held on to him for dear life, shell-shocked. "I love you,
Travis."

In the past week her life had, somehow, changed from a boring late-night TV show to a glorious old black-and-white film,
where she was the gorgeous star with the to-die-for hero lusting
after her. But although it was amazing and wonderful, it was
also weird. Not to mention terribly hard to comprehend, as if
she were going to wake up any minute, and it would have been
no more than a ridiculous dream.

She heard her name being called out, more and more frantic
each time.

"Lily! Lily!"

Oh no, she thought, *I knew this was a dream!* A really, really
lifelike dream, but unreal nonetheless.

Travis's arms were strong and warm around her. His lips
tasted of sugar and lemons. Was it possible to taste in dreams,
she wondered? And then there was a small hand on her back,
and Lily knew that she wasn't dreaming.

Even so, she had just been woken up with a splash of ice-cold
water.

Two very familiar voices beamed through the happiness-
filled, lust-laden haze clouding her synapses.

Janica and Luke had come to Tuscany.

And she had a sinking feeling that she knew why.

Project Save Lily had begun.

"LUKE?" Travis stared at his twin with equal parts disbelief and distress.

His brother's usual smile was gone, replaced with a grim stare. "Travis." Luke's voice was clipped and filled with unmistakable disapproval. And, if Travis wasn't mistaken, a fair measure of loathing.

Travis scrambled for something to say to his brother who had traveled five thousand miles to surprise him in Tuscany.

"What are you doing here?" It wasn't exactly gracious, but it was all he could manage at the moment. After all, he had just gotten married to Lily in a spontaneous Italian ceremony. Considering the changes he'd been through during the past several days Travis was amazed that he was still standing. Over Luke's shoulder, Travis could see Lily talking to a small dark-haired girl.

His worst fears were realized. "Janica?"

Lily's little sister spat his name. "Travis."

He barely resisted taking a step back. If the look in Janica's eyes was any indication, the little sprite was gearing up to kill him. Slowly and painfully.

Janica advanced on Travis. "What was going on up there on the stage?"

Lily grabbed Janica's arm and tried to pull her away from Travis. "I'll explain everything to you guys later. Right now Travis and I have to—"

This time Luke was the one taking menacing steps toward Travis. He poked him in the chest. Hard. "You'd better explain this right now, 'cause I'm itching to break something on you."

Travis felt like he was falling deeper and deeper into a hole that he hadn't seen until it was too late. He looked at Luke, his twin's anger palpable. Janica speared him with a glance of ultimate fury. And then there was Lily.

Travis badly wished he could read the look in Lily's eyes. Was she angry? Was she sad? Had she wanted to marry him? What did she want him to say?

For the first time in his life Travis was at a complete loss for words. He didn't know what he should do. He didn't know what he should say.

So, in a moment that would live on in his nightmares for months, he fell back into his usual modus operandi: He made a joke out of everything.

Forcing his muscles to ease up, he chuckled and waved his hand in the air. "We were just messing around up there," he said, effectively dismissing not only the marriage ceremony between him and Lily but their entire relationship.

Lily's mouth fell open. Then closed. He was dying, couldn't she see that? Didn't she know how hard it was for him, to love her, need her so much, so quickly? He wished they could be alone to try and figure out how to get through this, how to deal with making their relationship public. But instead of pulling her away from Luke and Janica, Travis stupidly filled the silence with more garbage. "We were giving the locals a good show, right, Lily?"

He didn't look at her to see if she nodded or not. He couldn't bear to. Not right then. Travis had felt so calm during the ceremony, even after he realized that it was for real. But that was when he'd been able to pretend that it was just the two of them, that no one knew them. That no one was going to judge Lily for being lush and round. She was so beautiful to him, but he knew firsthand how important bones and angles were when it came to treating a woman nicely. Just because he had faced up to being a shallow excuse for a human being, didn't mean that his friends and coworkers would behave the same way. If anyone said anything to hurt her . . . he couldn't stand to even think about it. And even though he knew that Luke and Janica loved Lily for who she was, just seeing them made all of his fears rise up. He didn't have a plan in place, and this was all happening so fast that he couldn't hack it under the pressure.

"But she's wearing a wedding dress," Janica said. "And you were kissing her like . . ."

Travis forced a snort, and in that moment he hated himself far more than anyone else could have, even as he said, "So we got a little carried away. It doesn't mean anything."

The minute Lily walked away, Travis felt as if his heart had been ripped out of his chest.

It didn't mean anything? Had he actually said those words? But she would understand, wouldn't she, that he had been put on the spot by their siblings? That he hadn't known what else to say?

Travis badly wanted to run after her, but even if Janica hadn't been standing directly in his path, he knew he couldn't. Right then everything he said was wrong, and he'd just make it worse. But Lily loved him enough to give him another chance, to let him explain later. Didn't she?

"You go after her," Janica said to Luke. "You're taller so you can find her in the crowd. I'll stay here and deal with this prick."

Luke shot Travis one more deadly glance, then plunged into the crowd where Lily had disappeared.

Travis ran his hands through his hair and girded himself to

deal with a protective sister who was out for his blood. And rightly so.

LUKE RAN through the crowds after Lily, confusing her several times with other women in white wedding gowns. "It's like the Twilight Zone for weddings," he muttered as he slowed down his pace to let an elderly lady walk past him. "I'm losing her," he said, impatiently scanning the crowd for a flash of red hair. Up on the steps above the square Luke saw red curls. He couldn't believe the joke his brother had just played on Lily. Innocent, naive Lily. Luke felt like scum of the earth for ever suggesting that she continue her relationship with Travis. The minute he had found out about their one-night stand he should have told her to stay away from his twin.

Their whole lives Travis had been no good where women were concerned. What had possessed him to think that Lily could ever play the same kind of game that Travis played?

A flash of white on the stairs disappeared behind the trunk of an old cypress tree. And that was where Luke found Lily sitting on a tree stump, staring blankly off into the distance.

As his footsteps pounded up the old stone steps, Lily looked up with surprise, hope etched into the lines of her face. It was painfully obvious to Luke that she wanted Travis to be the one coming after her. The next time Luke saw his twin he was going to pound Travis's face in until he did such permanent damage that no girl would ever want to look at Travis again.

Lily forced a wobbly smile. "Luke," she said, standing up to give him a hug. "I can't believe you and Janica came all this way. It's so nice to see you," she said, but Luke had a feeling that she wasn't the least bit happy he and Janica had come to Italy.

"I'm so sorry, Lily," he said, as he gently rocked her in his arms.

To his great surprise, Lily pushed out of his arms and stared at him. "There's nothing to be sorry about."

Luke didn't know what the right words were. He gestured down to the square. "But what about what Travis did?"

Lily shook her head at him, her mouth in a tight line. "Travis didn't do anything to me. We both did this together. He was right. The mock-wedding didn't mean anything. We were messing around, having fun in Italy."

Her words were firm, but Luke felt in his gut how hard it was for Lily to act so nonchalant in the face of Travis's less-than-gentlemanly behavior.

Linking her arm in his, she started them back down the steps. "Let's get back down to the square. There's a big party going on tonight, and if I'm not mistaken, I'm at the center of it."

Luke did as she wished, but as he stole a sidelong glance at Lily's composed face, he couldn't help but feel that she was more hurt that she let on. He had to let her confide in him in her own time, he knew that.

But at the same time, Luke got the sense that Lily was really and truly changed by everything that happened since the fashion show. No longer weak—not that he had ever thought her weak, soft maybe, but full of caring and love— she carried herself with an inner poise that he had never seen in her before.

Luke was confused by Lily's sudden changes. She had always been the one person he could count on just to be. He told himself that it had been a long flight, and he supposed he was suffering from the effects of travel and the beginning of jet lag. Maybe things would even out and go back to normal once he got something to eat and closed his eyes for a few hours.

JANICA ADVANCED ON TRAVIS. Between clenched teeth, she said, "You are the lowest of the low. How dare you mess with my sister like this! If we weren't in public, I'd kick you in the balls so hard they'd be black-and-blue for a month!"

Travis backed up and almost knocked over a couple in the middle of a passionate embrace. What the hell was he going to say to Janica? Worse, what the hell was he going to say to Lily?

His marriage to Lily did mean something; he didn't want to pretend it didn't, but he'd been so completely thrown off by Janica and Luke's appearance, he'd choked.

Plus, there was one other uncontestable fact. Based on his rough translation of the Italian language, he and Lily had just been legally wed under an antiquated law.

Janica poked him in the chest. "Don't you even have anything to say for yourself?"

Travis swallowed and nodded, trying to find his footing in the mess that he'd created for himself. "Yeah, I've got something to say. But Lily's the one who needs to hear it." He looked over Janica's shoulder at Luke and Lily, who were making their way through the square.

Janica crossed her arms across her chest and narrowed her eyes at him. "This better be good, or I swear I'm going to make the rest of your life a living hell."

Travis held his breath as Lily and Luke got closer and closer. He was sure Janica had plenty of ideas for the kind of tortures that a man would never want to endure. But, frankly, right now he was more scared of Lily's response to what he had to tell her than he was of the little she-devil with the big claws who was burning a hole into him with her hatred.

Unable to stand it another minute, Travis pushed through the crowd. Ignoring Luke, he grabbed Lily's free hand and said, "We need to talk."

He didn't know what he had expected from Lily—tears maybe? Accusations?—but certainly not a raised eyebrow and the steady voice that said, "Okay. Go ahead."

Trying to tune out Luke and Janica, who were huddled protectively around Lily, Travis took her other hand in his and said, "According to Italian law, you and I are married."

Lily's blank expression never wavered. "For tonight's festival, maybe."

"It's no joke, Lily. We're legally wed. The ceremony was binding."

Lily swayed back on her feet ever so slightly, and although Luke reached out for her, Travis pulled her closer to him. *Lily is mine now, not yours,* he thought as he glared at his twin. Luke was going to have to get used to the fact that he came second now. His twin had had his chance all these years as Lily's friend, but it was Travis who loved her like a woman.

"But I thought it was all just for fun up there." Her voice was faint.

Travis squeezed her hands. "The Festival of Weddings is special." He stared into her eyes, willing her to read his apology for what he had so stupidly said in front of Luke and Janica. He wanted to be alone with her, to explain his fears, to say that he still loved her. But everything was too raw, and he didn't feel like he could say "I love you" to Lily in front of their siblings.

Lily blinked several times, and he thought he saw the sheen of unshed tears in her eyes. "So, you're my husband now?"

He swallowed hard and tried to infuse the two words, "I am," with every ounce of love he possessed.

That was it, he decided, he was going to get down on one knee and profess his undying love to her right there, right then. She'd see how much he loved her, and everything would be okay. But there was no more time for talking as the music started up again, and, for the second time that night, they were pulled into the center of the celebration.

13

LILY WANTED TO SHUT OFF her mind to let the magic of the celebration draw her in again. But it was difficult—no, impossible—after what Travis had said.

"*We were just messing around,*" he had said. "*It doesn't mean anything.*" His careless words had hurt so much, and she had run away from him, in more pain than ever before. But when she saw Luke coming up the stairs to console her, she realized that she couldn't stand to play the victim again. This was between her and Travis. She would somehow manage to play along, even as her heart tore into a thousand pieces.

And when Travis had taken her hands in his and told her that they were actually married, it had been such a shock. But an even bigger shock had been the vulnerability she saw in his eyes. As if he expected her to throw the marriage in his face.

If he had said that he loved her in front of Luke and Janica, she would have forgiven him. But he didn't. And it would be all she could do to get through the night in one piece.

Travis was given a tray filled with small glasses of grappa. The man who handed Travis the tray spoke rapidly in Italian, gesturing to Lily. How she wished she knew the language. Lily, who had spent so much of her life feeling powerless, had never felt quite so helpless before.

Softly, Travis translated for her. "I'm supposed to hand these glasses out to everyone, but first all of the men are supposed to kiss you for good luck."

Woodenly, Lily went along with the ritual. She greeted first one man, then the next, letting them kiss her on the cheek in congratulations. Travis followed close behind her handing out grappa to the men and women. By the time she made it through the crowd, Lily felt like she'd been kissed by every man in town. And then everyone had their drinks raised high in the air as they yelled, *"Per cent'anni"* throwing their drinks back with gusto.

Travis's eyes pierced her. "For a hundred years," he translated and she shivered in response, her heart bruised and battered.

How she wished they had never come to the festival. Why couldn't they have gone back to their room and just made love instead? Then none of this mess would have ever happened.

But then Lily remembered Janica and Luke and knew that the mess would have happened, if not in the square after their impromptu wedding, then at the hotel. Lily could hardly believe it, but she was actually mad at them for ruining her fantasy. For thinking she needed to be rescued. Whether she did or not was beside the point.

At the same time, Lily knew that even if they hadn't come to Italy, something similar would have happened in San Francisco.

Travis would have acted like she didn't mean anything to him, and she, being lily-livered as always, would have hidden her broken heart and played along.

Long wooden tables were being brought into the square. It was chaos as they were draped with tablecloths, candles were lit, and huge, steaming platters of food brought in.

The priest directed Lily and Travis to share the head of the table, plush velvet seats that seemed fit for a king and queen. Overwhelmed by it all, Lily swayed on her feet.

Travis reached out to hold her steady. "Are you all right?" he asked with concern.

Lily couldn't bear to look at him. "I'm fine," she said as she tried to pull away from him. He was so close to her and so hot, so incredibly hot she was burning up, but instead of giving her room to breathe, he drew her closer. "If you want to leave, its okay, Lily. We need to talk about what just happened."

That was all she needed to hear to get back on her feet. "No," she said, desperate for any reason not to hear what Travis had to say about their impromptu wedding. "I don't want to ruin the celebration for everyone." She needed to buy some time to plan her escape so that she wouldn't have to hear Travis say the awful words she already could imagine.

"*I never meant to lead you on this way.*"

"*I got caught up in the heat of the moment and that's why I said I loved you.*"

"*I thought the wedding was a joke. If I had known it was for real, I would have stopped them.*"

"*We both know that you and I could never be together.*"

Stiffly, she made her way to the seat of honor. Travis followed behind her, with Janica and Luke close on their tails. Dinner was endless, with at least a dozen courses of meats, cheeses, fruits, and breads. Lily didn't have any appetite at all. It wasn't that the food didn't look delicious—it certainly did, given the way all the celebrants were stuffing themselves—but she was on pins and needles and could hardly breathe.

Even so, Lily didn't want the celebration to end. Because as soon as it did, she was going to be cornered by Travis, or Luke, or Janica. All three of them wanted to pick her brain, or worse still, *talk* to her about things. She didn't have anything to say to anybody right then. All she wanted to do was lock herself in the hotel room and go to sleep and never wake up.

As the tables were cleared, Lily's heart raced faster and faster. A grand procession announced the arrival of the wedding cake—a glorious concoction at least three feet high, decorated in pinks and blues.

"Oh my God, Lily, look at that cake!" Janica gaped in amazement and elbowed Luke. "I want one exactly like that at my wedding," she said to him, but Luke was busy watching Lily's face. She looked sad and tired and different. Luke couldn't pin down what it was about her that had changed. There was a new strength in her certainly, but that wasn't it.

Was it love?

Luke cast a glance at his brother and shook his head. How could she possibly be in love with Travis? Why were people always attracted to the people who were the worst for them?

Janica was still making noises about how glorious the cake looked, and he grimaced, wishing she would be quiet for once. She had been chattering away since they'd boarded the airplane in San Francisco. He'd always thought that she was spoiled rotten, walked all over Lily, and was far too cute for her own good. Between her looks and Lily's endless support, Janica had never worked for anything. The world had always been handed to her on a silver platter.

Luke shook his head in consternation. For once he wished somebody would hand Lily love on a silver platter. Too bad that Travis didn't seem to be up to the task.

THE TOWNSFOLK CALLED OUT for the cake to be cut. Travis brushed a lock of hair from Lily's face, and she trembled at his touch. He so badly wanted to say, "Do you still love me?" but instead he said, "Looks like it's time to cut the cake, sweetheart."

Lily visibly flinched at his endearment and an ice pick pierced his heart. He held his hand out to her, praying that she wouldn't reject him. When she put her soft hand in his he was struck, yet again, by what an incredible woman she was. And he was about to lose her.

Just days after finding her.

They walked together to the center of the table, where the cake stood in all its glory, waiting to be devoured by all the newly married and remarried couples in the piazza. The silence between them was painful, and Travis desperately wished he could think of something to say to ease her tension.

"Nice-looking cake, huh?" he said. Without looking at either him or the cake, still staring straight ahead, Lily nodded. Travis felt like a bumbling fool.

"I wonder if everyone will get a piece," was her reply, and Travis felt like they might as well be discussing the weather. She was a million miles away, and it killed him.

The priest handed them an oversized silver cake cutter and wrapped both of their hands around it. Travis's heart beat wildly as their bodies pressed together, and Lily's heat seeped into him. He wanted to throw her over his shoulder and lock her in the bedroom with him. He knew he didn't have the right words to show her how much he loved her, but he could worship her with his body.

And then she would know.

In one fluid stroke they cut the cake. The cheers were loud and raucous, fueled by copious amounts of local wine and good food.

"*Bacio, bacio, bacio!*" the townsfolk sang.

"*Bacio, bacio, bacio!*" Louder and louder, the words became more insistent, more passionate.

The chanting was impossible to ignore. From the deep red flush across Lily's cheeks Travis knew that she had already translated the word into English. Vowing to do at least something right that night, Travis turned Lily in his arms until she was so close to him that he could smell the sweet grappa on her lips.

"I love you, Lily," he whispered. She sucked in a breath and struggled to escape him, but Travis refused to let her go. Threading his hands through her hair he captured her lips, leaving no doubt in any bystander's minds about his possession of his new wife. Wanting to pour everything in his heart into the kiss, he loved her lips like he had loved her body so many times in the past week. Lily took her breath from his body as he tasted every inch of her sweetness. His lips a hair from hers, he whispered, "You're mine, all mine," then took her mouth again tenderly in a final kiss.

Lily's eyes grew wide, and this time when she tried to escape his embrace, he let her go. Off into the night she fled. Travis tried to keep his face steady. But the crowd was clamoring for cake and more wine, and the music had started up again, so no one seemed to notice that anything was wrong with the groom.

෨ ෨ ෨

No one, that is, except Janica and Luke.

"What is going on here?" Janica asked Luke as they sat stunned by the kiss they'd just witnessed. "I used to think that black was black and white was white, but now I don't know what to believe."

Luke ran his hands through his hair, making them stand up on end in a particularly rakish way. In his logical way, Luke laid out the facts. "All we know so far is that they got married, and evidently it's legally binding."

Janica snorted. "You're forgetting the most important part. Men!"

Luke looked confused and not a little disgruntled. "And what's that?"

"The kiss!"

This time Luke snorted dismissively. "You're reading too much into it. It was just a kiss. They didn't even want to do it. They *had* to do it."

Rolling her eyes at his cluelessness, Janica said, "Give me a break. Even I couldn't miss the heat between them. They practically lit the table on fire." Poking Luke with her index finger, she said, "And don't you dare try to argue with me when you know I'm right."

"Okay," he conceded, "maybe they have some chemistry, but that doesn't mean that Travis has changed. You know he can't commit to one woman."

"But what if he has changed?" Janica said. "There was something in that kiss." She wrapped her arms around herself and shivered. "Something that I don't think anyone here can deny."

"You're being too romantic," Luke said, obviously unwilling to see what she had seen so clearly.

Janica looked up at the moon, trying to figure out what it was about the kiss that got to her so much. With a snap of her fingers, she said, "I've figured out what it is."

Luke already looked unimpressed. "Go ahead, I'm listening."

Her eyes bright, she said, "Travis was pursuing Lily, not the other way around."

Luke started in his chair. "Are you sure? I mean, Lily's the one who's always had a crush on him."

"I know that," Janica said, annoyed at Luke for going back to the obvious.

"So how could things have changed so much in a week?"

Janica shook her head and stared up at the moon again. "I don't know," she said softly. Looking back across the table to the wedding cake, she stood up. "But I think we'd better go find out because lover boy is gone."

DAMN HIM FOR KISSING ME *like that.* Lily ran barefoot down the winding cobblestone streets, her skirts raised, her shoes in her hands. She had nearly convinced herself that she had imagined Travis's feelings for her, that the week had been nothing more than her imagination running away with itself, when he went and shattered every ounce of self-preservation she had left with that kiss.

His kiss had stolen her very soul. Even if she had wanted to fight it, she couldn't have. No one could have. His will to possess her was too strong.

You're mine, all mine, he had whispered against her lips.

She had longed to hear those words from him her whole life. But now that Travis had finally said them, it was all wrong.

Travis was Travis and would always be. Lily wanted to kick

herself for forgetting that for even one moment. These few days with him had been incredibly precious, but nothing had really changed.

Her feet were killing her, but she was afraid to put her shoes back on. The heels would slow her down. She gave a passing thought to her real clothes and shoes, which were still back at the square. Right now all she wanted was to get back to their hotel room and lock the door. Her instincts told her that Travis was close on her tail, so she ducked into a narrow alley and picked up the pace.

She couldn't see him again tonight. She couldn't talk to him. It was impossible. When he had apologized for hurting her hadn't he vowed never to hurt her again?

The saddest part of it all, Lily knew, was that she had wanted so badly to believe that he truly did love her. She had trusted him.

Even though she knew better.

Even though she knew that trusting Travis, that loving Travis, was a one-way trip to a severely broken heart.

TRAVIS TOOK EVERY SHORTCUT he could find back to the hotel. If he didn't get to the room before Lily, she'd lock him out and he'd never be able to convince her to listen to what he had to say. Truthfully, he didn't know exactly what he was going to tell her, but hiding from what had happened tonight would only make things worse.

The hotel was deserted when he burst through the thick wooden door. He took the stairs two at a time and when he turned his key in the door to their room, he half expected the locks to be changed.

The rooms were dark. Not bothering to turn on any lights,

he pushed through the patio doors to the balcony. Looking down to the moonlit fields below, he wondered where Lily was. What if she had been so distraught that she got in a car with a strange man? Terrible visions of Lily, his Lily, being overpowered by a burly Italian made his blood go cold with fear. If she had come to any harm tonight, he was never going to stop blaming himself.

The door opened behind him, then closed with a click. He heard panting and turned around to see Lily doubled over, trying to catch her breath. He wanted to run to her, but if he did, she'd bolt back out the door. It was hard, so hard, to wait for her.

She turned and dead-bolted the door. Unable to wait it out any longer, Travis softly said, "Lily," not wanting to scare her. She jumped back against the door, uttering a high-pitched scream.

"You," she stuttered when she finally got her breath back, "you scared me.

"I didn't mean to frighten you, Lily," he said as he took cautious steps toward her. If he could just hold her in his arms, then she would—

"Please leave," she said.

"Lily. Let me explain."

Her eyes were as blank as her words. "I can't do this right now." Her voice grew wobbly. "I'm tired. I want to go to bed. *Alone.*"

The word "alone" slapped Travis across the face with its finality. "I understand," he said quietly, and he did. "And I'll go."

Lily's face contorted with such relief he almost cried at the pain of knowing how much she didn't want to be near him. Feeling weak, so horribly weak, he said, "But please, let me say one thing first."

Her eyes glittered in the dark and he hated himself even more than he already did for making her cry again. "Go ahead," she said emotionlessly.

Travis swallowed hard. It was now or never. "I didn't mean those things I said in the square, Lily. God how I wish I could take them back." Lily closed her eyes and leaned back heavily against the door. "I saw Janica and Luke, and I don't know what happened. I freaked out. I acted like an idiot. But I didn't mean any of it. We weren't just messing around. This isn't a joke to me. I know you don't want to hear it right now, but I do love you. I really do, Lily."

When Lily was silent, Travis asked, "Do you believe me?" and hated himself the minute the words left his tongue.

Lily opened her eyes. "I don't know what to believe anymore," she said sadly. She flipped the dead bolt open and turned the knob, opening the door to the hall. "Good night."

Knowing it was no more than was his due, Travis did as she asked. "Good night, Lily," he said as he walked through the door and back down the stairs.

Travis sat heavily on the couch in the lobby, just as Luke and Janica pushed through the wooden door. He stared at them blankly. He no longer cared what they thought, what they said.

The only person whose opinion he cared about was upstairs hating his guts. And there wasn't a damn thing he could do about it.

LUKE TOOK IN his brother's dejected state immediately. He'd always been able to read Travis, and right now Luke was reading something he'd never seen in his brother before: self-hatred.

Travis had always been unfailingly self-confident in everything he did. His very presence was infused with assurance that he knew the right thing to do, the right thing to say, the right way to feel at all times. Could it be that Lily had done this to him? Could Lily have broken his brother apart?

It was impossible for Luke to swallow. The Lily he knew, who had been his best friend since grade school, couldn't hurt an ant, let alone his unbreakable twin brother.

"She's upstairs if you want to see her," Travis said heavily.

Instead of heading for the stairs as Luke had expected her to do, Janica sat down next to Travis on the couch, her legs folded beneath her. "Have you talked to her yet?" Janica asked and Luke was shocked by the concern he heard in her voice.

"Not really," Travis said, his throat sounding tight with emotion. "I wanted to, but she's so worn-out and sad, and I'm the bastard who did that to her."

Janica reached over and patted Travis's hand. "It'll be all right," she said, and this time Luke wasn't the only one shocked to the core by the direction of her sympathies. "I think you just need to give her some time," she said, unfolding herself from the couch. "What room is she in? I think I'll go see how she's doing."

"Room 305."

As soon as Janica disappeared up the stairs, Luke sat down across from Travis. The two brothers sat in silence, until Travis broke it with, "I really messed up this time, didn't I?"

Luke started to nod, but then stopped himself at the last second. After all, hadn't he been the one who told Lily to rip Travis to shreds? Luke hated to see his brother in pain, and guilt overwhelmed him. A week ago at the Fog City Diner he'd been giving Lily his brilliant advice on how to play Travis like a fiddle. But he had underestimated both his best friend and his brother.

And look where it had gotten the two of them: married and suffering.

Luke didn't like himself very much all of a sudden. *And here I always thought I was the nice brother.*

Travis was waiting for Luke's response, so without either agreeing or disagreeing with the question of how much of a screwup his twin was, Luke said, "Do you want to talk about it?"

Travis pushed his palms into his eye sockets. "No," he said. "Yes. I don't even know where to start. I mean, I've been horrible to Lily since the very beginning, since we were kids . . . but now, *this . . .*"

Luke swallowed past the lump in this throat. He'd never seen his brother in pain like this. "You really are afraid of losing her, aren't you?" Luke didn't mean for there to be such disbelief in his words.

Travis glared at his brother. "You don't think very much of Lily, do you?" His words held the promise of danger.

"Trav, no, it's not that. Lily's amazing. I—"

Travis cut Luke off. "Here I thought you were her best friend all these years, but now I'm finding out that you don't know her at all. Lily is the most incredible person I have ever met. There's nothing about her that I don't love." Luke's eyes widened at the word "love." Every muscle in Travis's body readied for attack. "What? You're surprised that I'm in love with Lily?" Travis laughed, but it was an ugly sound. "You should have expected that. After all, who wouldn't be in love with her? It's me who doesn't deserve to be loved."

Luke tried to reply, but Travis wasn't finished yet. "That's right. I'm a sorry excuse for a human being, and if Lily never wants to see me again, I'd understand it. What the hell can I give her? Lessons in selfishness?"

Luke couldn't watch Travis rage at himself any longer. "Yeah, you've been selfish and arrogant and condescending more times than I can count," he said. Travis deflated like a pinpricked balloon at his words, sinking into the sofa, looking smaller than Luke had ever seen him. "You've done some things that I can't condone. And you've treated a lot of woman like dirt over the years."

"Don't let me stop you now that you're on a roll," Travis said dryly.

Luke slid over next to Travis on the couch. "Look. You've finally faced up to who you've been all these years."

"I've been the worst to Lily," Travis said into his chest, his neck slumped down like a drunk.

Luke nodded. "I know you have. But what I'm trying to say, Trav, is that it's not too late to change. It's never too late to change."

Travis looked up from his chest. "You're not just blowing smoke, are you?"

Luke laughed. "Trust me, the last thing I'd do is build you back up if you didn't deserve it. But you do, Trav. Look at how you've already changed since you and Lily connected. You've got something to fight for now, someone who's more important than your pride or ego or even how much you might hate yourself right now."

A glimmer of the old Travis poked through. "Hate's a pretty strong word, don't you think?"

Luke laughed, and said, "Gotta call 'em like I see 'em." Sobering, he said, "Now the question is, what are you going to do to win Lily back?"

Travis looked up at the frescoed ceiling. "What if there's nothing I can do? What if she doesn't love me anymore?"

Luke gave his brother a rare and spontaneous hug. "That's not how love works, Trav. But it's up to you now to prove that to her." A little uncomfortable with all the sharing they were doing, Luke got back to the nitty-gritty details. "Got a place to sleep tonight?" Travis shook his head, and Luke said, "Didn't think so. Why don't you crash with me and Janica? She sweet-talked an old lady in town into letting us use a guest room."

"Thanks, but I'd rather stay here."

"Just in case she comes down?"

Travis nodded and looked bleak. "Just in case."

SOMEONE KNOCKED on the door and Lily groaned. "Go away," she said, hoping Travis hadn't come back to talk to her again. She couldn't deal with him tonight, but she didn't know if she had the strength to send him away a second time. The knock came again, and this time Janica said, "Lils, it's me. Let me in."

Lily climbed out of bed and slipped on a silky robe, then padded over to the heavy wooden door and opened it an inch.

Janica stood in the hall, looking unsure of herself. "Hi."

Out of the blue, Lily was overwhelmed with love for her sister. "Come here." She opened the door wide and wrapped her arms around Janica's slender frame. "I love you," she said, and Janica said, "I love you, too."

Lily felt tears well up in her eyes so she let go of Janica and turned around. "Isn't this room amazing?" she said with forced gaiety.

Janica made a perfunctory glance around the room, which wasn't like her at all. "Yeah, it's great," she said dismissively. "I wanted to make sure you're okay."

Lily was so touched her bottom lip started to tremble. She sank down on the nearest couch in the living room.

"I can't believe you came all the way to Italy," she said. "For me."

Janica bit her lip. "Luke and I thought we were doing the right thing, but maybe . . ."

Lily squeezed her sister's hand. "You came to save me, didn't you?"

Janica nodded, and a lone tear fell. "Maybe you didn't need saving after all. Maybe everything was going just fine until we came along and ruined everything."

"It would have happened anyway. San Francisco, Italy, it doesn't really matter."

"He loves you, Lil," Janica said fervently. "I know he does."

Lily sucked in a breath. "Did he say something to you?"

Janica shook her head and Lily's face fell. "No, but that's not the point. I *know* he loves you. And you should have seen him down there in the lobby. I've never seen anyone look more pathetic."

Lily crumpled, and Janica hugged her. "I don't know what to do. What to think. He said he loved me, but then he said it didn't mean anything. And I love him so much I hate myself. And now he says we're legally married."

"Shh," Janica crooned against Lily's hair. "Remember when I was a little girl, and I'd be really upset about something?" Lily nodded. "And you always said that if I went to sleep when I woke up in the morning everything would be so much better?" Janica reached for Lily's hand and helped her to her feet. "It always worked, Lils," Janica said as she walked her sister toward the bedroom.

"I'll never be able to sleep," Lily protested, but Janica had taken control and was flipping back the covers, smoothing down the crisp, clean sheets, and fluffing the pillows.

"Hop in," Janica said, and Lily looked at her baby sister,

glad that she didn't have to do all the worrying by herself anymore.

"Jan," she said, "will you stay with me for a while?"

"Just like when we were kids," Janica said.

For the first time, their roles were reversed as Janica curled herself up around Lily and rocked her to sleep.

14

After spending a long sleepless night on the couch in the lobby waiting and hoping for Lily to come down the stairs, and say, "I forgive you. I love you. Come to bed," Travis was glad to see the sun finally shining on the cobblestones outside. She obviously hadn't forgiven him and he still hadn't figured out any way to win her back. Where, he wondered desperately, was the guy who could talk his way out of any situation? What had happened to his smooth words?

Their plane was leaving the following morning and Travis was running out of time. Somehow, he knew that if he couldn't convince Lily that he loved her there in Tuscany, he'd never be able to. Real life in San Francisco would, without a doubt, intrude and stomp all over his flagging hopes of being with the woman he loved.

Stubbly and haggard, Travis stretched his arms and legs out. Maybe an espresso would kick-start his brain and help him feel halfway decent. He headed out onto the quiet streets, down to the corner café. Standing at the bar, Travis downed three espressos, cutting himself off when his head started to buzz in a rather unpleasant manner.

A well-polished woman came in off the street and signaled to the waiter. Travis didn't spare a thought to the woman's abundant breasts or perfectly made-up face. Instead, he noticed the way the light played off a huge sapphire on her right hand.

"That's it," he said, filled with sudden anticipation. "I need to buy her a ring!"

Throwing down several coins on the polished bar, Travis asked the café owner where the nearest jewelry shop was located. Changed from a pathetic loser to a man on a mission in a matter of seconds, Travis's long legs ate up the distance between the café and the jewelry store. Given that it was barely past sunrise, the store was dark and deserted. He paced back and forth in front of the store, his impatience growing by leaps and bounds with every moment that passed.

And then he noticed the sign, translated to read, "Closed on Mondays."

Travis had to restrain himself from punching the glass in on the door as he snarled, "What am I going to do now?"

He pushed through the front door of the hotel and was greeted by Giuseppe, who was just starting his shift at the check-in desk.

"Signor Travis! What a beautiful wedding it was yesterday." Giuseppe winked. "I saw that you and the signora left the celebration as soon as the cake was cut." Noting Travis's wrinkled and weary appearance, he said, "You are up early after such a night. Is there something I can help you with, signor?"

Travis figured he was out of luck, but he'd never forgive himself if he didn't give it one last try. "I need to buy Lily a ring," he said, getting straight to the heart of it. "Will any stores be open today?"

Giuseppe shook his head. "I'm sorry, with the festival everything is closed because of the celebration."

Travis nodded and closed his eyes in defeat.

"All hope is not lost, signor. I will make a phone call if you will wait a moment," Giuseppe said as he picked up the phone at his elbow. After a short, colorful conversation that Travis was too tired to try and follow, Giuseppe smiled broadly. "My sweet mother has a small business selling antique jewelry. Would you like to see her?"

Considering that he would have bought a dime store ring out of a bubble-gum machine at that point, Travis was thrilled by this option. He ran down the street to retrieve their rental car where they'd parked it during the festival and an hour later, Travis looked at the ring in his palm. Now that his initial panic had receded, Travis realized that the store down the street being closed had been a blessing in disguise. A new, shiny platinum diamond ring wouldn't have fit Lily at all. Not like the ring that had so lovingly been given to him by Giuseppe's mother.

Thick, soft gold, the band had weathered time and was beautifully imperfect. A three-carat sapphire sat in the center of the band, while red rubies and green emeralds surrounded the sparkling blue gem that reminded Travis so much of Lily's eyes. It was a ring like none Travis had ever seen, rippling with color and character.

Just like Lily.

As Travis drove up the winding streets back toward the hotel, he prayed that Lily would wear the ring. Unfortunately, Travis knew that at this point not even an addicted gambler would have bet on it.

∽ ∽ ∽

LILY OPENED HER EYES as the first rays of light streamed in the bedroom window. Janica lay next to her on the large bed, snuggled up tight with a pillow. Lily's first sensation was delight at the beautiful blue sky. And then she remembered how every one of her dreams had come crashing down around her last night.

Travis's words jumbled together in her head.

"Have I told you how beautiful you look today?"

"We were giving the locals a good show up there, right Lily?"

"I love you, Lily Ellis. I always have."

"It didn't mean anything."

"You're mine, all mine."

"It's no joke, Lily. We're legally married. The ceremony was binding."

Lily no longer had a clue what to think or feel, especially after Janica's heartfelt, and unexpected, vote of confidence *for* Travis and his profession of love. She sighed and curled up into a tight ball on the bed. She wished she could cry to release some of the pain inside, some of the confusion, but the tears refused to fall.

On a day when she should have been preparing herself to head back to the dull life she had always lived, Lily couldn't escape the feeling that she was waiting for something else to happen. She closed her eyes, but she knew sleep was a distant memory.

Married? It was impossible for her to grasp. How could Travis have known that it was a real ceremony and still gone through with it? Especially if he was going to denounce everything the first chance he got?

Pulling on her robe, she headed for the bathroom. A bath, that was what she needed to clear her head. Lily leaned over to turn on the faucets on the side of the luxurious tub and her hands stilled on the bronze fixture. Memories of masturbating while Travis watched were impossible to push away. And then that night in the olive field when he had made love to her. It had been so perfect.

No, she couldn't get back into the bathtub, the memories were too fresh. She opened the shower door and willed herself to forget having had naughty sex with Travis on the small ledge. Turning the water on full blast, she closed her eyes as it streamed over her face, plastering her curls to her head. She brushed her hair out of her eyes and reached for the shampoo. But as she poured some onto her hand, the smell reminded her so strongly of Travis she nearly cried out.

He was everywhere. And Lily knew he wouldn't stop haunting her once she had left Italy. Especially if the marriage was really legal, and they had to deal with an annulment.

No, he would continue to haunt her in San Francisco, as he always had before. Only this time, she knew the reality of Travis. The glorious, sensual Travis. The funny, sweet Travis. The infuriatingly macho Travis.

But most of all, she'd be left with the part of Travis that made her hurt so much. The man who claimed to be in love at 5:00 P.M., and then changed his mind at 8:00 P.M., then back again an hour later.

She rinsed the shampoo out of her hair and lathered up with soap. She needed to get out of the bathroom and fast, before she became a whimpering idiot. Finally finished, she toweled off and headed back into the bedroom to get dressed.

She and Travis had planned to visit one final antique dealer that morning. Lily wanted nothing more than to hide in the room all day under the covers, but no matter how screwed up her personal life was, she was committed to doing her very best as an interior designer for Travis's clients. She was going to the antique store, and she was going to look beautiful and professional.

A wispy blue sleeveless dress called to her from the armoire. She hadn't felt nearly bold enough to wear it before, but now that it didn't matter how she dressed, she fingered the beautiful material. She sat down on the bed and bent over to towel-dry her hair.

I can do this, she told herself as she took a deep breath. Her hair nearly dry, she pulled the dress out, stepped into it, and closed the side zipper. Taking another deep breath, she turned to look into the full-length mirror on the armoire in the corner of the room.

She gasped with surprise. The dress outlined her full figure beautifully, lovingly cupping her breasts before draping to her waist, then back out at her hips. The hem brushed the bottoms of her knees.

I wish Travis could have seen me in this dress, she thought, then grimaced. Who cared what Travis thought? From that moment on, she was going to dress to look good for no one but herself.

Slipping into a pair of strappy sandals, she grabbed her purse and went downstairs to catch a cab. Giuseppe whistled from behind the front desk.

"Good morning," she said, hoping against hope that he wouldn't bring up last night's wedding.

No such luck. "You are *bellissima* this morning," he exclaimed as he kissed his lips.

"Thank you, Giuseppe."

"But of course, what bride is not beautiful?" he asked, grinning from ear to ear. "I saw your signor here earlier, and I think you will like his surprise very much." He slapped his hand over his mouth. "But I cannot say any more."

Lily's heart started racing, and she reached out for the counter to support her shaky legs. "Surprise?"

Giuseppe waggled his finger at her. "Not another word."

Lily nodded, but the buzzing in her ears was so loud she couldn't remember why she was standing at the reception desk in the first place. She merely had to hear Travis's name, and she could barely remember her own. Oh yes, it dawned on her, she needed a cab. For her appointment.

Forcing a smile, she said, "Could you please call a taxi for me, Giuseppe? Thank you."

He nodded, and she went to sit outside on a stone bench. What kind of surprise did Travis have in store for her? She wasn't up to any more surprises. What she wouldn't give to go back to her old boring life. Sure, it had lacked spark, but at least it had been peaceful.

But even as she thought it, she knew she wasn't being honest with herself. She wouldn't give up this week with Travis for anything. Because no matter how much he'd hurt her, at least she'd finally gotten to find out what it was to truly live. Every moment in his arms had been glorious. Every laugh they'd shared had been a flower blooming in the sun.

Soon enough she'd go back to her old life. But in this incredible blue dress lay her last chance to be the new sexy, fun, adventurous Lily. Even if she had to try to do it without Travis by her side.

TRAVIS SHOOK GIUSEPPE'S HAND. "I owe you one. You're a genius." He bounded up the stairs without waiting for a response. He knocked on the door to Room 305. "Lily? Are you in there?"

The door opened and his heart soared—Lily was actually going to listen to him, which must mean she didn't hate him after all—but then he saw Janica's face and went cold as ice.

"She's not here," Janica said as she lounged against the doorframe. "But geez," she said with a smile, "nice room, huh?"

Travis stared at Janica uncomprehendingly. He had to find Lily. "Did she say where she was going?"

Janica shrugged. "Nope. Her note said she'd be gone all morning." Her eyes narrowed. "You're not going to do anything stupid are you?" Rolling her eyes, she added, "What I mean is, I hope you're not going to do anything even stupider than what you did yesterday, because she was pretty upset last night. A little romance wouldn't kill you, you know."

Something wasn't right. Janica wasn't ripping him to shreds like she normally did. But right then, Travis didn't have time to find out what game she was playing. The ring was burning a hole in his pocket and he was dying to slip it on Lily's ring finger.

If she let him.

He headed back down the stairs, his mind racing. Where would Lily be? Like a lightning bolt, it hit him. She was keeping the appointment they had made with one last antique dealer.

"That's some good work ethic," he mused as he headed for his rental car. Lily never ceased to surprise him. Even when he had treated her like dirt, when most women would be moping and feeling sorry for themselves and planning his downfall, she was out briskly taking care of business.

Not that she couldn't be planning his downfall at the same time, he supposed with a wry grin.

"Good luck!" Giuseppe called out, and Travis almost laughed. Giuseppe had no idea how much luck Travis needed.

He drove like a madman. Thankfully, the streets were deserted so no one had to jump out of the way to save him- or herself. His heart was beating a million miles an hour when he pulled up in front of the antique store. He sat in the car to regain his composure. Through the leaded window that faced the establishment he saw a flash of blue.

It had to be Lily.

He cursed himself for being such a wimp. *Get out of the car and go win her back you idiot,* he told himself determinedly. Travis stepped out onto the pavement, already warm from the early-morning sunshine. He walked around the car to the front door and reached for the handle but didn't turn it.

It killed him to admit it, but he was scared. What if she saw him and turned away as if he didn't exist? What if she looked right through him? He would rather have screaming than coldness. At least then he'd know that she still felt something for him.

Shaking his head at the way his doubts were running away with themselves, Travis took a deep breath, turned the knob, and entered the store.

The front room was empty, so he closed the door behind him quietly and headed for the large room at the back of the building. He stepped into the open garden area. And that's when he saw her: a goddess in blue, her red hair flaming in the sun, running her fingers over a pile of brightly colored tiles.

Travis's breath stilled as she lifted a heavy tile up to the light. He remembered watching her at the furniture store, dusting the dining table. She had been so sexy then, but now that he knew Lily intimately—how she liked her coffee in the morning, what made her laugh out loud, that she was afraid of spiders and snakes no matter how small or harmless they were—she was infinitely more beautiful to him. Had it only been one week since he'd woken up to the one thing he'd been missing his whole life?

Only to lose her now if he didn't play his cards right.

He heard a sound like an animal getting caught in a steel trap and only when Lily whirled around with her hand on her heart to look straight at him did Travis realize that the awful noise had come from him.

"What are you doing here?" she exclaimed as she took a nervous step back into a pile of tiles.

"I had to find you, Lily."

Her eyes were wide as she stared at him. In her eyes Travis saw hope and sadness and fear and, how he wished it was still true, love.

The old Travis would have slickly laid out all of the reasons why she should be with him, why she should love him, reasons she wouldn't be able to deny. But the new Travis flat out didn't have the words. Not when he looked at Lily and saw her goodness.

Moving slowly toward her, trying not to frighten her away again, he went down on one knee. Lily gasped when she realized what he was doing, and Travis took advantage of her surprise by taking her hands in his.

"Lily," he croaked, his throat full of emotion. One lone tear slid down her cheek. "There are no words to make up for what I did last night. There's nothing I wish I could take back in my life more than my thoughtless words." Lily's tears were falling in earnest now, as Travis said, "You're so important to me, sweetheart, and it doesn't matter how hard I have to work to win you back or gain your trust. I'll do it. You're the most important person in the world to me, and I love you. Please, if you can ever forgive me"—he reached into his pocket for the ring, and Lily gasped again in shock—"would you be my wife?"

INSTINCTIVELY LILY FOUGHT the reality before her. But the man she loved, the man she had always loved, the man she knew she would always love regardless of whether it made any sense or not, was kneeling at her feet begging her to forgive him.

Begging her to marry him.

The silly, naive girl inside Lily who still believed in fairy tales and heroes on noble steeds wanted to be swept into his arms. If only she could erase the past twenty-four hours, to rewind the tape so there wouldn't need to be any more apologies.

Watching the open book of emotions pass across Travis's face with each passing second, a small voice of hope whispered inside of Lily's head, *Look at him. Hasn't he changed? Hasn't he done everything he can to apologize? Why are you denying yourself what you want more than anything else in the world?*

That little nudge was all Lily needed. She didn't have it in her to reject Travis. She never had, and the truth was she never would.

The dam broke inside her heart, then Lily was on her knees, kissing him, saying, "I love you, Travis," over and over until Travis's tears mingled with hers.

"You're crying," she said, and she reached up to wipe away his tears. He was brushing her soft skin with his thumb, looking like he could hardly believe that she had actually forgiven him.

He kissed her again, soft then hard. "Will you?" he asked softly, and she nodded.

"Yes, Travis," she said, her words trembling as he kissed her lips softly. "I want to be your wife. I want you to be my husband."

Travis held out her hand and slipped the ring onto the third finger of her left hand. "You're mine, all mine," he said, "forever."

She stared at the ring in wonder. "It's the most beautiful ring I've ever seen, Travis. Where did you find it?"

Travis scrambled to his feet and reached for Lily to help her up. He hugged her tightly, "That's a secret that only Giuseppe and I know the answer to, I'm afraid," he teased.

The dealer returned with a bottle of champagne and two glasses. "There is something to celebrate, yes?" he asked, with a charming grin.

"Yes," Travis said, "yes, there is." He intertwined his arm with Lily's so that they could drink from each other's cups, while Lily tried to convince herself that she felt safe and secure in the knowledge that she and Travis would be together for the rest of their lives.

THE REST OF THE DAY and the early morning flight back to San Francisco on Tuesday was a blur for Lily. Janica and Luke had been stunned by her new ring, but pleasantly so, which was a relief. She hadn't wanted to defend her relationship with Travis to her sister and best friend, partly because she hadn't had a clue what she'd say.

Luke and Janica slept in their suite that night, so Lily got a tiny reprieve from being all alone with Travis. It wasn't that she didn't still crave him. Of course she did. But she was glad to have a little space to process everything that had happened before she fell back into his arms.

Yes, she'd always been in love with Travis, ever since they were kids. But in retrospect, Lily could see that it had been infatuation, not real love. Real love was so much more complex. Had she even scratched the tip of the iceberg yet?

Everything had happened so fast—one week was simply not enough time to process the changes in herself, in Travis, in their relationship—and Lily's head buzzed with it all. Professionally, the trip had gone amazingly well, and the crates would soon begin to pour in with treasures for the house. She had vague thoughts of getting her own business up and running, but thinking of the future hurt her head. Maybe, she admitted, that was because she wasn't completely sure what the future held with Travis.

Even after hearing his vows to her as he slipped the incredible ring onto her left hand, she felt unsure. He couldn't know what trials lay before them in San Francisco.

Worry turned into bleakness as her doubts ran away with themselves. What if she couldn't fit into his real life? Or worse still, what if she couldn't handle the realities of his past? What was she going to do when confronted with stunning ex-girlfriends? What if his friends didn't think she was good enough for him? What if she never felt like she measured up compared to Travis? Could their love really last if she always felt inferior to him?

Lily took a large gulp of white wine. She just needed to shake herself out of this weird funk she was in. She glanced back toward the laughter flowing in from the in-flight bar behind the seats. Unlike her, Travis had been in great form since she had accepted his proposal. He was all smiles, and Lily didn't detect even the slightest bit of worry or doubt. He and Luke had been hanging out at the bar, and even Janica had joined them when Lily feigned sleep. She wished she could find the energy, or the will, to partake in the merriment, but she didn't have it in her. Here she should be celebrating the one thing she had wanted all her life: Travis's ring on her finger and promises of forever. It was probably just fatigue, she thought, drifting off into a restless nap.

The next thing she knew they were landing in San Francisco and picking up luggage. Travis was so solicitous, carrying her bags, keeping his arm around her, kissing her cheek and the top of her head. God, she wished she didn't have such a headache. It was pounding through her brain like an anvil.

In the parking garage she kissed Janica and Luke good-bye and climbed into Travis's Jaguar. She closed her eyes and leaned back against the headrest, glad that he didn't want to talk right at that moment. If she could just take some deep breaths and get some oxygen to her brain, maybe her headache would be gone by the time he dropped her off at her apartment.

But when she opened her eyes they weren't in front of her unassuming Noe Valley apartment. Instead, Travis was standing in front of his loft. "Welcome home, sweetheart."

Lily blinked back tears. What the hell was she doing crying? Wasn't this her ultimate dream? Why was she longing for the peace and quiet of her homey living room and kitchen, instead of the cold steel and hard lines of Travis's loft?

"Oh," was all she said in reply, but when he looked at her with a question in his eyes she made herself smile, and say, "I guess I hadn't really thought about our living together." His eyes clouded over, and she fumbled, "I mean, obviously we're going to live together, but I hadn't really thought about where we'd live."

He rubbed her arm gently out on the sidewalk in the morning light. "I thought we'd stay at my loft until we found something to buy together," he said.

For some crazy reason the words "something to buy together" tied her stomach up in awful knots. Travis was so sure of himself, so sure of every decision he made, and it was one of the things she had always admired about him. She had always been so wishy-washy, so afraid to make the wrong decisions that she pretty much never made any decisions at all. Lily desperately wanted to be the bold new her that she had cultivated in Italy, but she couldn't fight the feeling that something was going to go terribly wrong in the near future.

When would Travis wake up next to her and realize that he had sold himself short? Tomorrow? Next week? Next year? Every time they went out he would see the kind of beautiful, perfect women he could have had, then he would look at her and wonder why he had made such a rash proposal.

Travis was waiting for her to say something again, and she didn't want to disappoint him. After all, why make their eventual breakup happen immediately by her own sullen behavior? She wrapped her arms around him and hugged him tight. He lifted her up off the ground, spinning her around. Forcing a playful wink, she said, "Let's see how long it takes me to girly up your bachelor pad."

Travis laughed, and said, "Have at it." Lily was surprised. He didn't seem the least bit dismayed by the thought of having her in his personal space.

Trying to be lighthearted, she said, "Bet you won't feel the same way once the boxes of tampons are under your bathroom sink." She cursed herself for being such an idiot. *He's not going to think tampons are cute and funny. Way to remind him that you're ruining his perfect bachelor life.*

He laughed and made the appropriate face. "It's either that or babies, right?" he said with a straight face, but when Lily's mouth dropped open he hugged her again, and said, "You should have seen the look on your face," laughing at his joke. In a loud voice he declared, "Bring on the tampons. I'm man enough."

Travis lifted their bags from the trunk. Lily threw her purse over her shoulder and followed him to the front door. A large pile of mail sat on the floor to the right.

A pink-and-red envelope caught her eye. Lily's fingers tingled with the urge to rip it open. It was no surprise to her that women wrote Travis love letters. Frankly, she would have been more surprised if they didn't. Women had always chased Travis: At least she hadn't been alone in her obsession. She stared at the poisonous letter on the floor, her imagination hurling images at her of naked photos, lightly perfumed, slipped in between expensive sheets of stationery that declared true love and endless sex. The women who wrote these letters were beautiful women with perfect figures. Twenty-one, probably, and barely legal enough to be sipping a chilled glass of white wine in between rumpled bedsheets.

Maybe he could turn a blind eye to these love notes if the way he said he felt about her was real, she thought with a smidgeon of hope. But after ten or twenty naked pictures floating into his mailbox from the postman, wouldn't he realize that he was missing out on all of that young, decadent flesh? Wouldn't he long to touch round, firm breasts and kiss pink, pouting lips?

Travis dropped their bags in the foyer and bent down to pick up the pile of mail. He grabbed the pink envelope and Lily's heart fell to the floor. He turned to her with a smile. "Looks like Janet had her baby."

Lily stuttered with surprised. "That's a birth announcement?" Her voice was breathless and shaky.

Travis raised an eyebrow. "What did you think it was?" Lily

turned red with shame at her awful assumptions, and Travis chuckled. "A love letter?"

Lily shook her head too fast in denial and felt so dizzy that she leaned against the oak table near the door to steady herself.

Travis dropped the mail as he reached out for her. "You're exhausted, aren't you?" he asked, the concern in his sea-green eyes making her feel like a traitor.

"A little," she said in a small voice.

His arm warm around her, he led Lily into his living room and got her settled on the couch by the window. "Why don't you relax here while I unpack, then I'll rustle us up something to eat?" He lowered his voice to a sensual pitch. "And then, if you're feeling better, we can officially have our wedding night."

The beautiful ring he'd given her felt heavy and cold on her finger until Travis kissed her lightly once, then twice, the third time slipping his sweet tongue into her mouth. Lily responded instinctively, and when his forearms brushed against her breasts she gasped at the sensation.

"Hopefully that'll give you something to look forward to."

When he'd taken the bags into the bedroom she held her hand up to the light. The huge sapphire sparkled wildly, casting colored shadows on the walls.

Lily couldn't hide from the feeling that she didn't deserve to be wearing the exquisite ring. What about her was good enough to win Travis's love? She wasn't pretty enough, wasn't charismatic enough, she wasn't even a dynamite businessperson, no matter how well he seemed to think she had done in selecting furnishings for his client.

But Lily's fears went even deeper than her usual insecurities about her looks. When would Travis see that there was a big difference between falling in love with someone during a wild trip to Italy and actually living with that person in the real world?

Lily sighed and curled up into a ball on the couch. She knew it was her old lack of confidence rearing its ugly head again, but even though she knew what the problem was, it didn't mean she knew how to fix it.

The only thing she knew for sure was that when Travis took her to bed that night, she was going to knock his socks off. Maybe the amazing sex they shared would keep Travis by her side, at least for a little while.

TRAVIS HAD BEEN PLAGUED with the nagging sense that something wasn't quite right with Lily all day, but her response to his kiss on the couch banished his worries. She was likely tired, and he couldn't wait to get into bed with her again. They hadn't made love since the morning of the festival. Making love to Lily ranked number one on his list of the most satisfying things he had ever done, and he looked forward to a lifetime of as much wild sex as they could fit in.

Starting with tonight.

He called for some Chinese food to be delivered, then dumped the contents of their bags into the hampers in his laundry room. Maria, his cleaning lady, would be in the next morning, and she would take care of their clothes.

Heading back into the kitchen, he pulled a bottle of Chardonnay out of the fridge and uncorked it in one smooth motion. He poured two glasses and handed one to Lily who had risen from the couch and was leaning on his steel-topped kitchen island.

Seeing her in his environment, soft and round against the

sharp, flat metals and plate-glass windows, he felt bad about assuming she'd live with him until they found another home. Taking a sip of wine he said, "I never realized what a bachelor's pad this really is."

Lily's eyes widened in surprised. He leaned against the other side of the island, and said, "Cheers" as he lightly bumped his glass into hers.

"Cheers," she repeated, but she didn't drink. Instead she said, "It's a wonderful space, Travis. So full of light."

Travis was warmed by her compliment, yet he couldn't miss what she didn't say. He prompted her, "But?"

"Don't take this the wrong way, okay, but your loft is a little sparse."

Travis choked on his sip of wine. "Sparse?" he said. "That's quite a politically correct way of putting it," he said with a laugh. "I can see that you're going to be great with clients."

Lily blushed at his compliment. "Thank you," she said, her words tinged with a measure of surprise.

"A woman's touch, your touch, is precisely what this place needs."

The doorbell rang, and he went to collect the Chinese food. As he paid he realized that he really was glad to have Lily in his house. For a brief moment he had worried that he would feel cramped by her, but it was just the opposite. She was so warm.

And beautiful.

And sexy.

Travis's cock grew hard, reminding him, very firmly, that he and Lily hadn't yet had a wedding night.

He carried the take-out cartons into the kitchen, utterly starving, but not for food. "Are you hungry?" he asked. When Lily shook her head it was all the invitation he needed. Reaching for her hand, he drew her back toward the bedroom.

Just outside the door he pressed her up against the wall. "I want to do what we did after the fashion show. Exactly what we did. Do you remember?" His voice was husky, and his dick was so hard it felt like it was going to burst. Lily nodded, and he slipped his thighs between her legs, the silky material of her skirt no barrier at all. "But today," he said, "I want to do it all naked."

Lily bit her lip, her white teeth leaving an impression on her plump red mouth. "Good idea," he said, leaning over to suck her bottom lip into his mouth at the same time that he unzipped the long zipper at the back of her dress. The dress had a built-in bra, so when he slipped it off her shoulders, her breasts were bare and beautiful.

"Oh God, Lily," he said, "I've been dying for you."

He bent his head down and tongued a nipple. She moaned and pushed her chest into his mouth. He slipped the dress all the way off her shoulders, then slid his thumbs into the thin waistband of her lace panties, shoving them down her hips. All the while, he tongued her breasts, first one sweet nipple, then the next, until they were stiff points.

Once Lily was naked, Travis tore off his own clothes, never taking his mouth away from Lily's soft, hot skin. He sucked at the pulse point on her neck, relishing the rapid beating of her heart, loving the musky smell of her arousal.

He kicked his jeans off and pressed his nakedness against Lily. Pinning her wrists above her head, her back arched against the wall, her full breasts pushing into his chest, he slid one thigh between her legs.

He groaned with pleasure when she began rubbing her wet pussy against him. "That's it, Lily," he urged. "Come against me, sweetheart," he said as he pushed his muscles hard into her clit.

With a gasp her eyes opened wide, then fluttered shut. Frantically, she rocked against his leg, and Travis pushed back even harder. He needed to suck her tits more than he needed to breathe. Without breaking rhythm he bent his head to the succulent flesh and nipped at her.

"Travis," she gasped, as his mouth closed over her nipple. His cock was sliding against her thigh, and he had to force himself to hold on, not to blow all over her leg.

As soon as she stilled against him, Travis slid down to his knees and buried his face between her legs. "No," she protested, "I can't take any more," but he ignored her as he lapped at her, loving her taste.

He pushed her open with his finger and tilted his head so that he could slide his tongue in, hard and pointy. Lily sat down onto his face and he held her up with his thumb on her clit. He rubbed tight circles on the sensitive nub, moving his tongue in and out, first slow and shallow, then fast and deep. When she began to convulse, he slipped two fingers into her and latched on to her clit, sucking hard and fast.

She cried out, but he couldn't make out what she was saying as she came hard against his lips and fingers, clamping down on his fingers with each contraction.

Even though he really wanted a repeat of her masturbation performance on the night they'd first hooked up, he couldn't wait for it. Standing back up he said, "Wrap your legs around me, sweetheart."

Her eyes were unfocused at first, but as comprehension dawned, she said, "I can't. You won't be able to—"

"Just do it," he growled.

"What about protection?"

"We're married now," was all he said, and she blinked in surprise, then, thank God, when he didn't think he could take it anymore and was about to drag her to the ground, she lifted one thigh around his hips. Roughly, he pulled her other leg up and slid into her pussy, hard and hot. He couldn't remember the last time he'd been inside a woman unsheathed. Lily clenched around him, and the sensations were incredible. She wrapped her arms firmly around his neck and pushed her pelvis into his, taking him even deeper.

"Lily," he groaned into her neck. He reared into her again and again, his orgasm so overpowering that he forgot everything but the feel of Lily's hot cunt sucking his cock. He shot deep into her. "I love you," he groaned, as she cried out his name. He held her up, panting and sweaty as he waited for his heart to stop beating doubletime.

"I love you, too," she whispered into the hollow of his shoulder. They untangled their damp limbs. When Lily's feet touched the floor again, Travis felt bereft of her comforting heat, her solid weight in his arms.

"Ouch," she said as she pointed her toes and flexed her leg muscles. "I think I'm cramping."

"Need a massage?" Travis asked, his wicked intent clear.

Lily ran into the bathroom. "You've got to catch me first, big boy."

Travis pretended to chase her and by the time they were standing under the dual showerheads of his shower, they were giggling and tickling each other. Teasing touches turned into full-blown caresses, and even though he thought he'd eased his intense need for Lily in the hallway, Travis realized that he'd merely taken the edge off.

"Come here, you." He soaped Lily up from her shoulders to her ankles. He'd never felt so at home before. Not until Lily. Pulling the nozzle from its holder, Travis washed her off, spending extra time between her legs.

She swatted him away. "I think I'm clean now, Travis," she said sternly, even though her eyes were dancing.

Travis pretended to give it careful consideration. "Open your legs a little wider," he said, and when she obeyed he shook his head. "No, I'm afraid I've missed a spot." He hit her clitoris with a stream of water, sending her into an instant explosion. She opened her legs wider, pink, wet, and all his. Travis couldn't stand it another moment. Sitting down on the tiled seat of his luxurious shower enclosure, he pulled her down onto his cock. And as she rode up and down, calling out his name, sending him into another spiraling orgasm, Travis knew that he'd never love anyone as much as he loved Lily.

15

LILY'S LIDS WERE HEAVY as she opened her eyes. For a moment she didn't know where she was. And then she remembered: Travis's loft. Not because of a one-night stand. Because they were married.

Married.

It was still too much for her to take in, even though she wore his ring, and he'd shown her the Italian paperwork last night when they were sitting in bed eating chow mein and kung pao chicken.

"We're married," he had said in the hallway when she'd asked him about a condom, as if that answered everything. And she'd been so stunned she hadn't been able to do anything except give in to the moment.

Everything had been such a whirlwind the past week that she didn't have a clue when she was supposed to get her period, so she didn't know if she should be worried about getting pregnant or not. She wished they had thought things through a little better, instead of getting wrapped up in the heat of the moment.

A baby. What if she got pregnant, and that was when Travis decided he'd had his fill of her?

She noticed a note on the pillow. "Had to get into the office for an early meeting. Meet me at noon at the office and I'll take you to lunch. Can't wait. Love, Your Husband."

Lily held the note to her chest as she looked out at the oak tree beyond the bedroom. She couldn't believe how well Travis was taking their accidental marriage. Previously a con-firmed bachelor, now he was slipping the word "love" and "husband" into his notes? She wished she had the nerve to ask him about the big change, but she was too afraid of what he might say.

What if he laughed in her face and said, *Gotcha!* like it was all some horrible practical joke?

Lily closed her eyes. She had to stop doing this to herself. Every day with Travis would be a slow death if she kept waiting for the axe to fall.

The clock on the bedside table said 10:00 A.M. How could it have gotten so late? After showering she realized she didn't have any clean clothes left in her suitcase. Travis's walk-in closet beckoned, and even though she told herself she was just look-ing for something she could wear until she picked up some clothes from her apartment, what she was really doing was snooping.

Inhaling his potent scent, she fingered his Prada suits and Ralph Lauren ties. She buried her face in his T-shirts and opened up all of his drawers to see what he had hidden.

"What was I expecting to find?" she said aloud, hating herself for being so suspicious and negative. "A dead body? A marriage certificate to Miss America?"

Thoroughly sick of her bad attitude, she grabbed a starched white shirt and pair of black slacks that looked like they might fit her. "Please don't be too tight," she prayed as she slipped them up over her hips.

They were snug, but when she examined herself in the full-length mirror, Lily was surprised by how good she looked in Travis's clothes. Sexy, yet classy. She knotted the shirt at her waist and turned up the collar. The legs of the slacks were a couple of inches too long, but when she slipped on her sexy red high-heeled sandals you couldn't really tell. She applied mascara, swiped on some lip gloss, and the look was complete.

She rushed out and hailed a cab, incredibly nervous about going to see Travis at his office. She'd never been in the large, glass-fronted building, but she'd driven past it many times.

She paid the driver and took a deep breath before pushing through the large front door. One look at the lithe blond secretary with enormous breasts who sat at the reception desk and Lily was tempted to tuck her tail between her legs and run.

How had she thought she could ever compete with the women in Travis's world?

"Hello?" the young girl said.

Lily hated how meek her voice sounded in reply. "Hi," she said, having to swallow before continuing. "I'm here to see—"

Travis leaned down from the railing above and whistled. "Wow," he said as he took in her improvised outfit. "Don't you look sexy? I'll be down in a second."

Lily blushed at his compliment and walked on trembling legs toward the leather couch by the stairs. She smiled at the receptionist, but the girl had a glazed, stunned look on her face and didn't smile back. Lily studied her hands on her lap, not knowing what else to do with herself.

Even though she was pleased that he thought she looked good, she wished he hadn't called it out for everyone to hear. She could hear them thinking, *Her? He thinks she looks good? Where have his standards gone?*

Before she knew it Travis was down the stairs and had pulled her into his arms. "Hi, gorgeous," he said, before giving her a thoroughly distracting kiss.

Coming up for air, Lily said haltingly, "I hope you don't mind that I borrowed your clothes."

His eyes hot, Travis said, "You can wear anything of mine that you want." He leered down the front of her button-down shirt. "Especially if you don't wear anything underneath it."

Lily reddened again, but managed to tease him, saying, "I was wondering how long it would take you to notice."

"The minute you walked in the door," he said with a wink. He grabbed her hand and pulled her up the stairs. "I want to introduce you to everyone before we go."

Oh God, it was going to be Italy all over again, an instant replay of the humiliation and hurt that she had gone through when Travis had been confronted with Luke and Janica during the festival. Lily wanted to run. This was never going to work. She couldn't face the embarrassment that was bound to be on Travis's face when he realized that playing a husband in a foreign paradise and actually being a husband in the real world— at the office, no less—were two very different things.

Lily looked down at her clothes, desperate for an excuse to postpone the inevitable fall. "Like this? Maybe we could do it later?"

"I want them to meet the brightest new interior designer in town," he said, ignoring her protests.

Lily numbly shook hands and smiled so much her lips felt

like they were going to crack off. She cast a sidelong glance at Travis, watching for dangerous signs—a little stiffness, nervous laughter maybe—but he was as cool as always. Could that possibly be pride she was reading in his eyes?

"Now that everyone's here, I think it's time to make the announcement that Lily and I were recently married in Italy."

He held her hand tightly, which was a good thing since she nearly fainted. Travis's behavior couldn't have surprised her more. Not only was he claiming her as his own, but his joy radiated through her. His employees cheered loudly, and another round of handshaking, hugs, and backslapping ensued. But through it all, Lily couldn't help but think that the women were giving her the evil eye and the men were wondering what kind of magical sex tricks she had up her sleeve to land a guy like Travis.

Finally, they were out on the street in the blinding sunshine. Lily was glad for the excuse to slip on her sunglasses so that Travis couldn't see the confusion and terror she couldn't hide. Right around the corner from his office, he opened the door to a French bistro.

The man behind the podium beamed. "Monsieur Carson."

"Jean-Luc, I am delighted to present my wife, Lily, to you." Travis's formality was enormously cute, and it helped Lily to relax a slight bit.

Jean-Luc fell all over himself to welcome Lily, and she felt much better by the time they were ensconced in a romantic booth with a chilled bottle of champagne. She gulped from her glass like the wine was water. When she looked back up at Travis his smile was wide and relaxed.

"Guess what?" he said, looking like a happy schoolboy who had gotten out of class early to go play.

"Um . . ." Lily said, her mind having gone completely blank.

"I have just rented the perfect space for your new business. Retail up front, office in the back. Great demographics."

All the wind knocked out of her. "My new business?"

Travis was so thrilled by his announcement he didn't notice her rapidly paling complexion. "James had remodeled the space for a previous client, but since they moved to the East Coast, it hit me how perfect it would be for you. And you know what's even better?"

Lily took another huge gulp from her champagne glass before saying, "What's that?" in a remarkably steady voice.

"It's down the block from my building. We'll practically be working together. And of course I'm going to turn all of my clients on to you, honey."

She croaked, "Great," and this time Travis paused and seemed to notice that everything wasn't right. Covering, she smiled. "I think I'm still a little dehydrated from the flight." She gulped down more bubbly. Feeling woozy and somewhat drunk when Travis insisted on showing her the new storefront, she didn't have the strength to resist.

Two blocks away, there it was—an old storefront that had been beautifully fixed up, like the fashionable stores on either side. It was a sunny street, with mature, leafy trees, and for a moment, the big city disappeared. The first waves of excitement pushed through her shock.

"Oh Travis," she breathed, as they got closer. "Can we go inside?"

Stopping in the middle of the street he swung her into his arms and hugged her tight, kissing the top of her head. "I knew you'd love it."

Lily's eyes misted. How did he know her so well when she hardly knew herself?

A second later he slipped the key in the lock and Lily saw her dream business in full color, 3-D. "Antiques up front, from France and Italy. I can't wait to travel all over the world to find the perfect treasures." Travis held himself back so that she could lose herself in the space. "And a design studio in the back." She turned to the man she loved. "It couldn't be more perfect, Travis. You're amazing."

His face lit up. Lily threw the lock on the door. "You don't have to get back to your office right away, do you?" she asked as she began unbuttoning the top buttons of Travis's dress shirt.

Staring at the curve of her breast that was now revealed, Travis drawled, "I don't own the business for nothing." Their wild, yet sweet, lovemaking was the perfect way to christen the building.

AS THE WEEKS FLEW BY Lily was busier than she'd ever been. Between looking for a house with Travis and setting up her own design business, she barely had time to worry about their relationship. Their nights were filled with lovemaking, and they often met at lunchtime for a quickie before grabbing something to eat.

Travis had insisted on throwing a huge postwedding party for everyone they knew at his loft, but by the evening of the party, Lily wanted nothing more than a hot bath and a good book. At the same time, she was glad she was too exhausted to care about whether his friends liked her or not. She just plain didn't have the energy to worry about it. Because although she still felt like an alien intruder in Travis's perfect world, she had learned to roll with it during the past month. And oddly enough, he didn't seem to think there was anything weird at all about having her in his life, day and night, either as a coworker on their design projects or as a wife.

But while Travis was clearly taking all of his life changes in stride, Lily felt like she was barely staying afloat. Hopefully things would settle down to normal soon. In any case, she was looking forward to seeing Janica and Luke that night at the party. She had barely exchanged three words with either of them since returning from Italy.

She propped a large houseplant under one arm as she turned the key. Putting the plant down in an empty corner of the foyer, Lily walked into the living room and surveyed it with pleasure. She had brought several pieces of furniture into Travis's home and with some colorful uplifting artwork and bright, puffy pillows everywhere, the loft was starting to feel like home. The caterers were hard at work setting up buffet tables.

"It looks great," she said to the manager. "I'm going to take a shower and get dressed, then I'll come out and help."

"We've got it under control, Mrs. Carson," the lovely woman said with a smile.

Lily smiled back calmly, but on the inside she was a wobbly mass of Jell-O. *Mrs. Carson.* She still hadn't gotten used to it. Maybe it was because they hadn't had a proper engagement. Or a formal wedding.

Or maybe it was the fact that up until a week before their wedding day Travis had barely even acknowledged her existence. How had everything changed so fast?

Lily got in the shower, knowing better than to look for answers for something she would never understand. Travis said he loved her. Again and again he said it, every time they made love, sitting across from her during breakfast, holding her hand as they walked along the marina. Why did she keep fighting it?

She heard the door to her bedroom open and whirled

around as Janica peeked her head into the bathroom. "Hey, Lils," she said, perching on the edge of the tub, not the least bit embarrassed by Lily's nakedness.

Lily wished Janica had the slightest sense of modesty, but given the slinky dress she was wearing, which looked to be held together by pins, Lily knew it would be a cold day in hell before Janica changed her ways. More power to her, Lily decided. She dried off with a huge, plush, forest green towel.

"I'm so glad to see you," she said to her baby sister. An onslaught of emotion threatened to bubble over as she watched Janica fix her hair in the mirror. She longed to tell her sister all her doubts about Travis and their marriage. After all, Janica had never liked Travis, so she wouldn't try and put a false lovey-dovey spin on things, would she?

Janica turned back to Lily and looked intently at her. "You look great, Lils. Have you been working out?"

Lily shook her head. "Too busy to work out," she said, bending over to twist a towel into her unruly hair. With a laugh she straightened up, and said, "Not like I'd need an excuse to be lazy. You know me."

Janica ignored Lily's dig at herself. "I know what it is," Janica said with a sigh and a twinge of envy. "It's true love."

So much for not getting all lovey-dovey on me, Lily thought as she gave up her plan to dump her worries on Janica's lap.

"Or all of the marathon sex," Janica added wickedly.

Lily almost dropped her towel. "How do you know about our sex life?" she sputtered.

Janica burst out laughing. "I didn't until now," she teased. "Between you and me, how is Travis in bed?"

Quickly recovering from her sister's trick, Lily lowered her voice and said, "Between you and me . . ." She made a show of looking out the door to make sure no one was listening.

"Go on," Janica said breathlessly.

"Like I'd tell you, you little twerp," Lily said, with a grin.

Janica groaned. "Shoot. I was just wondering how the Carson brothers are in the sack is all."

Lily raised an eyebrow. "The Carson brothers? As in Luke?"

Janica got up and changed the subject. "I brought the most incredible dress for you to wear tonight. I've been working on the design since Italy."

Lily took in Janica's flushed complexion and decided to do some more probing later. Luke and Janica? The thought had never occurred to her before, especially since she'd been so wrapped up in her own whirlwind romance. Guilt weighed her down, and she sat down heavily on the edge of the bed, deflated.

"I'm sorry that I've been so busy lately. I'm going to cut back so that we can spend more time together."

Janica whipped around, the pretty dress floating from her fingertips. "Are you crazy? I'm so happy for you! A new business and a new husband! It's about time you got off your butt and did something with your life."

Guilt turned to irritation, even though Lily knew her sister was right. "Well excuse me," she said sarcastically, starting to riffle through her makeshift lingerie drawer in Travis's dresser. "I didn't realize I'd been such a lump of coal in your stocking all these years."

Lily blinked back tears. Even her own sister thought she had wasted her life. Up until a month ago she evidently hadn't been worth much to anyone.

Janica's giggles were the last thing she expected to hear. Lily whirled around and threw the lacy bra she had selected at Janica. It landed right across her open mouth, and this time laughter gurgled up from Lily's throat. "What are you laughing at?"

she demanded as she threw one bra after another at her sister, followed by a thong panty that sat like a hat on Janica's dark hair.

Janica launched herself at Lily and hugged her tightly. "You're wonderful, Lily," she cried. "Did you see the way you stood up to me?"

Lily blinked with surprise. "I guess I did sort of do that, didn't I?"

Janica nodded fervently. "You did. It was great. You've changed so much in all the best ways. I never thought I'd see the day when I would say this, but Travis is the best thing that ever happened to you."

Lily held a fistful of panties to her chest and leaned back against the dresser. "Do you really think so?"

Janica smoothed out the dress and handed it to Lily. "Put this on. It's gonna look fabulous. And yes," she added, with a feline smile, "not only is Travis a changed man, but he's made you a changed woman." She put her chin in her hand and fluttered her eyelashes. "Ah, the wonders of true love," she said dramatically. Having caught Lily off guard, Janica whipped her towel off. "Now get dressed, and let's party."

Two hours later the party was in full swing. Travis's client meeting had gone late, so they barely had time for a quick kiss before the doorbell started ringing. Even so, thanks to Janica's vote of confidence, Lily felt much more positive about everything. Who knew, she thought with a smile as she refilled the wineglasses for a group of Travis's sleek, fashionable friends and coworkers, maybe everything would work out after all. Why had she wasted so much time worrying about things falling apart?

She looked across the room at Travis, who was cracking up the circle of people around him with a story. He looked up and winked at her midsentence, and Lily's heart filled with love. For her husband. She couldn't wait for the party to be over so that she could rip off his clothes and attack him. Maybe she'd tie him up again. Or maybe, she thought with a delicious shiver, he'd tie her up.

He walked toward her and wrapped an arm around her waist, smiling down at her. Reaching for a spoon from the table beside them, he clanked it on his wineglass several times. "Everyone," he called out in a strong voice, "could Lily and I have your attention?"

Faces turned expectantly in their direction, and Lily could feel herself turning pink. "What are you doing?" she whispered.

He kissed her on the forehead. "Just making a little announcement," he whispered back. Squeezing her hand, he said, "Thank you for coming on such short notice to our party. As you all know, Lily and I got married in Italy last month." A loud whooping went up in the room, and someone started a chant of "Kiss, kiss, kiss."

Travis grinned. "Good idea." He pulled Lily to him, and she gasped as his lips found hers, hard, then soft, his tongue sweeping into her mouth possessively. The cheers grew louder, and she was reminded of their wedding at the festival, when all of the locals had cheered for them.

Someone yelled, "Get a room," and Travis finally let her come up for air. She clung to him limply as he joked, "You won't miss us for a little while, will you?" He pretended to drag Lily back to the bedroom.

Everyone laughed, including Lily. "What I really wanted to say in front of all of our friends," he said, his expression serious, "is that I love this woman with all of my heart." Lily didn't hear the sighs of "ahh" and "isn't that romantic?" as she stared into Travis's eyes. It was down to the two of them, and she was lost in his incredible declaration. This time she pulled Travis down to her and had her way with his sweet mouth.

Everyone cheered again. "Anyway, thanks again for coming. We're glad you could be here to celebrate with us."

A million voices started talking at once, then Travis was pulled off for a round of backslapping congratulations. Walking on air, Lily spotted some jackets on one of the couches. Picking up the coats, she headed to the back bedroom to put them with the rest of the pile. The sound of malicious, cutting laughter stopped her dead in her tracks. She pressed herself into the shadows in the corner of the hallway.

"Can you believe what a cow she is?"

"Oh my God, she's huge," a second woman said.

"No kidding. I remember once when Travis said I needed to spend more time at the gym. And I'm a size four!"

"He told my friend Jenny that she needed to get rid of her love handles."

The first woman let out an angry snort. "How do you think that red-haired bitch got him to marry her?"

A man's voice chipped in with a faint British accent. "Probably got knocked up, and poor Travis felt like he had to do the right thing."

"It's awful," agreed the second women. "He's so beautiful, but her! Can you even imagine what their kids are going to look like?"

All three of them laughed nastily. "When she was filling our glasses earlier I barely stopped myself from accidentally spilling it down her dress."

They all laughed again. "Oh, I wish you had. That would have showed her. Oh good, the bathroom's finally free."

Tears streamed down Lily's cheeks as she walked away from Travis's awful coworkers. Why had she thought for a minute that she could fit in with these people? Each one was more polished, better-looking than the next. None of them had ever spent a moment worrying about their clothes, or their hair, or whether they were going to say something stupid if they opened their mouths in public.

Just as she had suspected, the past month with Travis was nothing more than a dream.

A dream that she was finally going to have wake up from, like it or not.

Sniffling, Lily fixed her makeup and wiped her eyes in the mirror. She had to make it through the party in one piece. Once they were alone, she would tell Travis that things weren't working out. Surely, in no time at all, he'd find a perfect woman to fall in love with and marry.

A knock on the door startled her out of her misery. "Sweetheart?" Travis poked his head around the door. "Oh good, I was hoping I'd find you in here. Alone." He waggled his eyebrows and grabbed her, stealing a kiss. "Have you been crying?"

Lily shook her head and forced a smile. "No," she insisted.

Travis ran his tongue over her lips. "I could swear I taste salty tears," he said quietly. "Is something wrong, Lily?"

"I had something in my eye," she lied. "We should probably get back out there, or people will be wondering where we are."

Travis still looked concerned, but he was kind enough to leave the reason for her red eyes alone. Moving into teasing mode, he said, "They'll know exactly what we're doing, us being newlyweds and all."

Lily's heart clenched with sorrow. He was so precious, but he deserved so much more than she could ever be. Someone who could stand beside him, beautiful and self-assured, not some dumpy girl with nothing going for her. Not some loser who wouldn't know how to be a good wife and companion if she had an instruction booklet printed across her thighs.

He kissed her softly, then pulled back. "Are you sure you're all right?"

Lily pressed her face into his neck and breathed in his wonderful, masculine scent. She wanted to stay like that forever, but such embraces would soon be nothing more than poignant memories. She just wasn't strong enough to fake it. Not with Travis.

She let go of him and took a step back. "No, I'm not all right."

He reached for her, but again, she stepped away. Hurt flashed in his eyes. "What's going on, Lily?"

She swallowed hard. What was she supposed to say when she was about to push away the only man she'd ever loved? The only man she ever would love. "This isn't going to work out," she said softly.

He looked like he didn't know what language she was speaking. "What isn't going to work out?" Each word ground from his lips like gravel.

She forced herself to look him in the eye. "Us," she said, barreling ahead before he did or said something that would make her change her mind. "You've been so good to me this month. The job, the trip, the marriage."

Travis exploded. "Do you actually think I married you to be *good* to you?"

A tear slipped down her cheek. "I'll never forget these past weeks. They were incredible. All my dreams came true."

He grabbed her shoulders hard. "I didn't marry you to be nice to you. I married you because I love you. Haven't you heard anything I've said to you? Do you think it's this good between everyone?"

Lily ignored the throbbing in her shoulders as she struggled to finish what she'd so foolishly started. "Even if you think you love—" she began, but Travis cut her words off as he pushed her away from him. She stumbled into the corner of the bed and fell back onto it.

"What else can I possibly do to convince you that I love you?" he roared.

Angry at everything and nothing at the same time, Lily struggled to get back on her feet. "I'll never be a size two. I'm never going to be able stand next to you without people laughing and wondering how you got stuck with me. You'll hear soon enough how I tricked you into marriage by getting pregnant, and how our children are going to be fat and ugly like me," she yelled in fury, hating herself more with every word that spilled from her lips, but unable to stop. "I'll never be able to fit into your world. Never! Can't you see what you married? Can't you see that it's just going to be like it was with Janica and Luke in Italy over and over again, forever?"

Travis made a move to comfort her, but she stopped him by blurting out, "Give me one possible reason why you should love me."

Travis went completely still. "I can think of a thousand reasons, Lily." Her heart stopped beating altogether as she waited for him to tell her what they were. Instead, his sad words were like a slap across the face.

"If you ever realize what those reasons are, Lily, let me know. Because I'll be waiting."

With that Travis turned and walked out of the bedroom, not bothering to close the door behind him. Lily sank back down on the bed, his words echoing in her head. She'd never been more at a loss for reasons to love herself than at that awful moment.

16

TRAVIS WENT BACK OUT to the party, feeling as hollow as an empty warehouse. He'd thought he'd found real love, the kind of love that would never leave, never go away, never hurt.

How could he have been so wrong?

He poured himself a glass of whisky from the open bar and pounded it in one gulp. Lily was leaving him. Never in a million years did he think Lily would leave him. When he looked at her he saw forever. Little girls with red curls and little boys with big blue eyes.

The hardest thing he'd ever done was to walk away from her. He had wanted to shake her until she started talking sense. But somehow he knew that all the pleading in the world wouldn't change the fact that Lily didn't love herself.

And even though he wished he could change it simply by snapping his fingers, he couldn't.

Until Lily learned to love herself, there was no hope for the two of them.

Travis prayed that it would happen soon. Because even a minute without her love was too long.

SHE COULDN'T BREATHE in his bedroom, in his apartment. Slipping out the sliding door to the private terrace, she awkwardly maneuvered over the railing into the neighbor's yard. A gate led out to an alley between buildings. She stood in the cool, damp passageway gasping for air. A cat jumped out from behind a Dumpster, and Lily jumped. Blindly, she started walking. She needed to get as far away from Travis as she could. Every cell in her body screamed for her to go back to him, to beg him to take her back. But even in her despair, Lily remembered the resolve in his final words.

"I can think of a thousand reasons, Lily. If you ever realize what those reasons are, Lily, let me know."

God, it was hopeless! Any reasons she could come up with would sound like a bad joke. Like some quasi Miss America contestant trying to say what her best feature was. *I've got a big heart,* she thought, that's the best she'd be able to come up with. Oh yeah, and she had big boobs. So what?

She raged at the unfairness of it all as she hoofed it past light after light, barely noticing when she crossed at a red and several cars skidded to a stop inches from her thigh. She looked up and realized she was at the cemetery. Her parents' cemetery. Guilt washed over her. She had intended to bring flowers to their graves ever since she'd come back from Italy. But one thing had led to another, and she'd never had the time.

No, she corrected herself harshly, she'd never *made* the time.

"I suck," she said loudly, confident that at least in that assessment of herself she was correct. Feeling ashamed for her hands being empty of blooms, she walked over to the large bay tree.

Beneath the thick canopy of leaves lay her mother and father.

All of a sudden she was sobbing and on her knees in front of their graves. "I really blew it this time," she said as her chest heaved. She felt like she was going to throw up. "Do you remember Travis?" she asked. "I had such a crush on him, even as a little girl. Mom, you used to say I'd never be able to pick between him and Luke." Her sobbing intensified. "But I did, Mom, I picked Travis. It was always Travis. I never thought he'd love me back, though, not in a million years. And now that he says he does, I can't believe him," she cried.

When no one answered Lily realized she had been expecting some sort of counsel from her long-gone parents. If only they could have solved the problem for her with a cup of warm milk and a fairy tale that would make her fall back to sleep after a nightmare. She gulped for air and tried to calm down.

"I loved you both so much," she said. "And I've missed you so much. I used to wish . . ." She stopped, feeling selfish for thinking it, let alone saying it out loud. "I wished that you hadn't died so that you could have helped make me pretty and tell me you loved me. Travis says he loves me. But I won't let him because I don't think I'm good enough."

In a flash, Lily realized the truth behind what she'd said. Apart from Janica and Luke, she had never let anyone close enough to hurt her. But Travis had crept right in.

"We got married," she said to her parents, as her tears dried on her cheeks and the beginnings of a smile curved up the edges of her lips. "In Tuscany. Oh, you would have loved it. It was the Festival of Weddings. Mom, they dressed me up in a lace wedding gown. Dad, he was as handsome as you, I swear."

Suddenly, she knew the truth in her heart. "I don't want to lose him," she said softly. "He's a better man than he lets on, Dad. Don't be fooled by his act. Because he was never fooled by my act," she said, pausing to take in the weighty realization. "Even though I was," she whispered into the wind.

Leaping to her feet, she kissed her palm and pressed it to the joint cement gravestones. "Mom, Dad, I love you, and I promise to bring flowers next time, but right now I've got to go and win my husband back."

"WHERE DID YOU GO?" Janica asked later that evening, concern marring her smooth brow. "Luke and I couldn't find you anywhere, and Travis looked like the walking dead."

Lily closed the door to her sister's apartment. "We had a fight," she said. "A bad one."

"Oh no!" Janica exclaimed, running across the room to throw her arms around Lily. Fiercely she spat, "Here I was saying how good he is for you and then it turns out that he's . . ." She stopped midsentence. "What'd he do?"

"*He* didn't do anything wrong," Lily said fervently.

In her surprise, Janica backed away from Lily and tripped over a stack of fabrics. "If Travis didn't blow it, what were you fighting about?"

Lily walked over to the large window seat near the door and sank down into it. "I'm the one who blew it, Jan. The one who's been blowing it this whole time. I told Travis I didn't want to be married to him anymore."

"You what?" Janica yelled. "I can't believe this. You told the guy that you've been in love with since forever that you wanted a divorce? What's wrong with you?"

Lily laughed, but there was no humor behind it. "So many things, Jan. Too many."

Seeing the hurt on her sister's face, Janica came and sat next to Lily on the window seat. Rubbing her knee, she said, "Lils, you're the best. Why are you the only one who can't see it?"

Tears clouded Lily's vision as she looked up at her sister. "I'm trying to," she said, "I swear I am. I was talking to Mom and Dad today at the cemetery and I finally saw how I've been hiding behind my fear all these years. Fear of not being pretty enough, for starters."

"You're beautiful!" Janica protested.

Lily smiled fondly at her. "Thank you, honey, but I always thought I needed to look like a magazine cover to matter to anyone." Janica was shaking her head in passionate disagreement, but Lily barreled on with the words she needed to say aloud. "After they died I was so worried about anything happening to you. I could never stand to lose anyone else. It was so much easier to hide away from everyone. That way no one would want me. It'd just be you and me until you found someone else."

"I'll never find someone else," Janica vowed.

"Yes, you will. And he'll be everything to you . . . Like Travis is to me." Lily's eyes blazed with purpose. "I'm finally ready for life with Travis in the real world, Jan, even if the real world has ex-girlfriends and arguments and size-sixteen dresses. Even if it isn't always the perfect fairy-tale world that I want it to be. I want my husband back," she said, "but I need your help if I'm going to do it right."

Janica readily agreed. "Anything. I'll do anything to help you. Just like you've always done for me."

Lily smiled at her baby sister. "You know that fashion show you've got planned? Do you think we could make some last-minute changes?"

THE NEXT MORNING, Lily called Luke. "Lily, where are you?"

"At Janica's design studio. How's Travis?" She had been unable to think of anything else all night. "Is he okay?"

Luke grunted. "If completely drunk is your version of okay, then yeah, he's fine. What happened between you two? One minute everything seemed perfect, then you were gone, and he was downing whisky shots two at a time. Come back, Lily," Luke pleaded. "Travis is a mess without you."

"There's something I've got to do first."

"What could possibly be more important than Travis?"

"Nothing," she said quietly. "And that's why I need you to do me a favor." When Luke didn't respond, she said, "Please, Luke, help me with this. I'm not going to hurt him anymore, I promise."

Reluctantly, Luke agreed. "What do you need me to do?"

FORTY-EIGHT HOURS LATER, Lily was once again backstage at Janica's fashion show. Only five new designers were presenting their lines, and as the newest one on the block, Janica was opening the show. The theme was young, hip clothes, the kind of thing that thirty-year-old women and teenage girls would be comfortable in. She and her sister had spent every waking minute working on the outfits to Lily's specifications. Lily knew her idea was crazy, but for once in her life she was going to go for what she believed in without reservation. Without fear.

Not that she wasn't scared, of course, because she was. But since she realized that losing Travis was scarier than risking it all, she'd stayed the course.

She prayed that Luke had made good on his promise to get Travis in the audience. If he didn't show, all of her plans would be for nothing. And then she didn't know what she'd do.

But she couldn't think about the possibility of failure. Hope was all she had to hold on to, and Lily wasn't going to let go of it, no matter what.

Janica was brimming with excitement as the models walked

past one by one. "Lils, this is going to be the best show ever. Your idea was fabulous. I don't have to give you credit, do I?"

Lily laughed. "Not as long as Travis forgives me."

"He will," Janica insisted.

The music amped up a notch, and Lily was about to explode with nerves. The moment of reckoning had come.

TRAVIS HAD NEVER SEEN Luke so determined before. He'd practically picked him up and thrown him into the cab. And that was the only reason Travis was sitting in a plastic chair waiting for a stupid fashion show to start. Hadn't Luke seen that he was busy with the bottle? He ran a hand over the stubbly mess that was his face. As soon as this charade was up he'd head right back to the neighborhood liquor store to stock up on supplies. Thank God for booze. It was the only thing that could numb his emotions since Lily had walked out on him.

He wished he didn't feel so helpless, stuck in some sort of time warp while he waited, praying, for Lily to wake up and realize that she was worth something. Something amazing and wonderful and the best thing that ever happened to him.

The loud, pounding music was making his eyes water. He'd give anything to take a shower and slip under cool sheets. With Lily.

He looked up at the runway. He could still see her in that incredible dress, the mask of feathers and sequins covering her eyes. So beautiful and so sensual and so lush. And his. He'd known it from the moment he'd seen her on this very stage that fateful Saturday night that she was meant to be his.

His heart clenched, and he gladly grabbed a beer from a passing waiter. Luke shot him a worried glace, which Travis ignored as he slugged from the bottle. There was nothing else for him.

Lasers opened fire on the stage. Two huge video screens

dropped into place on either side of the runway. Techno music swirled and pulsated. And then the first leggy blond model hit the stage. The screens flashed the word SEXY and the music hammered home the same message that the sparkles on her tiny shirt spelled out. She paused at the end of the runway and mouthed word. "Sexy."

Travis swallowed hard. Why did everything have to remind him of Lily?

The crowd applauded and the next model appeared. The screens flashed PASSIONATE as pink sequins spelled out the word across the girl's ample breasts. She acted out the word with a definite flair and the crowd ate it up as her big pink lips formed the word. "Passionate."

Visions of Lily's breasts in his mouth, of her riding his cock like a she-devil, assaulted Travis.

A third model emerged as IRRESISTIBLE flashed on the screens, mirrored by the words on her chest. Everyone in the audience laughed, happy to play along with the game. "Irresistible," someone shouted, and the hair went up on Travis's arm.

"What the hell?" he said, more to himself than to his brother. Was this more than just some random fashion show? Was all of this meant for him?

Another model followed closely on her heels, her hair in little-girl pigtails. SWEET declared the video screens as the girl sucked a lollipop with an ardent tongue. Hoots and hollers and whistles filled the room.

Travis sat up straighter in his chair. "She couldn't have," he said in a low voice.

A model skipped out in a plush white faux-fur coat. She turned her back to the crowd as the word WARM slammed onto the screens. Furry red letters were laid across her back over the picture of an igloo.

"I need to find her," Travis said, but Luke pulled him back down to the chair when he tried to get up.

"Just a little longer," Luke said.

Too stunned to argue, Travis sat back against the chair.

Sexy Lily.

Passionate Lily.

Irresistible Lily.

Sweet Lily.

Warm Lily.

She had finally figured it out. And she had done all of this for him. He thought he'd never love her more than he already did at that moment. But he already knew he was wrong. He was going to love her more every single day for the rest of their lives.

The models cleared the stage, and a hush fell over the audience. Finally, a gorgeous redhead with big blue eyes emerged from behind the curtain.

IN LOVE.

Travis couldn't have stopped the grin that stole across his face even if he'd wanted to. He watched the woman he loved walk down the runway, slowly and sensually. His eyes never left hers as the previous models danced back onto the runway.

And then she was running down the steps, and he was pushing past the row of chairs in front of him, and she was in his arms.

"I love you Travis. And I'm sorry. For everything."

Travis took her lips in a fiery kiss. "Don't you ever apologize to me again," he growled.

She stared openmouthed at him in surprise, then threw her head back and laughed. "Never again," she promised.

This time he took her lips gently, overwhelmed by the love he felt for this woman. "And never leave me," he said, not caring for once how pathetic or needy he sounded.

"Never," she said softly, as one lone tear fell down her cheek. With a sassy grin, she added, "That's not the kind of woman I am."

Travis hugged her to him and laughed with joy. Thank God they had both finally found out who the real Lily was, because Travis could no longer imagine a life without her by his side.

Love a good romance?

So do we...

Killer Curves
Roxanne St. Claire

He's fast. She's furious.
Together they're in for the ride
of their lives...

One Way Out
Michele Albert

Suspense crackles as two
unlikely lovers try to outrun
danger—and passion.

The Dangerous Protector
Janet Chapman

The desires he ignites in
women makes him the most
dangerous man in the world...

I Hunger for You
Susan Sizemore

In the war between vampires
and humanity, desire is the only
victor.

Close to You
Christina Dodd

He watches you. He follows
you. He longs to be...close to
you.

Shadow Haven
Emily LaForge

She followed her heart home—
and discovered a passion she
never dreamed of.